A Sliver of Silver

Ines C Rothen

For Nina Micheleine

The people and characters mentioned in these pages are freely invented
and any resemblance to real people and life are purely co-incidental.

A Sliver of Silver

Content:

Title		page no.
Chapter 1	'Shavany'	8
Chapter 2	Damatina Easterwood	14
Chapter 3	Fenella	30
Chapter 4	Karl Gettevan	41
Chapter 5	Akwase And Lightfoot	52
Chapter 6	Longhorn And His Casino	59
Chapter 7	Birri	70
Chapter 8	Suni's 'Magic Powers'	75
Chapter 9	The Notters	87
Chapter 10	Jock	103
Chapter 11	Max	109
Chapter 12	Woody Divulges His Secret	117
Chapter 13	Time Moves On	124
Chapter 14	Amethyst's Concerns	128
Chapter 15	Konrad Is Caught Out	139
Chapter 16	Fenella's discovery	143
Chapter 17	Shayne	151
Chapter 18	The Journey To England	156
Chapter 19	Konrad's Dilemma	166
Chapter 20	Fenella is Unhappy	171
Chapter 21	Dexter from Texas	175
Chapter 22	Shayne knows Max's Secret	185
Chapter 23	Ysenda	193
Chapter 24	Tina's worries	205
Chapter 25	Amethyst invites Dexter	211
Chapter 26	Max courts Ysi	217
Chapter 27	Brendan is asked to help	219
Chapter 28	Ysenda and Max	225
Chapter 29	Brendan has an idea	233

Chapter 30   Dexter puts his house in order   238
Chapter 31   Lala-June   242
Chapter 32   Max and Ysenda decide   255
Chapter 33   Tina weeps   257
Chapter 34   Ysi and Max need Money   262
Chapter 35   Fate takes a hand   266

Epilogue   274

I will break open
the story and tell
you what is there...

Chapter 1

'Shavany'

Max sat at a long table in the living room and drew with a pencil on a large sheet of white paper, the expression on his face one of utmost concentration. In front of him on the table were two large boxes of coloured implements; one containing a colourful pallette of crayons and the other felt tip pens in no less colourful hues. Currently he was using the pencil to sketch a house.

Max was the ten year-old adopted son of Brendan and Damatina, aka Tina, Easterwood. At length a picture emerged, that of a big house with pillars by the front door and some ten or twelve steps that led down from the entrance to ground level. Max was happy with what he had sketched and now concentrated on what selection to make to fill in the drawing with colours that matched his imagination.

Below the stairs in the drawing on the left was a sign, in elaborate writing, that said *Shavany*. This he traced with a black felt tip pen. Underneath the lettering but left in pencil was a dwelling that resembled a rather untidy wigwam. The house in the drawing was complimented with a massive conifer to the left which received a dark green and brown treatment and some privet hedges to the right in the same colours that gave access to an orchard. That it was an orchard could easily be seen because Max had drawn apples in some trees, boldly coloured in red felt tip pen, and pears in a shadier green and yellow. The trees themselves were coloured in hues of greens and black. There were about ten trees in that orchard, all depicting the one sort of fruit or the other.

When Tina came into the room, Max shoved his finished work of art under her nose with the words: „Mama, that is the house I have lived in and still keep dreaming about". Tina looked at the drawing in some amazement. The boy clearly had artistic talents, for the house was in perspective and the whole picture was one that would place the artist at much older than his ten years. Max had told his mother about the picture in his dreams and it was Tina who encouraged her son to make a drawing of it. So here it was. Tina wanted to know the significance of the sign *Shavany* but Max merely said that, as he remembered, it was the name of the house. At the bottom in the right hand corner Max had grandly put his own name in sloping capital letters; at the end of the ‚X' he had retraced that in a double wavey line, with green marks, back to the letter ‚M'. While Tina thought that *Shavany* was an odd name for a house, she was also bemused by the wavy lines and green marks under his name because it was sitting there oddly and did not seem to be part of what amounted to his signature. When she asked him about that wavey double line Max told her that it was not a wavy line but a very thin snake, a green mamba, of the sort that his gramps Liffet had given him and which he kept in a special box in his bedroom.

Tina had never seen this snake and asked her son to produce it. When he did so, Tina was astonished to see it was an exquisite little jewel; a small silver snake, long and thin with two emerald cabouchon-cut eyes which could be seen on the underside of the snake. The snake's tail, its tapered end was delicately exercuted in green enamel which crept up the snake's silver back. Underneath the silver snake was a clasp to fasten it onto something.

Max told his Mama that gramps Liffet had told him it was a green mamba, of the sort that had bitten Liffet's dad *Roote*r but who had not killed it but let slither away. He himself had immediately applid some root to the bitten place, of a kind that was secret but which had been known to the

Shavany for hundreds of years; the wound had healed and he had lived. While still looking at this jewel, Tina told her son that it looked a precious thing and he would have to take care of it always because his gramps had given it to him because he, Max, was meant to have it. Tina then also praised him for the splendid coloured drawing.

Max of course was the product of her younger brother *Pelham*, whom the family had called *Pelly*, but who had told Myra that his name was *Puck*, an amalgamation of his Christian name, Pelham, Uno, Codak, which became the illustrious Puck. The addition of the last name, *Halbard* would have made awkward reading, apart from being instantly recognisable everywhere, so he had left it out. So *Puck* it was. Myra had accepted that and it has been quite a few years now since Puck and Myra had come to grief in Puck's Knightsbridge flat.

Tina herself had fallen out with her parents over her brother's death, her mother in particular; she held her responsible for Pelly's demise because it was precisely because of his drug taking that Mother had decided that their standing in society would be lowered, not to say ruined, by the presence of their drug-taking son that could in no way be explained away or indeed made acceptable to their snooty friends. Besides it put a question mark about the raising of a son in such exalted circles, who turned out to become a junkie. Mother had had no inclination to field questions as to what might have gone wrong there. Much better to have got Father to agree to pay for a flat for their son, albeit in a very swish area of Knightsbridge, so Pelham would be absent and the family would not have to answer awkward questions from those who frequented their salon.

Mother was of the opinion that, having paid an unbelievable sum of money for the Knightsbridge abode, it made everything all right. To visitors who did ask after Pelly, his mother just explained in a perfunctory manner that he had his own flat because he did not like to live with the family anymore. Had Tina pointed out that the real reason Pelly had his own flat was because his addiction was seen to lower her family's standing, her mother would have been furious that her daughter told the bald truth about their son's drug taking

Tina for her part had thought it monstrous to leave young Pelly to his own devices without any supervision at the tender age of not yet 22. She had visited him in Knightsbridge in secret on numerous occasions while neither parent had ever done so; indeed they had also discouraged Pelly from visiting them in case their posh connections should come into contact with him while he was high and unpredictable. Upon learning of Pelly's death, Tina had yelled at her mother that her brother was simply left to rot, that it had been only a matter of time for an overdose to kill him and indeed he had come to grief in that way and, moreover, with a young woman as well. Yet, the true facts were never reported because Father's connections made sure that it was only reported that their son had died unexpectedly. Everything else was swept under their valuable Persian rugs.

*****

Tina looked at her son's drawing and was a little perplexed over the name of the house. Max could not tell her where that house was in America, but said that it was his ,nana's and gramp's' house. Max then volunteered that there were in fact two nanas but only one gramps. There were nana Akki and gramps Liffet whom he lived with. But there was another nana, Finelly, whom he had never seen because she lived far away but sent letters to him on his birthdays and a small parcel every Christmas. Max said he did not like the one that sent him birthday greetings and Christmas presents; he did not like the presents for which he had to say thank you even if he did not like them. Nana Akki had told him it was polite to say thank you for any gift, even if one did not really like it.

„Nana Akki and gramps Liffet were always very nice to me and gramps always came up to my bedroom to read me stories. Sometimes he talked about his own life and once, when he talked he gave me that silver snake: ‚This is for you, he said ‚I want you to always remember me'. The snake was of a species that had saved his own father's life. His father had had had a high respect of snakes and said it was wrong to kill them. He had accidentally trodden on a green mamba, one of the deadliest of their species, and it had bitten him. Yet, he had not killed the snake but caught it with a stick and then let it sligher away. Gramp's dad, Rooter, had used a secret root to draw out the poison. Gramps Liffet then also talked about his own large family.

He was a ‚*Shavany*', most of whom are still in Oklahoma, but many people have left and are now all over America. He said they thought of themselves as First Americans and that their chieftain had been a man whose name I can't remember. Also nana Akki told me to call her that. Gramps Liffet said that his name was a long one in *gonki* and Akki and he spoke gonki to each other. Nobody can understand it and when they spoke to me it was always in English. Nana Akki too had a longer name in gonki but it was hard to remember and Akki is a much nicer name.

Nana Akki was very nice and always said I had to be polite to nana Finelly; even if I did not like the presents she sent for Christmas I had to say thank you. One Christmas she sent a painted wooden horse with a bright red bridle. But it would not stand up, so gramps gave it to one of uncle Longer's children. I think *Longer* is gramp's Liffet's brother. I had not been sorry to see nana Finelly's present be given away. Nothing that nana Finelly sent was either nice or what I wanted, but Nana Akki said I had to say thank you all the same because people took time and effort to select a present even if it was not what one wanted. But Nana Finelly never asked what I wanted, she just sent stuff and I had to say thank you."

Tina professed herself to be happy with ther son's explanation but thought she would do a bit of figuring out herself, later. She had never heard of an Indian tribe that called itself *Shavany*, but thought light would be shed on the matter if she went through the papers with which Max came to her and Brendan. These papers had never been looked at because it had been such a business to acquire Max. The foster carers had been sad to let their little charge go, but it was *Fenella*, the boy's actual grandmother, whom Max called Finelly, who had made everything more difficult than it needed have been. The boy was certainly right about being wary of the second nana; there was no warmth there at all, with her it was all about money.

Chapter 2
Damatina Easterwood

After Max was tucked up in bed Damatina,/Tina fetched these papers and, going through them, was soon made aware that The Native Americans Max had been talking about were in actual fact the *Shawnee,* whose recognised prophet, Max could not remember, was *Tecumseh* who had lived in the seventeenth century. The people Max referred to as having ‚gonki' names, were in actuality an *Algonquian*-speaking ethnic group indigenous to North America. In colonial times they were a semi-migratory Native American nation. The house that Max drew was the home of the people Max called nana Akki and gramps Liffet. Looking in the papers with which Max came into the Easterwood household she found out that the proper name of Max's foster carers were *Akwase* and Lightfoot Wayne. They had named their house *Shawnee,* after their tribal connections. From what Max had been telling her, when he felt like talking about his nana and gramps, the latter in particular had been trying to teach him his native language, 'Algonquin, a kind of dialect somehow influenced by Canada's two tier language system. There are, it seems, several such languages in different parts of America: *Plains* to which belonged the *Cheyenne,* *Central* to which the *Shawnee* belong and there is *Eastern* by far the largest group comprising many tribes.

*****

Then there was that silver snake Lightfoot Wayne had given to Max for the latter to remember him by. The serpent of course is very ancient: it was even represented in the Garden of Eden, when The Lord commanded that Eve and Adam could have any fruit they liked bar the apples from *that* tree. That snake was *Temptation* which had urged Eve to try the fruit from that tree, because it tasted sweeter and Eve could not resist. So, the serpent existed even then. The old Egyptions also worshipped the snake and Tina wondered now about a connection between the *Shawnee* and the Old Egyptions. As to the latter, the priests in particular, worshipped the Serpent Goddess Niut-Shaes some 600 BC or thereabouts.

Snakes had always held a special reverence for all kinds of peoples not actually dissimilar to the history of owls. For some people owls brought luck while others claimed that on sight of one there would be evil visiting on those unlucky enough to have seen or been in their presence. Some people, even today, in different countries, believe too that breaking glass means seven years of bad luck, while in Germany and Switzerland the saying is that glass shards bring luck. And' *touching wood* is a recognised global belief that averts bad luck.

So it was with snakes. The ancient peoples of Mesopotamia believed snakes were immortal because they could shed their skins and in the Bronze Age artifacts were discovered that bore the unmistakable coil of the snake. Yet in Africa it was *Dahomey* – worship of the python. As to the latter it was the *Pithia* who dispensed her Oracles at Delphi while sitting on a tripiod chewing laurel leaves, near the cave where the serpent *python* lived. Legend has it that Apollo had to kill the python in order to take its place. Delphi only acquired that name later when it was derived from *Apollo Delphinios*, the Dolphin. Delphi was of course known for its oracle but *Homer* hardly ever mentioned the oracle.

Each question put to the oracle was accompanied by a compulsory offering and this was not without influence on the Pithia. But the Pithia's pronouncements were ambiguous to say the least; they could be interpreted in different ways, dispensing advice which was then interpreted by the enquirer as most positive.

Snake worship went through many cultures. Sumerians worshipped a serpent god named Ningishzida and before even the arrival of the Israelites, snake cults were quite well established in Canaan. So, it was entirely possible that the *Shawnee* for reasons lost in the mists of time had adopted the snake – species unidentified – as a symbol of luck. And Lighfoot, Max's Liffet, had given him a little specimen in silver to remember him by. This sliver of silver was covered in green enamel to represent the green mamba as his father, Rooter, had been bitten by one. Max was keeping the snake in a special box because he did not want to forget his Liffet, nor Akki for that matter. Both mattered a lot to the boy and Tina had no wish for her son to forget them. She and Brendan wanted to give their son a good life which did not mean that he had to forget the old one; for Max it was just a new chapter in his development.

*****

Tina sat in an overstuffed armchair waiting for Brendan, her husband, to come back from his office in the highrise. He did not go there nowadays as often as in the olden days when it was still of paramount importance to stay on the top echelon of success. These days, when he went to his office and came home on occasion a little later than supper time, Tina would always wait with the evening meal until he was home. Although there were two cooks that prepared breakfast and dinner, Tina always insisted on making up her own lunch which she ate by herself, or together with Max if he was not at school but for dinner she used the cooks as it gave her the longest time to enjoy her husband's company.

Now, while waiting for her husband's return, she sat in her chair and thought about Max. He was developing well and had adjusted nicely. He came as a five year old and was now ten, so five years had gone by since his arrival. Max was beginning to be the spitting image of her younger brother but the adoption process had been quite problematic. She herself had wanted the boy to grow up in England; he came after all from her side of the family. Brendan's children, Marcus and Amethyst were all grown up and had left the family nest long ago. She remembered being introduced to Brendan's daughter, Amethyst and on sight they had liked each other, but Tina had been apprehensive about meeting Marcus because Amethyst told her that her brother had insisted he wanted nothing to do with riches but wished to lead his own life in the way he saw fit. Amethyst said that in her mind she still held the picture of Marcus as he headed out of the door, shouting that they could keep their wealth, but as for him he wanted nothing to do with it as it had a corrupting influence on all who had it.

Much had changed in attitude to money since her marriage to Brendan but, nonetheless Tina was worried about meeting Marcus, since, looking around her, the house was furnished to the very highest and most luxurious standard that reeked of immeasurable wealth. Would he spurn the house too, even though he had been born in it? Amethyst had told Tina that until coming across him at the Pumphouse Theatre she had not seen him for quite a few years. Father had urged her many times to try and find her brother, to no avail. Though she regarded father's reason for finding him suspect as he was going on about some paintings the new step-mother had hung on the living room wall; she had thought there had to be more than his paternalistic reason for wanting to see his son, but was nonetheless pleased when her father had told her he was to marry again. Amethyst was now Tina's new step-daughter and they got along fine. She and her family came regularly to the house and Tina got on well with the whole family, her husband Konrad and their two children, the minnow Ozzy whose birth name was Oskar, and Margaretha, whom everybody called Minnie, But, since

Amethyst and her family came from Brendan's side she was apprehensive about how Brendan might feel about having Max come into the family, the boy being from her side and still a child.

Tina had discussed it with Brendan, but she need not have worried for Brendan was more than willing to be a father to the boy. Not only did Brendan raise no objection but was ecstatic at the thought of having a little'un in the house again. He had always felt guilty; when Marcus and Amethyst were growing up he had largely been, from their ages of five or six, an absent father. Here was a chance to make up for it by adopting Tina's nephew, Max, and be a proper father to him. And so the boy was acquired so to speak. The Shawnee family had been sorry to lose him but realised that Max would have better chances with his blood family than if he stayed with them.

The real problem though had been Fenella Davey Gettevan, the one that Max called *Finelly,* who was a blood relative as she was the grandmother, mother of Myra, who died along with Pelly, the illustrious Puck. Neither Tina nor Brendan knew anything about Mrs Gettevan, but soon got the measure of her; Fenella was money driven. By and by and in round about ways they heard various rumours, about this woman's ability to extract large sums from of stores in New York by way of litigation and how a set of attorneys, one of whom she married, had helped her to her riches.

Indeed, Fenella, upon Tina's polite request of wishing to adopt Max, sent long letters, each one more insistent, with demands of unrealistic sums of money to let the child move from America to England. Fenella had written that she was the natural grandmother to the child and had been very attached to the baby ever since he had come to the States with her daughter. Fenella had been never been used to being closely questioned about her various assertions but after Tina pointed out to her that somebody who gets attached to a grandchild would never allow that baby to be fostered out to a strange family, the letters got more realistic, yet still demanding money. One of her letters pointed out that such sums as she demanded were surely no problem for a rich family such as Tina's, inded she dared to say that what she wanted was surely only pocket money with a family name like that. She added that she read the papers too and was fully aware of how rich her family was.

Tina refused to be swayed by such assertions and answered with polite refusals for any kind of sums and, indeed, eventually Fenella seemed to have accepted the futility of her demands and had given in and so Max had come to them. He had settled into his new home relatively quickly although he talked with genuine affection of his gramps and nana. Gramps in particular because he could alwys tell him such wonderful tales of his tribe and how they lived a simple life and how at the beginning White Man had come and taken over their land, which over time had become smaller and smaller as tribe after tribe was allocated less and less space on which they had to stay and make the best of it.

The *Shawnee,* as already told, originally came from Ohio and Pennsylvania but left their traditional homelands there. In the late 18th century, European-American encroachment crowded Shawnee lands in the East, and one band migrated to Missouri. Three reservations were granted to the Shawnee in Ohio by the 1817.

The tribe went to Kansas and had their land reduced and broken up into individual parcels. During the American Civil War many of the Shawnee fought for the Union but instead of receiving compensation or honours for their service, they found upon return to their land much of it taken over by non-Indian settlers; they had been granted 130,000 acres of Shawnee land, while only 70,000 acres remained to for the tribe.

*****

In quiet moments Tina wondered if they had done the right thing in removing Max from the family Wayne in Connecticut. It had been a loving family that had fostered Max and his drawing of the house, which he called ‚Shavany‘ was the *Shawnee*, the name of their tribe. Tina's thoughts turned to Max's self-centred actual grandmother Fenella Gettevan and also thoughts about wealth. She herself came of course from an ultra rich family and the trappings of that wealth was for all to see. She only had to mention the name *Halbard* (before she became Brookman and after that Easterwood) and every door just flew magically open. Not knowing any better since, from childhood, she and Pelly were used to enormous wealth and the obvious advantages it brought. As children they thought it was all normal and everybody had what they had, but later, married to her first husband, Jackson Brookman, whom she called Jack, her name changed from the influential *Halbard* to the nearly as influential *Brookman*. The money supply increased, in fact added together it was more, way more than what she and Pelly had growing up as Halbards. She and Jack had so much in the way the could spend without caring about any price tag it was just like buttering bread.

In the way that she and Jack could spend what they liked without worrying that the kitty might be empty, Jack was a Brookman and she was a Halbard and between them they were so unimaginably wealthy for their kitty never to be empty. Whatever they spent or wasted – there was always more available. It was just money. They did not have to learn the hard way to save up for what they wanted. The word ‚saving‘ had no meaning for them.

For all that, it had not been a love match between her and Jack. It was Tina's parents who endlessly talked about the advantages of a marriage between the Brookmans and Halbards that eventually, when Tina and Jackson met, both found each other attractive enough to agree to the match. The marriage too was successful enough because there were certainly no money problems and sex was acceptable too. Jack was a good enough lover and Tina knew no different as there had been no lovers before him. Then there was the money. There was so much of the stuff that neither Jack nor she ever had to have time to reflect what they might mean to each other as people. Money gave lots of very superficial pleasures that *could* be satisfied and, indeed *did* satisfy. And what pleasures there were when money could simply buy anything; there was no time or even reasons to think about love.

Tina shifted in her chair, thinking back. How stupid it all was. There would of course come, eventually, a reckoning: her marriage broke up. At first she was sorry when Jack just upped and left, but after a bit she began to enjoy her new-found freedom. She could even understand why Jack left, and she too came to see that all that coveting of money what not worth much as it could not be used to buy happiness.

For all that she remembered the rows with him over her dresses from Paris; his not being able to see how a scrap of silk could cost thousands and even more for handbags and shoes, all probably made by sweatshops in the Far East by girls who had to use exclusive materials selected by the brand in question but had to toil away for a pittance because what *they* did put food onto *their* table. Tina was thinking of what these girls must have thought toiling away on fabrics and leathers taken from rare species of snakes and other wild life. On balance, for the girls who were not informed of the end price of the article they were working on, one material or fabric was probably the same as any other. But Tina wondered if they would have had a care about the animals forced to give their lives to end up on the bodies of snooty, uncaring women whose only reason was to show off to likeminded women how expensively dressed they were and that it was nothing to them, that they had lots of similar in their wardrobes.

Tina now thought it odd that, while married to Jack, she too had belonged to that elite that never thought about the cost of anything, But now, married to Brendan it had finally come home to her that it was all nonsense. Brendan too of course had money to burn and initially she thought it would be hard to convert him to her new way of thinking, that money was indeed a corrupting influence. Strangely enough she had found it quite easy to convert him to her way of thinking as he had come to similar conclusions ever since his first wife Lindsey had died of drink because he had not been there for her although that was what he had promised when they married.

Come to think of it the wastefulness of her life had started to come home when she still lived with Jack, when on the one occasion she pressed a bundle of notes into the hands of a harassed looking woman with a baby in her arms and two by her side and went on her way without looking back to see the astonished unbelieving face of the receiver. It was nothing to her, Tina, just money, yet she had felt *happy* having parted with it to somebody who plainly needed a bit of benevolence. It had come home to her then that money was important to people who lacked it in sufficient amounts in their daily struggle to pay bills and put food on the table. And which of the necessities they had to forego because their children came first and there was not enough to go round while she and Jack wasted millions without a care. Yet for this ordinary woman standing at the bus stop that bit extra had come in very handy.

She and Jack did not just have a bit extra, they had it in such abundance that it would have made ordinary people's eyes water and wonder how necessary it was to obtain such unimaginably luxury, or indeed spend it. Yes, realising that was the start of the change in her thinking and for the first time she thought about people who had nothing, while she and Jack had everything. All the same, she had told her husband that she would not allow any criticism of the price tags of her dresses, handbags and shoes, when she could see how he could buy an outrageously priced car one week just because he liked the colour and make, crash it the following week and buy the same again in a different colour.

*****

Tina shifted in her chair. Change in her attitude came slowly but it did come. All that money and what was the result? Her parents were delighted about the marriage to Jackson because to people who frequented their salon it was proof that money was not only important by itself, it also bought favours and willing helpers who, on flashing a bit of cash, were happy to do any heavy lifting. Oh yes, the money did all that for the two families but it brought the young couple only limited happiness. The spending or wasting of untold sums was fun for a while, but it did not satisfy in the long run, and so the marriage was bound to fail and did.

When Tina told her mother that her marriage to Jack was failing, the latter had been aghast and put the blame firmly on her daughter. She had not been tolerant enough, Mother wailed, had not done enough to make the marriage a success and she even told her daughter that she suspected, Jack possibly had a mistress and if that was the case she should turn a blind eye to it. Tina told her mother it was not a case of her husband having a mistress, it was a case of them having fallen out of love with each other. Mother of course could not understand any of it. What could one possibly want more than money and standing in society? No, Mother had no understanding of anything of this sort.

Jack left but did come and see her a few times after he had left to say that he had given himself a new name, one of anonymity: he now called himself just *Bert* and he lived in a squat. Tina had no idea what a squat was and Jack had to explain that to her, that it was a house where nobody paid any rent to any landlord since nobody knew who the landlord was. Tina found it odd that people actually had to pay rent to

23

somebody as, the way she lived, everybody owned their houses and mansions.

At first she refused to see him when he visited, but over time she did and eventually would come to feel the same way as he did. It dawned on her what had never dawned on her before because she did not have to think about it: that money was important only to those people who did not have any, to those people who had to scrimp and save to perhaps have enough for a modest holiday with the family.

But also true was the opposite, which was that for different sections of society having enough money was just never enough and one always had to have ever more of the stuff to keep up with whatever trend one had to keep up with in order to stay on the ladder, ready for the opportunity to acquire the next rung up. Like her mother who revered her social standing and was convinced one just could never have enough money to stay on the very top echelon of society. For her it was certainly what money *represented*: ‚the standing‘ in the circle she and her father moved. She had bought into that and was still thinking that in those circles money was what kept them being important and one could never have enough to prove one‘s importance. And important too was the name. Not even flashing the cash, but just mentioning the name *Halbard* was enough to make most people do their bidding. Always. Thackeray said that there were people who were striving very hard after what was not worth having. For Tina’s mother it *was* worth having. She was fully aware of being at the top of the tree along with the name and was also fully aware that other people not so rich were happy enough to know them in the hope that some of their gold dust would rub off on them too. She not only did not mind that, but was positively glorying in being so important that there were people eager to emulate them.

Tina herself was beginning to see that money could not bring other happiness, that which could not be bought with money no matter how rich one was. Moreover the more one had the more one was likely to lose what it meant to be human. She felt sad that her brother Pelly had met such a terrible end at such a young age: perhaps had he had more understanding parents it would never have come to the kind of drug taking that killed him in the end.

What of herself though? She had had the same upbringing, both she and Pelly had the same parents, yet she never had any urge to resort to drugs. So, maybe, being fair, it was in Pelly's genes to resort to a life of destruction yet the same upbringing did not bring for her the same end result; she realised that people had different characters and could be inherently different, even though they came from the same womb.

Nature was complex but one positive thing that did come out of her brother's untimely demise was that he did leave progeny and that was young Max. Tina was now married to Brendan and was very happy, a happiness she never had with Jack. And now there was Max. Brendan of course had a very wealthy background as well and she herself coming from a failed marriage had convinced herself that she would get Brendan to see that money was not everything. Even though between them they had more than plenty, it did not need much persuading for Brendan had been feeling guilty too about not honouring his pledge to the mother of his two children. That she had died an untimely death he never truly got over and his way of dealing with it was going to his highrise and making more money.

She and Brendan had been of one mind that Max, being her nephew would have to be brought up by her and Brendan. That Brendan loved her, of this she was certain and Max after all was her poor brother's child, so he was family. She knew nothing about poor Myra but she got the measure of Myra's mother and her impression of that lady was one of self-centredness and selfishness. No wonder Myra had turned to drugs with a mother like that.

That her brother was an addict as well she put at the door of her own mother being hell bent on maintaining her social standing no matter what. Tina now knew that it was a very shallow ambition of her mother that her main aim in life was not to suffer any embarrassment in the circles she moved by having a wayward son who was likely to do outrageous stuff in her presence that could not easily be explained away and make it presentable. Tina was amazed to think that for so long she herself bought into that aim, the aim that money was everything including the social standing. But she had woken up now.

Marrying Brendan had been the turning point. Her parents had been over the moon when she announced her intention to marry into the Easterwood family. Mother in particular had been horrible when Jack had walked out and had roundly blamed her daughter for not looking after her marriage better, but when Brendan came along and with him the name Easterwood, mother was effusive in her praise of the family and remarked that Tina had done well to garner such a man, since the family could be termed of as good enough in social standing though not quite as high as the *Halbards,* but then no family in this country was equal to that name, but the name Easterwood was to her mind near enough. Yet she let Tina know in no uncertain terms that she could count herself lucky to have found such a man as it was for Tina the second time around: she was a divorcee after all. Saying that she lowered her eyes in such a way that for Tina that meant only one thing: she was ‚damaged goods‘.

*****

Tina sat back in her chair and thought about Brendan. It was funny how that started. She had had no notion of a new relationship. She had already been deserted by Jack for nearly a year, had got into her own stride and started to like her new freedom. So any ideas of a new relationship, or even a second marriage, never entered her head. When she was

26

invited to a private viewing prior to the main exhibition of a painter of modern art she had not even wanted to go, as she had not felt all that well that day and had planned on a trip into the countryside as it was getting late in the season and Nature's Painter had started to spray his colourful palette in a wide sweep over all the trees and Tina, in any case, preferred autumn to summer.

Even so, when the invitation came along she went. Later on she would say that it must have been Fate that had changed her mind and she had accepted the invitation to the pre-view. There were not many people present and to her surprise she actually liked the paintings exhibited there. Yet she did not buy anything, but decided she would go again when the exhibition opened properly for the public. Brendan had been at the exhibition too and by way of conversation he came over and introduced himself, Brendan Easterwood. She had known the name of course because the name was very well known in her circles, but she had expected a man to act in accordance with the money he had. That had not been the case and it would not be the last time that this man astonished her.

And so it had started. After the exhibition he asked her for coffee and, having nothing better to do she accepted and they went across the road from the exhibition to a small cafe; nothing swish, just a small place with a couple of tables covered in formica. That was another thing that fascinated her. She knew the name Easterwood. That it was *the* Easterwood she readily believed because the price tags of the paintings would be beyond a normal wage earner who happened to have that name. So she accepted that this man had untold sums of money at his disposal, yet did not seem interested in impressing her by visiting an upmarket coffee place, but chose the one across the road.

It was true she had found the man attractive but that he chose not to impress her with money left a more lasting impression on her. Talking over coffee she found they had much in common and Brendan seemed in no particular hurry to leave. He told her about his work in Wapping, in a high-rise office. He also told her that, to begin with, he had not been interested in making money. His father had pressed him to see how he himself had made *milly-deals* as he had called them and so he felt he owed him something and spent a few months in his father's office. And caught the bug. He had wanted a simple life, a family life – he had two children and a lovely wife, but once the bug had bitten him he could not help but follow the money. So he added millions more to what the family already had and that in itself brought a certain pleasure. But his wife could not understand that she had lost her husband to money, took to drink and died when she was not yet forty years of age.

In time his son came of age and had talent and he had tried his level best to induct him into the world of high finance. Marcus, to please him, also did a stint in the city, but found it too hypocritical to be part of it and bowed out. He decided on becoming a *Gentleman of the Road,* the other end of the scale and it took years for him to come back home again and then only for a visit. That has been the status quo to date and he, Brendan felt that he had failed as a parent. It was only after his children left home had he realised that all that money-making was alien to family life, by which time a lot of it was too late to rectify.

Brendan told her that it had been many years since his wife had died and he had never found anyone he had wanted to replace her with. But in truth, he had not really been looking. At first when he was told about his wife's death he had taken off to the high-rise and immersed himself in work. The guilt came later. A lot later, but it did come, and it prevented him to enter another relationship. What he did find eventually was that the money that was in the family was enough for him to take it much easier and in so doing it had changed him. Living, though he was often lonely, was a lot more satisfying than all that pressure of adding more millions from people who were sometimes of quite dubious provenance. When younger he would take their money, but the older Brendan now refuses to have anything to do with money of dubious provenance.

Tina liked what she was hearing and they met again, in a park that time and the more she got to know him, the more she liked what he stood for and eventually they got close and Brendan asked her to marry him. And so she did. She never regretted it.

Tina then heard the door open downstairs and shortly under the frame appeared Brendan, her husband. She was happy to see him and together they went in to dinner.

Chapter 3

Fenella

Fenella Davey had become Mrs Fenella Gettevan, she having married her attorney, her demised daughter Myra's erstwhile lover. The marriage was not a success. It was not that Fenella regretted her intervention in her daughter's love-life when she was still alive, far from it, for she believed she had done her daughter a big favour by claiming the lover for herself. No she regretted the marriage to Karl Gettevan because she had miscalculated, had fondly believed that by marrying the attorney, she would be getting a better deal when suing diverse stores for 'injuries' sustained while slipping and falling on the smallest of imperfections in the stores' floors. Fenella was very money driven and it counted far more than having a happy marriage, the latter coming way down the line in her priorities.

Until the most recent lawsuit the law firm *Wewill Gettevan* had been stupendously successful in their endeavours to give Fenella and themselves a very handsome income. Fenella's discovery about the love affair between her daughter and Karl Gettevan was entirely accidental. She had telephoned the law firm to speak to Karl and was told by his partner James that Karl was away seeing a client out of state, in Connecticut somewhere; he could not say exactly where, but could look it up if she insisted. Fenella did not insist but had found it odd that Myra had also taken off, telling her mother she was taking a weekend away out in Connecticut. From New York to Connecticut was at least some distance and nobody went there unless there was a specific reason. Baby Max had been farmed out to Connecticut but Fenella knew that Mayra was seriously lacking maternal feelings and

Fenella felt it was very unlikely that she would pay the baby a visit. Yet she was going to Connecticut and was adamant that she would be definitely gone for the weekend.

*****

Myra had come back from Europe after an absence of some eighteen months with baby Max in her arms with the explanation that the father of the baby was conceived while she had been sitting on a contaminated toilet seat. Mother had scoffed:

„Do you mean to tell me that the father of your baby is a toilet seat?“ Fenella had known for some time of Myra's drug taking but at no time did she think it was because of her falling way short of having been a hands-on mother to the girl. Myra, irrespective of her improbable assertion that a contaminated toilet seat had resulted in a baby, had nevertheless stuck to her story and in the absence of a more concrete father Karl and Mother had to accept what they were told. Myra had invented the story about the toilet seat because she had, while in England, been conducting an affair with Puck, but had sent her Karl love letters proclaming undying love and telling him how she missed him and that she had been nothing if not absolutely faithful and true. So the real provenance of the baby could not easily be explained all things considered. In all her many letters to him she expressed her wish and hope that one day they would be together as man and wife. Being pregnant with Puck's child she named Max, was an unforeseen mishap not to say inconvenience which had been discovered too late to do anything about.

Clearly, by any stretch of the imagination, the father of Max could not have been Karl as, for one thing over 3,000 miles separated him and Myra and for another he could not have been around when the baby in question was conceived. So the contaminated toilet seat was the nearest thing to hand

31

that Myra could think of by way of explaining the baby's provenance.

She herself had not thought it very probable either that a contaminated toilet seat could produce a pregnancy, much less could result in a baby, but she held that conveyance of the belief was everything and if one voiced an opinion convincingly enough and looked for all the world that one believed it then it just simply had to be so. What was the fictional detective Sherlock Holmes's mantra? 'When all impossibles had been discounted then what remained had to be the truth'. Myra held on to the ‚remaining' bit and stuck by her story.

The reality was that Myra arrived back in the States from England with Max. She herself had not much of an idea about motherhood and Fenella too was less than interested in providing grandmotherly care. All the same Fenella had a controlling quality to her character and not wanting to be responsible for the baby, did not want to relinquish control of it either and so decided to take charge of a sort. That amounted to ‚farming' the baby out. In no time she had found, out of state, what she termed to be a suitable foster family for Max. As for Myra she was quite content to let her mother handle the specifics. For her it meant freedom to pursue renewed pleasures with Karl and press home more rigorously for her lover to leave Mary-Jane, his wife, and his children and marry her.

All the same, while continuing her affair with Karl, Myra still lived at her mother's house, since, back in America she had nowhere else to go, but the house was large and her own room was at the top of the house. This seemed to have suited both women, in particular Fenella whol liked to keep a gimlet eye on her daughter to check what she was up to. Yet for all her controlling nature she had had no idea about the clandestine affair of her daughter and Karl, though she had discovered Myra's drug taking when one day she had rifled through her daughter's handbag to look, ostensibly, for some keys and had found these suspicious looking packages in sliver foil. Myra was careless in the way she took her drugs and would leave tell tale empty little bag in her purse. It had never occurred to her that her mother was checking her purses.

Karl, for his part, having had nine years with Myra, decided that marrying her would mean a jump from the frying pan into a roaring fire and so, while promising everlasting love did his best to string it out and keep her as his lover and Myra's longed for ring on her finger was only a promise that would be made good at some unspecified time in the future.

Fenella may have been a control freak and surely was but she was far from naive or stupid and when she was told in that phone call that Karl was seeing a client out of state, in Connecticut and Myra had let slip that she was going to Connecticut too for the weekend with a friend, Fenella had put two and two together and eventually got it out of Myra that Karl was her lover and had been for near on nine years.

Upon being found out about her affair with Karl, Myra had asserted that Karl would leave his wife and children and marry her quite soon, such had been decided. But Fenella knew in the way she had got to know Karl as her attorney that he would never leave his wife and children unless he was forced into it and Myra was not strong enough to make him do that. All the same, Fenella was amazed that the love affair had gone on for nine years under her nose. Nine years!. My God! Who would have thought it! She was determined to put a stop to it in whatever way she could and top of the list was getting Karl to divorce his wife and marry her, Fenella. Yes that was definitely the best plan. Karl, she felt, was in any case far too old for Myra; he was better suited to her. That she and Karl were never suited as a couple either never entered her head. Whatever Fenella wanted and had set her heart on, Fenella would get, there was never any doubt of that.

Marry him she did, but the cracks began to show already on the honeymoon. A high point though was that she had relished her daughter's face when Myra had knocked on the hotel room door of the Dorchester, ready to melt into Karl's arms when she, Fenella had came out of another room and seen her daughter's face. Fenella had let Karl explain to Myra that he and Fenella had married the week before and they were now on their honeymoon; he felt that something so important could not be imparted in a letter to her and had to be told face to face. Myra's face had been a picture and Fenella would treasure that.

As mother and daughter they never got on. From the age of five Myra intruded far too much into her life and she found the little girl rather clingy As Myra got older she found Fenella in competition with her on many occasions on many things. But while Fenella had more important things to do than attend to the wiles of a small child, if was different when Myra reached her teenage years. Fenella suddenly felt that she needed to compete with her daughter in everything to prove she was still young enough to attract the opposite sex, notably the young men who took an interest in Myra. Even though she, Fenella was not interested in sex, if she could garner an early suitor of her daughter for herself it would confirm to her that she was still a woman who had the physical attributes that counted for something.

*****

Myra's father, Albert Davey, had left, never to return, when Myra was about five years old and Fenealla had actually been sorry to lose him. Albert might have been wanting between the sheets as Fenealla frequently threw at him, and she had certainly not wanted a second child with him, but the deficiency between the sheets was not what bothered her about her husband: it was Money.

To Fenella money was God, while to Albert money was to be worked for and if the salary obtained was a bit

34

short, one just had to want a bit less of life's luxuries. That did not suit his wife at all. She had wanted *all* of life's luxuries and if finagled properly, not to have to work to hard for it either. Albert was too honest about the money that came through their door. It was not that his salary was small. He was an engineer, engaged by Shell in the American oil fields and was handsomely remunerated; but he was on commissions and so the money was not the same every time. For Fenella it was never enough; in her view it was a pittance even with commissions paid and it was always nowhere near enough for what she wanted out of life.

For his part, Albert found his wife cold and if he was deficient between the sheets, well she herself did not do much to arouse his passion. When Myra arrived, he had tried to be a proper father to the baby but Fenella was too possessive to agree to any involvement. Obsessive though she was about the baby, she herself could not be bothered to do the chores of feeding and changing nappies and so, quite soon after the baby's birth, she engaged nurses to do that job.

In the end Albert stopped bothering and, realising how the land lay, felt there was no place for him in that cold home, and one day he left in the morning and never returned. When Fenella realised her Albert was not coming back she was at first furious because he had left without saying good bye, but as time went on, she had been pleased about gaining her freedom.

Yet it had been a whirlwind romance. Albert had been a handsome man, tall and slim in army uniform when she met him and she had been smitten the minute she saw him and wanted him for herself. He had a girlfriend, though not married, and in her wily ways managed to claim him for herself and making him dump the girl friend. She had seen a photo of her in his wallet and made a little tantrum about it. The girl was mousy and rather plain, Fenella thought and, Albert, upon her insistence dropped her. They had known each other only a month before she thought that they should marry. Albert, for his part had liked the wilful Fenella, yet when she pressed for marriage he had been a little uncertain and thought that they would have to know each other longer but Fenella was adamant and so they married. For Fenella Albert was a trophy on account of him being so very handsome, but for him, he found out quite soon after the marriage that Fenella's wilfulness did not translate into a happy marriage. There was never enough money as far as she could see. He was major in the army and when he came out of there and resumed his work as engineer for Shell and was handomely paid for the work he did, but for Fenella it was not sufficient to satisfy her desires. She wanted BIG.

After two years Fenella found herself pregnant and when Myra was born, Fenella proved to be a rather careless mother. Having constantly accused Albert of not measuring up between the sheets, he grew indifferent and when Myra was five daddy left one morning and never returned. By that time Fenealla had found the law firm Wewill Gettevan; she had a plan and found in Karl, one of the two partners a willing servant to her desires. He was married with a wife and children and his wife had high hopes of sending them to private school. The law practice while going well did not bring in the kind of money that Fenella was proposing could be gained with her plan.

And so it had begun. She found the stores in which she decided to slip and fall and Karl Gettevan, the attorney's job was to to the research to see if the selected store was good for the money without their recourse to legal steps. Also to check if the store had public liability. If it had it would be much easier to get the rquired compensation as the insurance company would largely pick up the tab. Fenella's ventures had been very successful year after year. The law firm Wewill Gettevan had discovered that the ceiling to avoid a defence of such a lawsuit was a precise $100,000. Stores would rather pay out with the help of their insurance company as they had public liability insurance, than defend any action. Defending such an action would soon turn out to cost a million and more. And since the insurance companies paid out the actual cost to the store was a small percentage of that, even if the premium for the following year would be higher, but could be offset with having less tax to pay.

Yet, with this latest law suit Karl had failed. Yes it was Karl who had failed, no question. It would never have occurred to Fenella to think that she had a good run in a fraudulent venture; it had brought her a good income over time and it was time now to close the system down. Fenella did not think like that. She could never bring herself to accept blame. It had to be Karl who had not done his research properly otherwise the money would have continued to roll in.

It may have been a rare failure but Fenella had no wish to close her beautiful system down. Another way just had to be found. Perhaps, not in New York, but out of state, with stores that had holding companies big enough but not so big that they were part of a chain. For that would never do, as word would get around very quickly and for Fenella to keep her income stream onside, it would have to be kept clandestine.

What to do about Karl though. Clearly, the marriage was not working out to her satisfaction, but she needed him still to carry out research on the viability of her selected stores. She did not mind driving from New York to the next State, maybe New Jersey. She would try and get Karl to do a ‚reccie‘; after all he had had many trysts with her daughter out of State, so she was sure he could accommodate her for that. In quiet moments she worried about distances; she and Karl lived in New York and she proposed to Karl to venture to New Jersey or Connecticut to carry on with the lucrative business of slipping, falling and suing for compensation.

Perhaps there was another way to carry on earning untold sums of money for doing very little; she would have to put her mind to that. For the moment nothing came into her head. As for Karl, she was sure that whatever she might come up with, she would be able to persuade him to do her bidding. But if all else failed it would be she, Fenella to come up with a plan. If she was really careful in working out the details, it might not even have to involve the partnership Wewill Gettevan. That had definitely merit because it would mean compensation that did not have to be shared with the law firm.

There was another thing to be considered. Fenella had allowed that the marriage with Karl was not working out but that was something she *could* rectify. It would be no hardship to divorce him and send him back to his ex-wife and children. From remarks he had made to her in unguarded moments was that he did indeed still miss family life. By that he meant his now ex-wife and his children and often wondered how they got on without him. His wife, while having finally had proof via Fenella, that he had been unfaithful with Myra, she had been so shocked she did not know what to say. Fenella then just told her to bow to the inevitable and divorce him and Mary-Jane had just meekly agreed to it. That Fenella wanted to marry him herself she was careful not to mention. However, when Mary-Jane had found her feet she had told her husband that he would never see the children again but that she expected decent monthly alimon payments from him for her and the children. Karl had said that if he had to pay for her and the kids he was surely entitled to have visiting rights, but Mary-Jane said that he had done so much damage to the family that she was astonished that he still felt he had any rights as a father.

As for Fenella, having managed to garner Karl for herself, the reality was that a large part of the fun had been being able to take the lover away from her daughter and claim him for herself. That was fine while Myra was alive, but now her daughter was dead that bit of fun had disappeared into the ether and with it the wheels of the marriage wagon. There was now nothing more to prove and living with Karl was, from her point of view, not the nirvana she had expected it would be. Whatever her daughter saw in Karl that had made their affair last nine long years, she, Fenella, could not see it. She found him lawyerly and dull to a fault.

When something did not work for Fenella, she made short shrift of it. As to her new marriage, it was not working in the way she had imagined so he had to go but not yet. For now she would perhaps still need him for her new venture. It would depend how it panned out. On the other hand, if she could devise a plan that would need no intervention from any attorney, it would mean she would have the full whack of the fee that was going to be paid to her alone.

She had always rather resented the fees that Wewill Gettevan, as a firm, had claimed for themselves and over time these fees has become ever larger. In the end, the sued for amount ended up in her bank account with one fifth of it deducted, that fifth being the fee which the law firm kept for facilitating the suit. Fenella thought about it. A whole fifth of the sum taken as fees for Wewill Gettevan. It was far too much. It had stated off as ten percent. And now it was diouble that. Honestly the greed of some people. They could obviously see the amounts they had to send to her bank and resented it and so over the years, their fee had increased. They had justified it by calling it disbursements. Whatever they chose to call it, it was way too high for Fenella.. All they had to do was a bit of research to ascertain that the store in question was worth the money claimed and that they had public liability insurance. And how long did that take? A child could really do it as they had all the information at their finger tips. No, it was too much money and it was not the firm that had the bruises and weals to show, it was she, Fenella. They could sit in their comfortable chairs and add up the sums, take out their considerable fees for not doing a lot and give her the rest and Fenella was convinced that both Karl and James *resented* that the larger amount that actually came her way, her, a vulnerable woman on her own. Entirely on her own; Myra was in England and the firm had taken advantage of her vulnerability. She felt she had to accept the doubled fee, but she had never been happy with it. Twenty percent had always been over the top.

Fenella thought about it all. If only she could find a way to bring her income stream back on line without the need of any attorney. That would be excellent. She felt there could be, she just had to put her mind to it, would have to apply her brain to think it all out. If she managed that she could not only cashier an unsatisfactory husband, she could also do away with the law firm Wewill Gettevan that charged her twenty percent. Yes, getting rid of a husband who in her eyes had lost his allure, that was the thing. Myra was dead and she was now on her own to figure it all out.

Chapter 4

Karl Gettevan

Karl had married Fenella who now bore his name. The marriage was in its infancy and already Karl was deeply unhappy with his new wife not least because he had been forced into a divorce with Mary-Jane he did not want. She had been an exemplary wife and, yes it was true, he had betrayed her for nine long years with Myra, abut he had never had any intention of marrying her. By his lights this had made the difference though it did not cut any ice with the wife.

Moreover, he had known Myra's mother only as a client and, together with his partner James Wewill, had helped the woman to astonishing riches, but on a personal level he had known nothing about her. Occasionally she had come to their office, affability itself; meetings he, Karl, had had with her had given no inkling that she might prove to be a difficult woman. He had accepted that she was forceful, certainly, but she had to be that given that she pursued these stores in such successful ways. James too, had given all credit due to her, but there was an undertone in his partner's remarks about Fenella. One time, when discussing a particular store that took a bit of persuading that it would be better to pay the sum demanded as otherwise things could get messy, the store had eventually capitulated, but it had taken the persuasive powers of Karl and James to make the store give in to their demands. That time James had said to Karl: "what a woman, so single minded about her pursuits of money. I admire her zeal but I would hate to be married to her". Yes, those had been the words of James and at the time he had thought nothing of that remark. Especially as he had planned a weekend with Myra, out of state. His wife had started to complain that neither she nor the children saw enough of him, but he managed to present her with a trinket and the words: "You know I love you and the children, but business has to come first, and you can see the proceeds pay for our children's private school and the fees are not cheap".

It worked every time when Karl wanted a bit of time away with Myra. Myra! She was an excellent lover, always so enthusiastic and exuberant and so easily sidetracked. She did of course, like all women, want the gold band on the finger but he knew better than to go down that avenue. He saw early that he would never be able to marry her because of her drug habit and although she swore that that business was dead and well behind her, he knew otherwise. When she was not looking he would go through her handbag and sure enough there were the tell-tale empty packets that had had contained her drugs. She had overdosed once in his presence as well and it had been touch and go but he had the presence of mind to walk her around the hotel room for a full two hours and that time she had come round. He had had the horrors of her dying in front of him and his having to explain it to his family. It did not happen, but, God, it was close.

And now Myra was dead and he found himself married to her mother. There was of course little Max. Karl still winced when he thought about how Myra had tried to convince him that the baby's provenenane was a toilet seat. Not for a minute had he believed in the possibility of that, but since she had looked at him so convincingly he had gone along with her absurd assertion. Hard on the heels of that they had had a weekend away somewhere in New York, he could not remember where and it had been like before. Fenella had taken charge of the baby; her solution had been to send the little mite to be fostered out in Connecticut somewhere and Myra, who had in any case no idea what motherhood meant, was free to pursue her pleasures with him. And now Myra was dead and he was once again a married man, married to a very unsatisfactory women. It had started on the honeymoon. He had not relished Fenella's insistence that he told Myra himself that he was now married to her mother and had liked even less to see how pleased she had been to see her daughter's crestfallen face when he had told her. He had watched her fleeing out of the hotel and into the street; he had felt sorry for her and he would have liked to run after her, fold her in his arms and tell her how much he loved her. And no, he certainly did not love Fenella, but she had been so forceful in her pursuit of him, it had put the kybosh on his marriage by Fenella telling his wife, Mary-Jane what had gone on between him and Myra for nine long years.

Understandably his wife had had enough and finally filed for divorce. Yet, she never told him, Karl, that it was Fenella who had told her about his love affair for all that time with Myra. How he wished he could have turned back time. He still loved his wife and, to add to his misery, he had heard through the grapevine that Mary-Jane was now in a new relationship. All the same, bearing in mind that he could not see a future with Fenella, he had not given up hope that his ex-wife might yet forgive him and come back to him; he realised he was no good on his own.

The rows with Fenella continued to make him miserable. She was never wrong; even when she was she had this knack of making him see that it was he who was guilty and he had to accept that she was right and he in the wrong. Only afterwards, when he thought about it could he see that once again she had managed to land him in whatever it was she landed him in. Sometimes, cautiously, he would talk to his partner in general terms. James knew of course that the relationship with Myra had gone on for nine years and also knew that Karl had felt that marrying Myra meant jumping from the frying pan into a roaring fire owing to her drug abuse, but marrying Fenella, well that was another thing altogether. That was not just jumping from the frying pan into a blazing fire, it was adding a good canister of fuel to it as well. James had told Karl as much and the latter had nodded his head miserably and mumbled yes he should have seen it coming.

Now Fenella as a client was lost to them both due to that last disastrous case, where the store manager told the firm that if it went to court it would be defended. The store, moreover, had video evidence to show that the whole thing was one big sham and they drop the matter while they could. James was the first to cotton on that that line of suing for compensation was now dead as more and more stores installed video cameras, primarily to stop the pilfering, but it could of course also stop being scammed.

There would be no further fees to collect from that lucrative seam and that was to be lamented. But even here Fenella had made it clear that, having had an unsatisfactory first husband, she was not about to believe that the second one might be any better. She had let him know that she had not married him for any shenanigans like sex. She had married him in order to increase her income and this now looked doubtful.

*****

The legal practice consisted of just two partners, James Wewill and Karl Gettevan. Both had wives and children, but James was the more steadfast in that he remained faithful to his wife. It wasn't that he was unattractive and did not appeal to the opposite sex, it was just that it was too much trouble for him to get hooked into an affair, then having to extricate himself from that as he could not conceive leaving his wife and children to whom he was quite attached. Apart from everything else he thought of the hurt all this would cause and that it would certainly jolt his equilibrium quite seriously. It was much easier to stay with the family he loved; besides his wife was, as he would say frequently, enough woman for him. There was one celebrity, he remembered, who said if one could have steak every night why go for burgers. Well, he had steak every night and did not even like burgers.

No, it was Karl who was always vain enough to try anything new and so fell for the charms of Myra when she was eighteen. He had liked her even when she was a lot younger but he oftentimes said to James that trying that would be jail-bait, but when Myra had turned eighteen it became a different story for him. To be fair Myra was a bit of a flirt and, though young in years, realised the magic she could weave around men and took full advantage of her sex. Karl though, being aware of his position as lawyer resisted any temptation to flirt with the young girl but when she turned eighteen and was still flirting with him openly, he took her up on it. To begin with it was just his vanity to be found attractive by a flirtatious young woman, but over time he actually fell in love with her. Even so, he had no intention of leaving his wife and children. For him it was just a bit on the side. He liked Myra's quirkiness; she could make him laugh in her funny ways and as time wore on, he found her simply irresistible. He did get wise to her drug taking though, when he found suspiciously small packets wrapped in silver foil in her handbag, but she made light of it and admitted that she partook sometimes of very light stuff because of the mother she had. He knew of course the sort of mother his young lover had, but decided to keep his own counsel because Fenella of course was one of his clients out of whom he did very well financially. Fenella brought a very handsome income for the law firm and for that he was more than grateful and so he decided to overlook the small silver foils and carried on with the affair with Myra.

Over time time Myra wanted more, wanted to be made an honest woman of but these were dangerous waters for Karl, and to pacify her would only promise that one day – one day – he would make her his own. Fenella knew nothing.

Had she been perhaps a little more perceptive instead of single mindedly pursuing the next source of income, she might have realised that her daughter and her own attorney were conducting a clandestine affair. That it went on for nine years had not been for Myra's want of trying to get him to divorce his wife, but Karl had played the long game. While promising to divorce his wife and marry her, over time he had realised that it would be foolhardy to do so. Karl had accepted Myra's persistent using, although she kept denying it, telling him that those days were behind her, that she had seen the light and had realised that raising a family and taking that sort of stuff was not the best way to have a happy marriage.

Karl had known more: he knew that what Myra said was not necessarily what she practised and the small packets in her purse kept being discovered by him. Besides she was a different character when she was high. So he played the long game, telling her he would divorce his wife so they could get married, while quietly deciding that he would stay married to the wife he had. Mary-Jane had been very acquiescent: she had of course known nothing about this affair with the daughter of one of their clients and wanted to believe the lies he told to see a client out of state when the truth was he took leave for a dirty weekend. Besides, however the duo worked for their clients, the result was that his wife was well cared for and her two girls went to an expensive private school and brought back the results that made her realise that she really had nothing to complain about.

Over Myra's unfortunate and no doubt accidental death alongside Puck, owing to an overdose Karl did feel sad, but he was also not a little bemused to be told that she had died alongside another man in that man's flat. Karl was far from stupid and wondered about the possibility that Myra's little boy Max in fact did have a proper and actual father and that man was Puck, rather than the improbable projected one Myra had tried to make him believe, the contaminated toilet seat. Better not go there, Karl thought since nothing could now be proved, not even via DNA as toilet seats were ineffective even if one knew the exact one.

Fenella coming into play while Myra was still alive, that had been an unforeseen thing. Of course he knew Fenella as his client but he had never had any amorous intentions towards her. When she proposed marriage he was astonished, while Myra fondly believed that Karl was hers and they would have a future together. Yet, Fenella had calculated correctly in one respect: Karl was not strong enough for the headstrong Fenella and after he had run out of excuses not to marry her, he felt browbeaten and gave in. After a while even he could even see the advantage of such a match. He was still loath to divorce his wife but to break the deadlock Fenella telephoned Mary-Jane, who had by then had one or two suspicions about the faithfulness of her husband. After Fenella had put the wife wise in the way of her husband having been conducting a nine year long affair with Myra – her own desire to marry him, she left out – the wife decided that enough was enough and filed for divorce.

Karl having never been much good on his own, agreed to the marriage with Fenella but it had been left to him to explain to an incredulous Myra in the hotel room at the Dorchester in London that he was in fact on his honeymoon with her mother. That had been the hard bit, to tell her, but Fenella had insisted and to this day Karl could never forget the look on Myra's face when Fenella had come from the far side of the room and he had to tell Myra the untellable, which he lamely said he could not put into a letter.

Well, what the hell did he expect? Flowers and good wishes for his happy honeymoon and marriage? He would never forget the way she flew out of the room, down the stairs and out of the hotel. Through the window he watched her vanish into the traffic. And now he was married to her mother and the marriage was not the success he had hoped for but the failure he had indeed feared. As characters they were very different in temperament and Fenella could never admit when she had gone wrong and would always lay the blame on a third party, in this case him.

Like that nasty business with the last store where video pictures threatened to be produced which showed that Fenella's catching an item of her clothing on a loose edge of the counter were not commensurate with the $100,000 dollars compensation her attorney, Karl Gettevan was demanding on behalf of his client. The firm was told that if their client pursued the claim it would be defended no question and the store was not afraid to produce video footage in court. As matters stood the store did not wish to pursue the matter but would be happy to have it in writing that their client would no longer pursue the case. Whatever the rantings of Fenella at her husbands failing to do the customary research, Karl, as was normal in their practice, had in fact discussed it with his partner James and both had come to the conclusion that the store would be good for the usual compensation figure.

Now that particular income stream had gone up in smoke, but Fenella was still thinking about continuing that line out of state, if at all possible. She was far from stupid and while ranting at her husband and laying this fiasco squarely at his door, she realised nevertheless that times had changed. Such stores as she would visit – even those out of state were like as not part of the same chains as those in New York; they would pool the resources and soon realise that it was the same legal firm who would repeatedly, in different stores,   make a claim each time for a precise sum of $100,000. Multiplied by a few times per year and it added up to quite a sum. Having lost that now meant Fenella would have to think of a different stream that could make up for this kind of loss. But, on the quiet Fenella had actually accepted that she had reached a dead end with this type of venture and would have to come up with an entirely new wheeze. Money seemed to go nowhere these days even though she loathed spending unless it was on herself. But she had come to rely on the very handsome income derived in such easy manner, with very little effort on her part, bar a vew bruises here and there. To start making do without such handy sums that came her way, after the attorney's fees were taken out, was not in her game plan.

Fenella was not short on imagination and had now a very vague plan in her head. Nothing concrete, still cloudy, but she would have to think about it hard, to turn it into something workable that facilitated an income stream commensurate with what she had up to now bar the last fiasco. Some form of blackmail perhaps could not be excluded.

*****

Initially anyway, at the beginning, it had been her idea of suing stores in New York. When she mentioned it to one Karl Gettevan, who had, with his partner, James started out on their own not so long ago, Mr Gettevan, one of the two partners, had heard her out then told her he would have to check it all out then get back to her within a week or two after he had done the necessary research to see what was feasible and what was not. Fenella's plan had been simple and after two weeks Karl had got in touch with her and said her system was ,doable' and he and his partner would take her on as their client. And it had worked for a few years, until this last business with that dreadful store and its manager. Bob Wagtail had presented the legal firm with video evidence that clearly revealed that if it did come to a court case the footage would be shown and their client would be the loser. It was on the cards that previous cases might be be dragged up as well and it could be one hell of a mess. Best to get out while the going was good. Fortuntely, this ghastly Wagtail only insisted she drop her case and the matter would be forgotten. While blaming it all on Karl, deep down she knew the game was up. Times had changed. More and more stores installed CCTVs, primarily to stop the ever increasing menace of people coming into stores with the sole intention of pilfering and the existence of cameras would not completely stop the practice, but at least minimise it and that could only be to the good. For Fenella it meant she had to change tack.

Briefly Fenella had told Karl Gettevan about about Max, that she had had a letter and it was another business that had to be tackled. The letter, postmarked England said it requested that the boy's family had wished that he be taken from the foster carers and removed to to England as he was the actual son of Pelham Halbard who had died along with Myra in London and whom she had known as Puck. Damatina Halbard- Easterwood was a blood relation of Max and it was the natural way of things that Max's future should not be with foster carers, but with his blood-family, who intended to start the legal process of adopting him.

So Karl had finally certainty that Max was the progeny of the man, Pelham Halbard, who with Myra had died in the man's swish flat. Fenella paid no heed to how Karl might feel about that, but, instead, she prattled on, telling him that she knew the family was filthy rich and by rights she should be able to extract a sizeable sum because of her ‚loss‘ of the baby.

Karl said nothing. It did register with him though that Fenella could not even manage a scintilla of sympathy of how he might feel about Myra having deceived him, not only over the baby but over the time she had professed undying love while carrying on with another man. That having registered he thought it would be pointles pointing that out to his wife and so he said nothing but instead stared at the table cloth while his wife's thoughts were as ever about the money she was going to extract from these people; that she hopeed that the sum could be large enough to compensate her for her loss of income from the various stores.

One thing was certein, she told Karl, she would not relinquish custody of the boy without being compensated. And decently compensated because the family was swimming in money.

Chapter 5

Akwase & Lightfoot

Max who called his erstwhile foster carers ‚gramps' Liffet and ‚nana' Akki had entered into a lively correspondence with them on a regular basis, encouraged by Tina who felt that it would be of benefit to the couple who lived such a long way away in America if they were kept abrest of news from their boy. When Lightfoot and Akwase realised they would lose their little foster child, they were quite upset for they had been fond of him and had cared for him in exemplary fashion. They had always known of course that they were only foster carers, but they had not thought that they would have to let him go again at just five years of age. In quiet moments Akwase had allowed herself to believe that little Max, who called her *nana* just as soon as he could formulate words, was theirs to look after until he had grown into a young man. They had perceived quite quickly from Fenella's first visit when she came to to offload the baby, that she would never take him back; she was just not the type.

That too was the belief of Akwase's husband Lightfoot, who was determined that the little boy would know the ways of the *Shawnee*. To this end he would read him stories about the ancestor *Tecumseh* and how White Man had come and – little by little – had taken their land away. There had been more of them and so the *Shawnee* as well as other Native Americans had no choice but to accept the very harsh terms from successive governments. The tribe might have lost their land, but they still could make a difference and Lightfoot was making sure that his little charge would know about the terrible and ongoing deceptions heaped upon his people.

*****

The American government, having first agreed that the Native Americans could live side by side with the new settlers soon did an about-turn and successively the different tribes were hounded out of their lands which was given over to the new settlers that had come mainly from Europe; the tribes were accorded what was known as *reserves*. Then even these got smaller and smaller. It was no different for the *Shawnee* but the more enlightened ones of that tribe realised which way the wind was blowing and went their own way. As Shawnee they felt that the only way to have any kind of life was to integrate into the new American Society and make the best of it. All became Americans who gave themselves first and last names. Max's foster parents became Lightfoot and Akwase Wayne. Yet in spite of these names they remained *Shawnee* at heart and kept alive the old ways inside the family. Lightfoot had kept his connection with the ancestors of *Tecumseh* and he and *Big Woodman*, his nearest neighbour, could often be found drinking a home made brew, made to a recipe from the old ways, of which Lightfoot in particular was very fond, because Big Woodman really knew how to brew it, but he would not tell him what went into the brew to make it go down so well.

And now the day and that horrible letter postmarked New York had arrived. Without opening it Akwase knew there would be nothing good contained in that envelope. In the past there had been letters with the same hand writing and postmark, but these were always addressed to Master Max Davey and so Akwase always knew that these letters contained greetings from Fenella, Max's grandmother, for the boy's birthday. And at Christmas time a small parcel would arrive for his Christmas present.

53

Looking at the letter that was now sitting on her kitchen table, Akwase knew that the letter was not about any birthday, for Max's big day was still months away; besides the letter was addressed to Mr and Mrs Lightfoot Wayne, so it was clearly meant for them. Akwase toyed with the idea of openening the letter, then rejected it because she felt that it should be Lightfoot who had to open it. In the end her curiosity won and she slit the envelope open to find out its content. She never liked Fenella. Sie was far too pushy for the self effacing Akwase but in her mind, opening the letter would show that it was about money. Akwase was firmly convinced the letter was yet again a demand for money; it was bound to be that. That woman could never have enough, yet she always, on the rare occasions that she did make the journey to them, was always expensively attired. Yet she moaned about how expensive the fuel for her car was these days – she drove a light coloured Lincoln Continental, a make not noted for fuel efficiency.

Akwase had got the woman's measure the first time around when she had dumped the baby, saying that she expected to be remunerated for the outlay of fuel on the way from New York to Connecticut. Akwase had told her that she never handled money and if Fenella was looking for compensation she would have to wait until her husband was here. In the end, when Lightfoot had come home, he gave her fifty dollars and his mien told Fenella that there would be no more and Fenella had departed with bad grace.

Akwase had slit open the envelope and gingerly removed the letter. She was as yet still sure the woman was asking for money, expected to read that she missed the boy dreadfully and had sleepless nights over it and some form of compensation of that ought to be in order. Akwase thought that it was something of this sort that was in the letter. If so, Lightfoot could deal with it. He was a lot firmer than she was. Left up to her, she would just send what was appropriate, something like a hundred dollars. Left up to

Lightfoot Fenella would get a stern reply in the negative, after which birthday greetings for the boy still came, but the Christmas present for that year would be more paltry still, as she would claim poverty. Whatever she sent she would always stress that the present in the parel was obtained through scrimping, hardship and penury.

Akwase never believed that because she could see that Fenella was far from poor, even though neither Akwase nor Lightfoot had even the tiniest inkling of how fraudulently Fenella swindled money out of big stores for her own gain. But they figured that somebody turning up in a car like that could not possibly be short of a dime or two.

It had been Fenella Davey as was, who had employed them as foster carers in the first place. The deal had been struck via telephone, but then she came in person to offload the baby. While on the phone it had been Akwase who had taken the call and she had not liked Fenella's peremptory voice. When she had sight of her, she had correctly summed up the voice of the woman and in the flesh she was exactly how Akwase thought she was; the impression had not been favourable.

Akwase now read the letter and realised that ist was not a demand for money but that Max was to be removed from their care. The letter said further that the matter was out of her, Fenella's, hands, that the father's family of the boy had requested adoption of him. Akwase had to sit down, shocked to the core and that was how Lightfoot found his wife, sitting at the table with Fenella's letter in her hand and tears running down her face.

Lightfoot took the letter from his wife's hand and scanned its content. Fenella had written that the boy's removal from their care was imminent and that Max was to travel to England with an escort, because his own father had died and that his family wanted to adopt the boy. Lightfoot finished reading, shrugged his shoulders and walked away.

And in the way he had walked away Akwase knew her husband was in turmoil too.

Lightfoot's ancestors were *Red Sticks,* which meant he himself was a also *a Red Stick* in his bones as had been his father, Rooter. *Red Sticks* had the reputation that they did not want to assimilate, which meant they were more isolated and formed a more traditional part of the Shawneee. Lightfoot still had many of the inherent traits in that he was unable to show emotions of any kind. He and Akwase had been together now for over fifteen years. Their marriage had been held by one of the elders in a wigwam who, for the occasion wore a splendid headdress of white feathers. But as Americans they still had to make it legitimate in a registry office, because that was the legal requirement and they had to comply with that.

There was a marriage dance which was held in the evening before onlookers who sat on the ground. It was quite a do. The dance participants entered barefoot, clad in costumes of the finest doeskin, bleached white and decorated with beadwork, and interwoven with feathers, shells and porcupine quills. Hair was worn loose so that the firelight reflected in the gloss of it. Instead of necklaces there were bracelets and bands of beaten silver and strands of painted shells on their ankles which clinked melodiously as the dancers walked. Lightfoot also wore a small silver snake, affixed to the doeskin. It was his personal good luck charm which had come into his possession in round about ways and it was that charm that he would later give Max and told him to look after it and remember him by, always.

The dances had gone far into the night and so Lightfoot and Akwase were married. For their first night they slept in the wigwam, kept snug and warm by the fire and by goat fleeces. The wigwam was kept for special events, like wedings and such like; most people now lived in houses.

Lightfoot and his bride had tried for a family themselves but Akwase could not conceive and Lightfoot after numerous years had accepted this but when the offer of fostering little Max had been made both he and Akwase had been of one mind, that of acceptance. They did not mind that Max was not a *Shawnee,* but from the first Lightfoot was determined that Max would grow up to know about *Shawnee* traditions and ways.

Their foster care for Max was in the sixth year, when that letter came that stated that Max's blood family wanted to adopt the boy and that he was to grow up in England.

And so the dreaded escort came, the boy was taken away and Akwase and Lightfoot grieved. Akwase had suggested that perhaps the pain might be less if they fostered or even adopted another child, even though she was always in fear that her secret, one that she had guarded since her marriage, might be dicovered. But losing Max had brought it home to her just how much she had longed for a child to nurture and raise and which was now denied her. But of her own daughter, now raised by her sister-in-law, Birri, she still said nothing to her husband. That was still a closely guarded secret and by the way he had reacted about adoption told her that that secret would have to remain in place, unshared.

On one of the reserves in Delaware were a number of children of all ages; it would not be all that hard to bring one of them up, boy or girl, it would not matter, to impart their ways onto a new offspring, although of course, since they were born on the reserve had already been brought up in the ways of the *Shawnee.* But Lightfoot would not hear of it. He told his wife that there was no one who could replace little Max and that she should busy herself with other chores that would make her stop thinking about what could never be. And so the Waynes lived without their Max.

Akwase had kept her secret but regretted her decision to let her baby be adopted by Birri. But in the way that her husband had vehemently opposed Max's replacement had shown her again that she had been right after all not to share it with him. What she had not factored in was that Fenella had somehow discovered her secret and would try and make use of it when the time was right. How she had discovered the secret was perhaps not so astonishing given that a woman of Fenella's character, wholly driven by money, would always be nosey enough to pry into other people's lives to discover things that might be of interest as a possible new income stream that could further enhance her bank balance. To Fenella nothing mattered so much as money and in the pursuit of that she would leave no stone unturned.

Chapter 6

Longhorn's casino

Longhorn Silvertip was the older brother of Lightfoot Wayne. There had been four siblings in his family, Rooter the patriarch and Ona the matriarch. The reason why Longhorn had a different last name to Lightfoot's name *Wayne,* i.e. *Silvertip,* was because in their algonquian language names were altogether different anyway. Both Lightfoot and Longhorn realised that if they wanted to get along with the new settlers, now called Americans, they would have to fit in and to that end they had to have a first name and a family name. Lightfoot chose *Wayne* for himself, while Longhorn, his older brother chose *Silvertip*, which possibly had a connection with the coins and cards he was dealing with on a daily basis in the casino, which he managed and ran. Although he too was a dyed in the wool *Shawnee* he was of quite a different stripe to his younger brother. He had also delved into the long history of the *Shawnee* tribe and the more he read about it the angrier and determined he became. The realisation that White Man had duped the First Americans by way of shunting them out of the way, simply because there were more of them, upset him deeply.

With his mother Longhorn spoke the Algonquian tongue but from his father he learned to speak English He also learned that the prophet of the natives was *Tenskawatawa* and that the tribe revered him, even though he had died in the nineteenth century. Longhorn also learnt that there were different bands of Shawnee and he and his brother belonged to the *Cherokee Shawnee.*

As children, he and Lightfoot and Akwase played together. They were more or less the same age though

Longhorn was the eldest of four brothers and sisters, two boys and two girls. It was not until the boys were in their late teens that Longhorn had fallen in love with Akwase, a girl on their reserve, which resulted in her becoming pregnant. Longhorn fully intended to form a family and be a father to the unborn child but his sister Birri had objected. The fact was she was very jealous over her darling brother, whom she loved very much. So when she realised that Akwase was pregnant with Longhorn's child she decided to do everything in her power to stop her brother marrying ,that girl'. It was true of course that Birri, being Longhorn's sister, could not actually marry her older brother herself, but neither could she accept that her brother might love somebody else.

Raising her vehement objections to the match had the result that Longhorn was feeling guilty, over what he could not say, but seeing his sister's angry and sad face, made his own feelings toward Akwase hesitant. He could of course not tell Akwase that the reason for the delay to get married was objections raised by his sister but his delaying the marriage had the effect that Akwase's baby, a girl she named *Shayne*, was born out of wedlock. Birri had won the first round. The next round was Birri persuading Longhorn that the baby girl should be brought up on the reserve. To that end and she had managed to convince a very reluctant Akwase that Shayne would be better off being raised on the reserve by her and Bigfoot and so Shayne was taken from Akwase and given to Birri and her husband.

Over time Akwase had come to regret that decision and could never understand how she ever went along with it. It put paid to the relationship between her and Longhorn and, indeed, not too long after this severance she had married Lightfoot, Longhorn's brother without ever disclosing to him that she had had a baby by Longhorn, who too knew nothing about it. It was a closely guarded secret which she would keep. She did not Longhorn that there had been a live birth, a baby girl and Longhorn never thought to question her about that, even though he had wanted to be a father to the child. He had simply assumed that there had been no birth at all. To add to Akwase's grief the marriage to Lightfoot remained childless and so, when Fenella had suggested that baby Max should be fostered by them, she had happily accepted. Finally, her mothering instincts were put to good use. She was fully convinced that Max would be staying with them until he grew into manhood.

Longhorn was not best pleased that he had lost Akwase to his brother, though he blamed himself for letting Birri spoil the relationship; he would have wanted to marry his sweetheart even if she had not been pregnant. But the fact that there was no birth that he knew of made it easier for Longhorn to get stuck in with the casino and in time marry Okonde.

Longhorn had come to suspect, correctly as it proved, that his sister had an unhealthy interest in him and although Akwase was now lost to him, having married his brother, he distanced himself from his sister as well and soon after married Okonde. Birri tried her best to get close to her brother again, but his bitterness over his lost love severed the relationship with his sister as well. Birri marrying Bigfoot was her last throw of the dice, to make Longhorn jealous, but that had failed too. Longhorn knew of course that Akwase had been pregnant with his child but he never made enquiries as to what happened to that pregnancy. Longhorn simply did not want to know. It was easier for him to concentrate on his marriage to Okonde which produced twin boys.

Fenella Gettevan who somehow had discovered the secret of Longhorn and Akwase and that Lightfoot knew nothing about it, would eventually try her luck to see if what she knew could be translated, through blackmail, into a good bank balance by way of replacement of the abandoned fraudulent income stream. The only drawback was that even if it worked she would still need her husband as attorney to make sure that a written contract could be established, termed in such a way as to not mention true reasons for the sums agreed, but couched nevertheless in legal jargon that would stand up in a court of law if it ever came to that.

Fenella, while absolutely serious about money and quite without scruples about obtaining it no matter how, had no intention of being party to having to fight anything of the kind in a court of law. Heaven forfend. She wanted everything to work as clandestinely as possible, in the hope she would get goodly sums of money for doing very little in return. And if it meant to stoop to a bit of blackmail to obtain that end, but there was nothing to prove how the money was obtained, well there was no harm in that as far as she could see. Also there was now nobody to look over her shoulder. Her daughter was dead and as to her husband, he was trained to find ways to make the illegal legal. That was his job.

*****

Lightfoot and Longhorn were close as brothers and each knew the other's business but the secret of the existence of Shayne was never aired; neither was the fact that Shayne was raised by their middle sister Birri; it was simply accepted that the girl was Birri's child.

Lightfoot worked in that casino as a croupier for a time, but he had found it too stressful. He had found it difficult to take the money from the losers and there were always more losers than there were winners, which was a fact of life. But he found that difficult to handle, especially when he thought of the families of the losers that had would have no food on the table and their kiddies would have to go without. He also had found it hard to reconcile the truism that a loser, instead of going home, would carry on gambling and losing more because his primary thought was always that he would win back what he had lost. Yet, there were a few highrollers that could afford to lose what they had lost, but mostly they were ordinary people who found the losses hard to bear. Lightfoot knew of course that the onus of

62

responsibilty lay with the losers; they alone knew they had family while the money was squandered on bets with no guarantee they would return a win. Though Lightfoot recognised that this was addiction and any loser would not start to rue his foolhardiness until he was outside the casino, making his way home trying to fathom out what his wife would say when he came back penniless.

A moralist might hold that losing is positive because it teaches you to stop, but gambling, being an addiction has no time for that kind of logic. No gambler goes into the casino thinking they might lose. They go there with the firm conviction that they will win ‚a packet' and in their head they had already decided how to spend the win. And when the losses come it does not teach them that this was a lesson to be learnt – far from it. They just think that the loss is a one-off and if they stay long enough their luck will change in their favour again. The thing was that being a Shawnee did not prevent losses because even in their tribe there were addicts that only thought of winning. Indeed Longhorn had one man there who had won over $100,000. Longhorn had told the man to take his winnings and go home. The man had agreed and collected his winnings, got as far as collecting his hat, then as an after-thought he still felt his luck might hold, that he had had a very lucky night and he would tempt fate for one more throw of the dice and so went back to the table. When he had collected his winnings it was midnight when Longhorn told him to go home. When he left it was five in the morning and Longhorn had to pay for a taxi to take the man home. He had lost absolutely everything he had won that night. His luck had not come back.

Lightfoot bowed out. Longhorn was a far more sober man who encouraged a big winner to go home but if he did not and insisted that he was sure his luck would hold, he would let him, then saw it as his sad job to pay for a taxi to take the loser home. While his brother Lightfoot found it difficult to handle that maybe the loser's family's children had to go without, he, Longhorn was pragmatic enough to understand that the players came into his casino of their own free will and if they had an addiction it was up to them to seek help. All Longhorn could do was to recognise that some people had situations they were either willing or not willing to tackle.

*****

The two brothers always conversed together in the Algonquian language. Indeed, the names of Lightfoot and Longhorn were a translation of the Algonquian tongue, a language of the Algic family of languages, descended from Proto-Algonquian, a divergent dialect. For the brothers English was a learned language, while their native tongue Algonquian was what they had been speaking from the day they were able to formulate words.

It was as a young man in his twenties, after the affair with his childhood sweetheart Akwase had come to nothing, that he went in search of some meaning in his life. He had found the casino and thought he might try his luck there. At first and for many years he was employed as a croupier and in that capacity he proved himself to be very talented in the way he managed to distribute the cards and collect the winnings for the proprietors who were also Algonquian speaking Native Americans. They had liked the quiet ways of Longhorn and kept an eye on him to find out how he would develop. Longhorn did not disappoint them. He was scrupulously honest and the casino made money. There were many games that were offered at this casino:

Baccarat (Punto Banco style) and "Mini-Baccarat", where a dealer handles the cards. In both variants the casino banks the game.
Bingo, with a bingo hall able to accommodate up to 5000 players.
Blackjack with 6- or 8-deck shoes.

Craps.

Mah Jongg

Poker (played against the house) including

   Caribbean Stud Poker, Casino war, Crazy 4 poker,
   and Three card poker.

Roulette and lastly:

Slot machines:

   It was not long before the Mafia came calling with various schemes that would make them money, such as skimming the receipts and walking out with suitcases of money which would never be declared. But the proprietors were having none of it. They told those Men in Black and a collectively sour mien that this particular casino was run on an honest basis and saw no reason to change that.

   Various threats were made like a few bricks through windows and when that did not work the casino would be set on fire – that sort of thing. But the proprietors looked blank and said in their quiet voices that they would consult Tecumseh and the prophet Tenskwatawa and whatever he would advise they would follow that. They would need about a week and if the gentlemen would like to call back they would be given the answer. They were polite to a fault in their quiet ways that the Mafia were not used to. They had been used to their wishes being adhered to without murmur, their terror registring in their eyes with total satisfaction, but this lot seemed intimidatingly different in a way they could not understand. Nevertheless they departed with some confidence that they would get another large slice of untaxed cash from that establishement and thought themselves already the receipients of sizeable amounts carried away in unmarked suitcases via the back door.

   Alas, when they came back a week later and were told that the prophet Tenskwatawa said that it was not only inadvisable to give cash for doing nothing but that if that advice was not followed and cash would depart in this fashion, untold miseries and viruses would befall the Mafia families as well. The Mafio honchos might have been murderers and thieves and usurers, but they all followed the catholic faith. All observed of course all the holy days and spent untold sums on funerals on their murdered own. But they were utterly uncomfortable dealing with an unknown tribe that used entirely alien methods to achieve god knows what aim. It was best for once to leave well alone which is what they did; they departed, leaving the casino to carry out its lawful and honest buesiness. As for Lightfoot, once he left the casino he became chief of his tribe and attended the business of looking after the dispossessed in whatever way they were forced to endure the hardships of life.

The casino did have its share of highrollers; people who did have the funds to lose; among them there were very clever people who had a high opinion of their own mathematical skills to try their luck and ingenuity to win large sums of money for themelves. One such skill involved the mathematical know-how to remember numbers and they resorted to a system called *edge sorting*. This method involved the spotting of the tiniest of flaws in gthe printing of the cards, the neutral reverse part of the decks usually printed with hatching. Occasionally, very rarely though, but it did happen that errors occurred in the printing process. The tell tale that a player was edgesorting was when frequently new decks were required and rejected. If that happened a croupier would tell management and one of their staff would stay at a discreet distance observing the player. However, the practice was discontinued when Longhorn had all the reverse of decks that printing companies procuced for the casino left blank using decks of cards that were printed on woodfree, opaque stock. In addition every deck that came into the house was opened up and checked for flaws and discarded. Then the checked decks were repackaged, sealed and stored for use by the players.

The casino ran an honest business and there were times when there were big wins by solitary players. But if the same player won big too many times, they were then asked to take their winnings and then face an exclusion order, the time of which would be based on the size of the wins.

*****

The Shawnee tribe consisted of many people belonging to the same tribe. Some of them were related, others only distantly so. Both Longhorn and Lightfoot had cousins they knew about and some they did not know. But one cousin they did know was a young man who was also a Shawnee He had been a son of a grandparent and he used to come often to the casino, not to gamble but to see Longhorn. Longhorn was around 40 while Lightfoot was two years his junior. The young man was in his late 20s and quite personable. Longhorn had plans for him in the casino but in order to see how he might shape up, engaged him as a croupier. Longhorn was nothing if not cautious. Having seen how it had effected his brother Lightfoot he knew that being a croupier was not to everone's taste. One had to have a certain detachment from real life in order to make a success of working the baize tables. That Shawnee man turned out to be a worthy employee once he was hired and he stayed with the casino until his retirement age.

Longhorn knew what nobody else knew which was that the current proprietors were ailing and indeed a year down the line both were dead. They had nominated Longhorn as the most reliable among their staff and, after consultations with Lightfoot had decided that he would take on the burden of running the casino, which also had a small hotel next to the site. The hotel proved to be a winner as it was nearly always fully occupied, not least by losers and winners who stayed at the hotel in order to carry on the following day – the ones to try to win back the losses, others to try and add to the winning streak.

Longhorn himself was a family man. In his forties he had a wife and two children. While on the reserves many

67

families had numerous children, Longhorn and Okonde had decided that two were sufficient. When his brother Lightfoot married Akwase, Longhorn took stock and realised that it was pointless thinking about what might have been and so decided to forget about it and concentrate on his own family. In this respect there was plenty to do. He now had twin boys, named *Achak*, denoting Spirit and *Kitchi* which meant brave. And quite soon the boys names were abbreviated to *Ash* and *Kit*, names which rolled off the tongue easily. Longhorn wanted to be a good father to his boys and so concentrated on his family. It was a full time job being a dad to the boys while at the same time he had his hands full running the casino.

Ash was the elder of the two and was indeed a lively character, while Kit, the younger one was the more reflective one, but once he had fixed on sometthing and had made up his mind, nothing would deter him from implementing it. The family called him brave, as his name implied.

In summer when the weather was fine Lightfoot, with Akwase and Max in tow would turn up at the casino's hotel where there were always a family room reserved for them. Max loved going there, not least because it was always fun to play with the twins who had new ways of amusing themselves and Max was happy in the tumble of anything the boys got up to. The twins were both a year older than Max but about the same height and at that age age itself meant nothing to the children. They were happy playing together. Then it would be Kit who led the trio into daring games, encouraged by Ash and clapped on by Max who found the twins very engaging in whatever they did. On occasion Max would be asked where he wanted to go on holiday and he invariable said ,to uncle Longhorn's casino'. Gramps Liffet and nana Akki were too fond of the boy to deny him his pleasure and the company of the twins.

Max's early childhood was carefree, not to say idyllic and he could not imagine that ever changing. In the way children, when they become adults look back on their childhood, always remember that the sun always shone, the day was ever so long and the sky had never any clouds, so Max saw the time with gramps Liffet and nana Akki as the most wonderful and he could never imagine that it would ever change.

Chapter 7

Birri

Birri had finagled it so that she was now 'in possession' of her darling brother's girl *Shayne*. She had won and had ended up with the baby. An added bonus was that neither Longhorn nor Lightfoot, her two brothers, knew about 'the secret' and clearly assumed that Shayne was their sister's actual daughter. So from that point of view she was happy. But Birri was despite this victory still not happy because she was in 'a loveless marriage'. She had married *Bigfoot* after an argument with her brother who had not shown her the necessary affection she felt was due to her, by calmly announcing that he was in love with Akwase and intended to marry her. Birri had been incandescent:

"You can't marry her", she had screamed at her brother, tears of anger and frustration welling up.

"But I am going to marry her, as she is carrying my child".

Birri had looked, momentarily dumbfounded at her brother, unable to take in what he was telling her. When the momentous words finally filtered into her brain, she realised she had lost her brother to another woman and not just another woman, but Akwase of all people whom Birri had always thought to be exceptionally plain. And now Longhorn was in love with her. That had not meant to happen. Birri had from infancy adored her older brother and would have done anything for him, including marrying him. But Longhorn did not return those feelings; for him, she was just the older one of his kid sisters, whom he liked, to be sure, but only as a sister, nothing more, certainly not what one would feel for a woman to make love to. Birri had stormed off after her argument with Longhorn and quite soon after had married *Bigfoot Teakwood*, a dark skinned hunk of a man who had been after her for some time.

"One day, my beauty, I shall make you my own" he had said and she consented after the argument with her brother, to show him that she had prospects too, but in truth she had only agreed to marry Bigfoot in the hope that Longhorn might now be jealous. But Longhorn was not jealous; he had been happy that Birri had found love.

Suni was the youngest of the quartet, some ten years younger than Longhorn. Father Rooter had told his youngest daughter early that she had *insight*, a very valuable perception. It was true that Suni could feel things about people long before they actually happened to them but she kept this insight hidden as she had not entirely believed that this was in any way special and not just a quirk of her character.

Bigfoot, as his name implied, had huge feet that were sometimes clad in some type of moccasins, but, since he claimed they gave him blisters he preferred to go barefoot. Over time his feet just got wider, but he did not mind, telling his new wife that they went very well with his size as man. So Birri had married the man, not out of love for him but out of miscalculation. Longhorn, for his part, was pleased for his sister to have found a man worthy of her wanting to marry him. He even came to the nuptials but had left early. Bigfoot was uncouth and a somewhat rough lover, but for all that there was a sweetness about him and Birri felt a certain security when she was with him, though the union remained childless.

Birri had only just got married when Akwase had produced Shayne in secret. Bigfoot wanted children and though, by the time of Shayne's birth, Birri had not become pregnant, he had been optimistic:

"Don't worry my sweet, you will be the mother of six children in no time if I have a say in the matter. But six children or even one remained a dream on the horizon, so the seed grew in Birri that she it was who would raise Shayne. Bigfoot proved no stumbling block. His take on the situation was that there was ample time to produce six children and if she wanted to raise Shayne first, well where was the problem. But in an unguarded moment Suni had let slip to her older sister that she somehow knew that Shayne would be the only child Birri would raise.

Birri had not liked to be told that and had harsh words for her little sister, after which Suni kept her thoughts to herself. She she knew what she knew. She knew for instance that if she could develop her 'powers' fully she needed that sliver of silver, the snake that their dad Rooter had fashioned from the larger picture in the living room. After Rooter had died Longhorn had taken it to give it as a present to Akwase because she was pregnant. Akwase in turn had given it to Lightfoot after she had married him. Lightfoot had found that odd that his new wife had been given the snake as she was not strictly family though she was also Shawnee, but he had accepted the snake and fastened it to his hat.

As far as Suni knew, Rooter had left the little snake to her and to find out that Lightoot had got it on his hat was not what had been promised. Moreover, she found out that Lightfoot had then given the snake to Max to remember him by and now that snake that was meant to come to her had left her family altogether, was in a different country and was not even in a Shawnee family.

Suni was determined to get that snake back. She had mentioned it to Longhorn but he had shrugged and said it was only, after all, a sliver of silver with emerald eyes and an enamelled back, really only a jewel and what was the fuss about? This was very unsatisfactory to Suni who remembered that her father had said that the snake would only keep family members safe from harm and although Lightfoot had told Max stories about his ancestry Max was most definitely not family and also definitely not a Shawnee.

Suni knew what she knew. That snake, that bejewelled sliver of silver was more than what it was carved out of. It was to her after all that Rooter was talking to when he explained why snakes were sacred and how he had cured himself after having been bitten by the deadliest of their number. It was after he had cured himself with those special roots that he had fashioned that snake in miniature from the picture on the wall in the living room. It was Rooter who knew about healing roots that only Shawnee knew existed. Rooter had cured all of his four children at one time of any ailment they might have had over their short lives and the entire reserve respected him greatly for that. So, Suni knew that her father did not just fashion 'that sliver of silver'; he knew what he was doing and he had told his youngest daughter that what ever happened, she was never to lose that snake, for it had certain powers and in the right hands it could do wonders, like it had done for him in time of great need. But, and here he had looked his daughter in the eyes, the snake was a Shawnee thing and would only bring safety to another Shawnee, which is why that snake should never leave the rightful family. Suni would never forget that.

*****

Meantime Birri was preoccupied with closely watching proceedings in the Lightfoot and Akwese house and was quite satisfied that no matter how long they had been married, no issue followed. When Max arrived, to be fostered by her brother and Akwese, she was not unhappy about it, for she knew that the baby was only fostered and there was no prospect of him being adopted by Lightfoot and Akwese. So far she had been proved right. Max had become a cute little boy and Lightfoot had tried hard to make him an Honour Shawnee . She could see that the boy hung on his gramps Liffet's tales and could never get enough of them and Birri thought for once that there could be no harm in that.

73

Birri had made it her business to learn that the Waynes had accepted Max to be fostered; she had made it her business to be near when Fenella arrived with the baby, bundled up to be left with the Waynes. Even though she herself was never introduced to Fenella she could see nothing good in that woman's face, as she was quick to dump the baby then make off again in her huge convertible. 'That woman means business' she thought to herself, and in that she was certainly not wrong.

But Birry had plans and when she had plans she would always go to any length to have them carried out and was quite single minded in that pursuit. It was how she had managed to persuade Akwase that her new-born daughter Shayne would be better in a secure environment. It had been before Akwase had married Lightfoot and so she had to agree that it was better to raise a child in a family setting and so had handed over her daughter into the care of Birry, who would now keep a close eye on that foster boy too.

Chapter 8

Suni's 'Magic Powers'

Suni, the youngest of the four siblings - Longhorn, Lighfoot and Birri - grew up in a house. While the family followed the customs of the Shawnee tribe, they were, after all, American Citizens and these lived in houses. It was true that there were only just over 2,000 of Shawnee members left and these were dotted around North America, but they all knew that in truth their ancesters had been the First Americans who were shunted off their lands to make way for the new white settlers that came from all over the place, but mainly Europe. As there were more of them, they collectively decided that they needed the Natives' space and so the latter were hounded out of what had been their land.

Suni's ancestors were originally farmers from Western Pennsylvania, Virginia and Ohio, who had migrated across northeast and southeast. The homes had been wigwams and birch houses. The tribe was removed from their native land due to the Indian Removal Act of 1830, so its members settled in Kansas in 1831. However they were not to stay there for very long, as thirty years later, 1861 Kansas was to decree that the tribe should be removed yet again and so the Shawnee joined the Cherokee in Oklahoma. In 1980 the tribe sought independence and the act of 2000 established them as a federally recognised tribe.

Because these people lived in the Eastern US and Canada they were considered to be an Eastern Woodland Tribe. But, while they had their own government, police service and also their own laws, its members were still citizens of the United States and so, when it came to it, all had to follow US laws.

As explained, Suni, along with her siblings grew up in a house. So did most of the members of the Shawnee as they had embraced the more comfortable living rather than the cramped ones in a wigwam of previous times, though the latter was still used for special occasions such as weddings and such. While this was the case and that in matters of mores and customs they insisted on having their own, they had been shunted into the modern age, which meant they not only lived in houses but drove cars as well. There were some things they refused to give up like having the same names as their forefares had; hence Suni's older brothers were named Longhorn and Lightfoot, while she and Birri had the names they had.

The house of the *Rooter* family, her family, the Red Sticks, had more or less normal rooms and facilities. But there was one striking difference and that was in the living room. There on the wall, large as life was the picture of a life size snake with green eyes and a green body. It represented the green mamba, the equivalent of the family's coat of arms. It had been handed down by their grandfather. It was only American visitors who came and commented on the unusual picture while the members of their own tribe never commented on it as they knew what the Snake represented. This family revered the mamba, the green mamba to be precise. So it was only ever to the American visitors to whom Suni explained that it was their mascot because their father, *Rooter* had been bitten by a green mamba but had lived because he knew the secret antidote, found in roots (hence his name), had applied some immediately and it had worked. He had lived to a grand old age of eighty-five. Revering a snake was of course as old as time itself.

Suni had inherited from her ancestors some of their traits. While still small, the little girl would sit on the porch with her father Rooter who talked about his life. He held that practically everything a human being needed to stay alive could be found in the forest under trees and shrubs, if one knew where to look. He also told Suni that it was important that she knew the history of the Shawnee because, although governments had now recognised that the tribe peoples had rights. But he also knew that the hidden agenda was to get them all integrated into American Society, the first step to becoming indistinguishable from the settlers. Indeed, in the early 20th century the American Government had insisted that all the children of every description had to go to school and, even more drastic, the Native Americans were singled out and forced to go to boarding schools where they never saw their parents again. So, he told Suni, nothing could be taken for granted as far as governernments of every stripe were concerns and she would do well to learn its history.

As for snakes – all snakes - were sacred and protected and should never be killed. She would do well to respect them as they only rounded on humans if they felt threatended but otherwise kept themselves to themselves. It would not do to kill them and people who did had bad things happen to them in their lives.Suni's father had realised that talking to his daughter was good as he recognised that she was not like his other children, that she had inherited his special trait of far-sightedness which was unusual in one so young. The two of them had many conversations on that porch about life in general and their tribe in particular.

Rooter told her to be wary of any American Government; whoever was in charge, none was to be trusted. While various treaties had been made that guaranteed the tribes rights and freedoms they were always quite short lived. Rooter was convinced that what all governments wanted was indeed integration. And there would eventually be a tribe known only in the history books. In real life there would be no such tribe as the Shawnee or any other tribe, including the First American People. They would all be integrated into the American Society and one could only read about what was in history books after they were re-written and the bad bits about governments shown in a bad light, taken out. Suni was listening hard. Rooter who had an interest in America's history now imparted a litte of what he knew to his daughter:

"To be fair to history, the beginning was not like that at all. The first Pilgrims had come over to England with the ship, The Mayflower, which had reached New England (they called it Plymouth) in a parlous state. The ship took 65 days to cross the Atlantic and the conditions on that ship were simply awful. A lot died of scurvy, dysentery and much else besides and some of the babies, born to women on the ship, were stillborn. When the ship landed and the pilgrims got off the ship, being still Europeans, they found nothing but barren land, so they started building huts so they had somewhere to live. Some huts were for families, other huts were for a small community to convene.

One morning though an Indian man in full native regalia, but otherwise only clad in a loincloth ambled up and exhorted the strangers to form a kind of alliance tht promised to refrain from attacks of each other's peoples. In truth both sides needed each other as the Indians had lost most of their people to some kind of plague.

The Indian man had departed but returned with some sixty men the following week and the alliance was put on a solid footing. But it did not last. Harvests failed and all grew despondent. What rescued the situation for a short while was that France had been at war with England and as a result of that the beaver trade was decimated. That presented a golden opportunity for the new settler who managed to send across an abundance of beaver fur. I am afraid, Suni, the rest of this history I have forgotten but I can say that the beginning had been hopeful for everyone. But with the successful beaver trade came a lot more Pilgrims who scented big profits to be made in the New World and the population of the settlers began to grow and slowly, without anyone much caring, they took over the land and the indigenous population, the Native Indians were allocated less and less land".

Suni had listened to her father's explanation. She had had no idea how badly her ancestors had been treated and she would remember that.

Suni learnt a lot that afternoon, sitting on that porch with her father. She also knew other things as well - stuff that Rooter had not told her because he did not know – but Suni knew that it had been Longhorn who had wanted to marry Akwase and that Birri had raised such a din over her brother's intentions that it was Lightfoot who married her. Of the baby girl that Akwase carried and Birri now raised, nothing was said and Akwase never told Longhorn, the father of her child that she had had given birth to a girl she had named Shayne. Suni felt it had not been her place to mention it to Lightfoot. And so the secret stayed and Birri raised Shayne as her daughter. But Suni knew what she knew and what she knew was that that little sliver of silver, that little bejewelled silver snake was meant to have come to her but was now in a different country, owned by no Shwnee but an ordinary boy, simply because Lightfoot had given it to him because he wanted the boy to remember him.

She herself had not realised that she was anything special until she was about ten years old, after Rooter had told her, but when she did know she could see what others could not, was rather frightened by it. She went to see the tribes' *shaman* who explained to her that such her specialness was a rarity and needed to be nurtured and that there was nothing to be frightened about it. She should embrace it but never use that power in a negative way.

*****

Suni of course had witnessed the rows with Birri over Akwase, that Longhorn had wanted to marry her and Suni

79

had realised at once that Birri had actually been in love with Longhorn and had been jealous that her brother could fall in love with another girl. In an unguarded moment Suni had tried to reason with Birri that it was unhealthy for her to love her own brother, but Birri had been angry and with her for mentioning it and so Suni had shut up, keeping her thoughts to herself. She was unhappy because it had actually been Longhorn who had parted with the silver snake in the first place and it had been wrong for him to give it away.

Suni never married. It was not that she was short on suitors, far from it. She was a good looking girl with raven black hair she wore in a braid down the back and many a man might have been proud to have her as his bride. But Suni did not want to know; she had a way of looking at the suitors with her slanted black eyes that somehow made it plain that she was not interested. Eventually they had got the message and stopped coming round. This suited Suni fine. People of her acquaintance credited her with magic powers but that was because they did not know better and some people in the tribe still believed in the *shaman* who had the ability to heal, avert disasters and keep bad spirits away. But Suni was no shaman and her powers did not so much lay in magic but in the fact that she was far sighted with instincts that seem to tell her unfailingly when matters around her went critical or when it was right to tell someone a truth. And in this sense, she had formed a close bond with Shayne, the daughter that now grew up with Birri and Bigfoot.

*****

Birri as a mother left a lot to be desired. She saw no reason to enlighten Shayne of her true provenance and so Shayne grew up thinking that Birri was her birth mother. As she grew her mother got less and less tolerant and while her father, Bigfoot was quite lenient, she did not form a very close bond with with either parent. When things got really out of hand, she would flee to Suni who was warm and

80

friendly and there she found sanctuary. Quietly Suni promoted that. It was when Shayne was in her late teenage years that, after a particulary hefty row with both parents, Shayne came to Suni in tears. So it was Suni who enlightened Shayne about her true parentage and Shayne was shocked, not so much because this had been an undivulged secret, but Suni also intimated, though did not spell it out, that her sister had had an unhealthy interest in their eldest brother and relations had to this day been frosty. While Suni did not exactly put it in those terms Shayne understood quite well what Suni intimated. The latter, in her far-sightedness, advised Shayne to avoid telling her mother that she knew. 'the time to do that would come but it is not there yet' she advised and Shayne saw in her eyes the seriousness of what she was saying and decided to follow that advice.

Suni's motive at that point was to get that sliver of silver, the snake that her father had fashioned, back into her family and to her in particular. In Shawnee tradition she was convinced that the absence of that snake brought ill luck and for that reason alone, if nothing else she had not been at all happy when she knew that her brother, Lightfoot had given it as a memento to remember him by, to little Max, who was not even family, but a foster child.

Now the silver snake was in England. That it would be treasured of that she had not doubt because Max had loved his gramps and his nana. All the same, the snake was now out of reach and she meant to use all of her powers, such as they werc, to get it back. She and Shayne were close and in a way she had replaced the mother she should have had in Birri, but Birri had her own motives and motherhodd did not really bring her the pleasure she thoought would come with it. Plus the fact that she could not conceive and Shayne remained the only daughter, adopted or otherwise. So Suni became Shayne's confidante and the two of them could be seen often at the kitchen table in conversation with each other.

*****

When Shayne got to nineteen, one afternoon she and Suni were sitting opposite each other at the kitchen table in Suni's house, an earthenware jug of squash between them, the drink made from the squash flower that grew in Suni's garden. When she was a child her father had made strong drinks from seeds and roots both from wild plants and those grown around the house. The resultant drink was very potent as it was made from fermented corn, agave and manioc, a wooden shrub.

Rooter let her have a small drink once one of his concoctions was ready and even a small sip had made her dizzy. She did not believe in such stuff because alcohol generally was only consumed for spiritual experiences rather than drinking the stuff to get drunk. Drink in her family was a quest for enlightenment, powers of healing, connecting with the spirit world and war making. It was the same with magic mushrooms that Suni knew her father used sometimes to calm him down when life got on top of him. Rootes saw this as his secret but Suni knew but told no-one except one afternoon when she divulged it to her niece, Shayne. It was Suni too who had enlightened Shayne about Rooter's partaking of the *magic mushroom* and while her niece knew about them, she said she would never try it out because she had seen her grandfather having a hangover the following day and it had frightened her.

Suni's favourite drink was non alcoholic, a concoction made from the squash flower and that was now in a large jug sitting on the kitchen table while the two women talked. Shayne always liked to listen to Suni's tales of her and her siblings childhoods and how they played with each other silly games in which she more often than not come out the winner. The boys would then stomp off saying that it was entirely unfair how their youngest sister always won and they were convinced she had used magic powers to deprive them of any wins. That was how she acquired the sobriquet 'Magic

Suni' to which she always protested that no magic was involved in winning a game, only cleverness and strategy.

Shayne loved to hear her tales of derring-do when they were children. Presently Suni was holding forth about her general view of human life and Shayne sat there, sipping her drink and listening to the older woman expounding on human life:

„It is only comparatively recently that America has acknowledge its collective guilt in the way the First Native American had been treated over the centuries and it is only now that school children learn about how White Man, en masse, has displaced the indigenous population to make *Lebensraum* for itself. It is pointless going into detail about that because in every school book the full horror story can be read about. It is a pity though, because White Man could learn a lot about our ways of life. Indeed, the medical profession has only now woken up to the fact that we have remedies for ailments and cures for humans that the medical establishement has for years refused to acknowledge, but has suddenly found that our ways of curing people from quite deadly conditions is more than useful. It has scrabbled for some time now in the undergrowth for plants and roots in which to effect a cure for this and that.

This brings me to mention our father, Rooter, who cured himself after being bitten by a green mamba. He had known exactly which root would prevent his dying and in no way had be put blame on the hapless creature that had bitten him, because the snake had only been using its natural defence mechanism, which was to bite when agitated and thinking itself in danger of attack. Rooter had let the snake slither away but still thought that it was the divine will of our prophet Tecumseh that allowed our father to live.

My father then took himself to bed with a good dose of his secret, *the magic mushroom* which he did not know I knew. He took it when he felt agitated about something. It must have worked, for when he came round he said he had

had a dream. He said nothing more but went about to fashion an exact replica of the snake which was in the living room, but in miniature. My father had very artistic tendencies, for it was a work of art, that little snake, an exact miniature copy of what has been hanging on the family living room wall for many years, and that snake has been our mascot.

That little jewel he made should never have left the family and it was wrong for our brother Lightfoot to have given it away to Max, their foster child, for no other reason than he wanted the boy to remember him. There would have been many other ways for Max to remember his foster carer. I have been thinking a lot about that snake and the more I think about it the more I am convinced that it has to come back to this family again. Of course it had been Longhorn who had given it to Akwase first, simply because she pregnant with the child that was you.

You, Shayne are now a young woman of nearly twenty and I am electing you to get that snake back on American soil and into our family again. As a tribe we have lost so much over the centuries; this is one little thing in which we should triumph, don't you think? Having said that it will be by no means easy for you to bring it back and I can see all kinds of trouble over it, but, even so, that silver of silver needs to come back, it has been decreed so."

All the time Suni had been talking over the kitchen table, Shayne had pretended to draw imaginary pictures with the long spooon onto the kitchen table. That spoon was used to stir the concoction in her glass but this did not stop her from listening attentively. Occasionally she let out a sigh, but carried on doodling and listening. At length she dropped the spoon back into her glass and looed at Suni:

„I understand what you are telling me and what is more I agree totally, but am nevertheless at a loss to fathom how I could get that snake back. I mean, Max is now in England and has been for many years and we are here in America and there is a lot of water between the two countries; how do you think I could get that snake back. I can't wave a magic wand to do that, so how do you think I should tackle this?"

Suni again: „ Quite simply, you will have to go there. I will ask our sister in law, Akwase who has the address where Max was taken and we shall write a letter to ask them if it were possible to reconnect with Max in England. Hopefully they will say yes, issue an invitation and you will go there on account of having a little holiday. The rest will be up to you as to how you use your ingenuity to prise that little jewel out of Max then beat a seemly retreat. It will not be simple, I can guarantee that, but you do have to try."

*****

The afternoon wore on and Shayne rose to leave. Between them they had emptied the large jug of squash flower cordial. Shayne had to be back to help her mother prepare the nightly supper and Suni knew in the way that she knew her sister, that there could in the foreseeable future be no variation in this. Her sister was lazy but professed to be far to busy to handle dinner on her own and since Shayne had grown into a handsome young women she saw no reason why her daughter could not help with the tedious preparation for supper. Even though the nightly meal was a simple thing to prepare, Birri wanted her daughter's handiwork in the preparation of it for no other reason that she thought to ease her workload. Besides, what else had a young girl to do but help her mother in that chore. ‚Bigfoot wanted his daughter present at the meal and Birri reasoned that as this was the case, their daughter could help prepare it.

Shayne had not committed to anything. She rose to leave Suni's house, but the latter, in the way that she knew what she said about the snake had hit home, smiled her enigmatic smile as her hand went over her niece's pitch black tresses to swat a strand of her out of her face then planted a kiss on top of her had as Shayne went out of the door. Suni

85

watched her leave but resolved to go over to her brother's house with a view to start the ball rolling. She would find out the whereabouts of Max's home in England. Even though nothing had been resolved between the older and the younger woman, Suni knew in the way she just knew things, that Shayne would go to England in not too long a time and she wanted to be ready with the address, so a letter could be fashioned that would guarantee an invitation. That such an invitation would be granted Suni knew for certain that this would be the case and knowing that, she watched ner niece walk down the garden path, while she softly closed the door, with a smile on her face. The afternoon had been very fruitful indeed, that she knew. For the rest she hoped fervently that Shayne would be able to bring the snake back, but of that she was less certain, but one had to try in life.

Chapter 9

The Notters

Myra and Happy having gone separately to the Great Void, there remained five members who still called themselves *Notters*. While the play over at the Pumphouse Theatre, *The Beggars Opera* had, after a run of nearly 8 years, finally closed, the Notters, who all had had active parts but had come to terms with the fact that their destiny was the scrap heap, found to their absolute delight, that that scrap heap had thrown out new shoots and they were very green.

It was through that play that the Notters had been catapulted into society again, which none of them had thought would accept them again. Previously they had convened in the backroom of Maisie's Den, then run by the eponymous owner of the vegetarian cafe, Maisie Carrington, who had helped all of them, in no small measure, with encouragement and free breakfasts in the back room. It was not because the breakfasts there were free, that as well as none had money anyhow, but Maisie herself had believed in them and never stinted with assertions that life would work out somehow, that the main thing was not to lose heart, that their mishaps, grave though they were, were simply temporary.

And now, Maisie of course had fallen in love with the quiet, brainy Voltie, who had once again become Louis Parnell and they were now living together on the top floor of the cafe's building. Stephanie had moved out; she and Maisie had occupied the second floor of the building, but Stephanie had moved to Marcus Easterwood's the erstwhile Woody's abode, 66 Bertram Close, Vauxhall. On the land Registry the new owners of that house was listed as *Rhinestone Distributions.*

Maisie had thought that perhaps Voltie (she still called him that on occasion) might want to live elsewhere, but Louis only wanted to be where Maisie was. And so Maisie had the top floor of the building redecorated and turned into a quasi penthouse flat for herself Louis.

Through sheer luck she had managed to see an advertisement for a post in IT for a large Company that wanted to update its mainframe computer system. The ad had said, only people dedicated to success need apply. Louis had been dubious, but Maisie had encouraged him and so he had applied and got the job much to his surprise. There were new people running the cafe now and Maisie did not want to interfere.

Moneywise she was comfortable getting a good whack from the takings and so she had time to preside over the remaining Notters meetings at the new place, in the backroom of Grant's pub. The reason of the shift from Maisie's Den to Grant's pub was one of space. Since Maisie had given over the running of her cafe to the two men these had requisitioned the backroom where the Notters had convened and altered it so more of the cafe's clientele could eat there.

The cafe was doing wonderfully well and and the Notters had to find another place to meet and they found that in the Pumphouse pub, downstairs from the little theatre, the stage of which was now dark since the Beggar's Opera had closed.

There was of course still the quiet Schubert, *Shuby,* who played the piano downstairs again in the pub since upstairs there were currently no plays but of late he had become, it seemed to the Notters, more lively and they had wondered why that should be. Bert reckoned - he was always first with any news - that Shuby had found love, he was almost certain of that. The rest of the Notters had been doubtful because they knew of his sad previous life and how his marriage had come to an end, but, on reflection they had to admit that maybe there was something of what Bert had said – they thought they would pay closer attention. Presently the Notters were all assembled, Shuby too who for once did not sit at the piano but had taken a chair and sat at the table.

The Notters now met only once a month, on the first of each month in the backroom of the Pumphouse pub, courtesy of Grant Walker who was more than amenable to have them there.

Grant Walker was still running the pub but there had been some changes of the girls that served behind the bar. Dezzie had left Grant's employ and so had Tara. Bert had wooed the lively Tara and the two of them got quietly married. Grant was in on the secret and gave her a wonderful wedding present of a crystal chandelier, which even Bert with his background found it just wonderful to look at. They had now been married for two years and last year a baby girl was born to the couple at 3 Millpond Close. They named their tiny daughter Aurora. She would be called Laurie. Later, growing up she was to complain about why she was given at birth the name Aurora, then get called Laurie; why not Laurie, or Laura to begin with. Alas, this complaint had not come about yet, as the cute little baby was lying in its crib oblivious of the name she had been given.

Two new girls were now serving drinks to a lively clientele, an Irish girl in her thirties, called Deirdre and a Scottish lass from the Borders, called Eilidh who hated the name because at school her peers called her *eyelid*, so she called herself Ellie. Deirdre too, while she did not mind the name, customers could not remember it and so just called her Dee. So the new girls behind the bar were Dee and Ellie.

After Dezzie and Tara had left, Grants daughters, Millie and Unity, now also grown into young women, lobbied their father to allow them to serve drinks behind the bar at least at weekends, but as before Grant had said no. He just did not want his girls there even though they were now grown up. For the theatre upstairs new troupes for one play or another had come and gone and none had been as successful as the Beggars Opera. With a twinkle in the eye Bugs used to say that it was only because the Notters had been such outstanding actors that their play had lasted so long. Bugs was still his old self, but these days he could be found in company with Jock whom he dragged to the monthly meeting of the Notters, telling him that they were a good bunch and worth getting to know. He would be drafted to become another Notter.

*****

Grant had had time for the people whom Fate had thrown onto the scrap heap. Little by litte, over the eight years that the play had been running they were telling him their stories and he had felt that society had been very unfair in the way they had all been discarded.

Myra and Happy had met a sad end and Maisie herself had taken up with Louis, who no longer used the sobriquet ,Voltaire, or Voltie, though the Notters found it hard to get used to his proper name.

So, the Notters usually met on the first day of each month in the backroom in the pub downstairs and none ever missed the date. Grant bemoaned the fact that the little theatre upstairs was rather unoccupied and he hoped that one day another successful play could be staged up there. He missed the old days of the Notters turning up to play their parts.

Presently they were all concerned that the theatre upstairs had been unused for a good while now. There had only been two unsuccessful performances by roving troupes. One had lasted a week and the other nearly two weeks. With poor attendance their actors could not make enough even to get by and so, called it a day. Now the theatre was dark and empty. All the Notters could not help but creep sometimes furtively upstairs when they met on their day, then shake their heads and come downstairs again, saying something should be done to light up the stage again with something people would come to see. All of them were of the opinion that if one such play could be found, it would definitely again have to be Bert to stage the whole thing. That *The Beggars Opera* had been the success it was, all had agreed, in no small measure had been down to Bert and his natural bent to stage the play that enjoyed such a stupendous run.

Presently the Notters were seated at a long table discussing the matter when Bert breezed through the door in a somewhat excited state.

„Friends", he shouted; „friends, I think I have found a play that would do for us and which would, if handled properly, give us a fairly good run. Louis looked at Bert. Marcus who had come with Steph wondered briefly if Bert had *Burlington Bertie* adapted for the stage, but something told him that it would be a far better play that his erstwhile partner had fathomed out.

Bert had become a respected actor in his own right and his *Burlington Bertie* Routine had long been consigned to history. These days he had a more or less permanent slot at one of the West End Theaters and, financially, did very well with nightly performances and the odd matinee. He still liked being member of the Notters though and now he flung himself onto a chair and, without further ado opened his brief case and took out some typewritten sheets, staples together to make 10 complete copies of the same thing.

„The name of the play", he stated, „is called

Hobson's Choice". Bert looked at all the faces. Some had heard of the play others had never heard of it. The play was by one Harold Brighouse, a nineteen century author who, along with two others had formed the Manchester School of Dramatists. In 1954 it had been made into a film, directed by David Lean and was shown in black and white. Bert now said it would be an ideal play for the stage.

Moreover it would provide an opportunity for ‚those of us‘ who had, while playing the *Beggar* caught the acting bug and wanted to do more of the same. However it was nothing like that play as the main protagonists consisted only of half a dozen players plus a few minor roles for people who would would get a look in now and again.

When it was made into a film Charles Laughton was cast as the tyrannical Dad of three daughters. Laughton plays a semi alcohol-dependent father who motions to his doctor after a severe dose of the D.Ts that, when asked about his wife, his finger points upwards, obviously denoting that she is dead and possibly in heaven. Brenda de Banzie as Maggie, plays the daughter who her father insists is on the shelf at thirty. The real reason is that he needs her in the shop while he imbibes at the Moonraker pub nearby. Maggie's two younger sisters have suitors whom they want to marry. The miserly father refuses on the grounds that it would cost him too much money for dowries. The gist of the play is an aristocratic woman who comes into the shop to demand the name of the person who made the boots she has bought from this very shop, whereupon it turns out that it is Mossop, played by John Mills, to is toiling away for peanuts in the basement of the shop, in questionable light..

The aristocratic lady hands Mossop her card with instructions that he is to tell her immediately if he were to have other employment elsewhere. Laughton as father who is present too says in a peremptory manner that there is no fear of that, that Mossop the boothand would never leave his shop, whereupon the aristocratic lady says „Why ever not? That man is a treasure".

Maggie Hobson, the ‚on-the shelf'eldest daughter, then decides she will marry Willy Mossop, teach him to read and write and together they are going open up a rival boot shop. The play has a twist in that Father (Laughton) has ended up drunk in the basement of the miller who comes to Maggie for advice. Maggie has the idea that he should sue her father, but instead of money changing hands, it would be settled for the amount his single daughters want for the dowries in order to marry.

At the end of the play father ungraciously pays the girls' dowries to keep his name out of the papers and Maggie and Willie come back into the shop that changed its name to Mossop and Hobson. Willy Mossop, under the tutelage of his new wife is a changed man, since he has learned to read and write and he shows a rare talent for management. The shop, it is intimated, is to be a success under the management of Maggie and Willy Mossop.

*****

This then was the play that Bert handed out in a sheaf of typewritten pages – one sheaf for each of the gathered Notters. Voltie was the first to scan and comprehend what the play was all about and he liked it. He was happy to play the ‚dipso' dad of the three girls. He suggested that Maggie should be played by Deirdre or Ellie. While neither of them were Notters, the play needed three girls.

Grant was given a typewritten version of the play and he, without looking at it said that he would certainly favour the theatre upstairs being operable again. He would do his part of making it a success. He also felt happy that Bert would take over the direction. Grant too had felt that if the previous lot of actors had had Bert as their director the plays that had come and gone would have been more of a success with him there.

The one Notter that had not yet turned up for the present gathering was Bugs, though those present did not have long to wait for the door flew open and Bugs came through the doors of the pub with Jock in tow. He still preferred to be addressed as Bugs rather than his real name, Arthur Thompson. He disliked his real name because it was – to him – far too burgeois. Bugs was still the only Notter who had refused to give up his pavement-way of life. He said he

93

saw no reason to change, just because he now had a few more pennies in his pockets owing to the success of *The Beggars Opera.* Besides, for some time now he had his new friend Jock and he liked him enormously because he was of the same stripe and they could see eye to eye and were much of the same mind in everything. And both had decided separately that society was not for them, that they preferred to stay true to their own beliefs

In moments like that Bugs would sneer and say, „There you have it. Fate throws a few spanners into Life's Works and everybody is depressed and thinks the world has ended; then come opportunities and they are grabbed quicker than you can say ‚how do you do‘, and you see them jumping up society's ladder in double quick time“.

When Bugs and Jock had come through the door, Dee from behind the bar had given a low whistle and could not help a jibe:

„My, Bugs you do look crisp today. New shirt, new jacket and swish belt. I fear YOU have gone ‚society‘ in spite of your claims to the contrary and have done your shopping in one of the *bourgeois* malls you so despise?“ Bugs looked at her and winked:

"I take it as a compliment about my neat appearance, but would like to state that just because Jock and I are residents of cardboard city, does not mean we have to look smelly and neglect ourselves in the hygiene department. Where we get our crisp stuff from shall remain a secret. As for neatness I have you know that both Jock and I are regulars at the baths over our way, regular customers, which means we frequent that establishments once a week. In fact the supervisor there has become a very dear friend, Paula, her name is, and we are treated in the most civilised manner, receive a rubdown after every bath and then she let us lounge in one of the deckchairs and brings us a cup of tea if you please. Imagine the luxury – we revel in it. It has the nostalgia of Maisie's backroom then. But the upshot of all that is that we are clean and sweet-smelling at all times. However, I have to explain why we were late. Jock and I were on a mercy mission. We had been to the baths this morning and were pampered with the usual treatment plus being given the customary cup of tea when one of the girls let out a shriek and came rushing in, having discovered a cockroach. She was so fearful about these charming insects that she felt she had to quit there and then because obviously the cockroach meant that the establishment had unhygienic facilities and she could not possibly work under such conditions. So we had to go and free her of it while at the same time giving the girl a lecture about cockroaches.

Everybody has the wrong impression about cockroaches. I know New York, a place I have never been to, is apparently overrun with them, even the swishest of hotels and New Yorkers have learnt to live with them. To exterminate them all is futile as there are gazillions of them. However, I have never understood why there is such a frenzy and disgust about these insects. Not only are they harmless but they are magnificent creatures if only one took time to understand them a little.

The cockroack, much maligned, is an amazing animal, it can survive under water for 30 minutes and endure freezing temperatures. In addition, since it can resist radiation numerous times better than humans, I would say that if there is a nuclear war, the cockroach will rule the planet. The species is 350 million years old, while humans have only walked the earth for some twohundredthousand years. I would advise that the next time you lot see a cockrach in the kitchen you treat it with some respect, because it might just have something to teach you. It behaves according to an elegant algorithm: it moves in the opposite direction of gusts of wind that might signal an approaching predator and I say that this is surely a very good strategy for survival.

Voltie, now Louis Parnell, was not having Bug's earlier assertion about grabbing double quick society's largesses and felt that some assertions of his own were in order:

„We *were* the dregs of society, Bugs" said Louis, „thrown unwillingly unto the heap that is nomansland and, sure, we all thought that life as we had known it was finished and one had better get used to it. And we did, somehow, and it wasn't because we were thrown so far down, but it was mostly beause of the unfairness of it all. We had worked hard for what we had and to be discarded in this fashion was hard to bear".

Bugs remonstrated with him: „So you see, that is exactly my point; you did not stay down out of *conviction* but because Fate had dealt you a bad hand. But now, that same Fate has dealt you a better hand you have discovered your self-worth and what did you do? You were unseemly quick to you exchange the Pavement for the cosy house that promised a cleaner way of living; everything society offered: hot water, central heating and all that etc. etc. I will not say that I am a better specimen of humanity, but I will say that I am more honest. I could live in a house if I wanted to but I have no urge to do so. However, friendship is very important to me and I am still very happy that all of you are still my friends, even though you have gone ‚too society' for me. Fortunately I also still have Jock and we sit at the same pitch outside the New Covert Garden und share out what we have. And when Jock has had a bad day, I give him money because I have it now".

Dee, however could not leave it at that but had to fling at Bugs another missile:

„But surely Bugs, there is an anomaly here. You and Jock are using facilities which are a burgeois construct. Animals need no baths and what they deposit in the prairie or the serengeti serves as fertiliser to grow new grass and trees and animals even use for themselves what bigger animals have deposited, looking for nutrients that benefit them. But you are using facilities paid for with the kind of taxes you despise, yet use those facilities for your own benefit. What do you say to that?"

Bugs looked at Dee and fiddled with his shirt buttons, then said:

"I cannot deny that you have point here. Still, you have to remember that we are forced to live in that social construct, *society*, and it was only less than a couple of hundred years ago that sewers were installed in the cities because waste from people had to go somewhere and an earlier way was to flush raw sewage into the rivers where it killed all the fish, not to mention the stink of it which made people who had to inhale the air, sick too.

After the sewers were installed, the fish recovered and the air on the rivers improved. Where people live in close proximity to each other the state has to do something. As to public baths, its facilities Jock and I use with some frequency, fall into the same category. You are wrong about animals not needing batths, they do too, but use rivers and lakes. As for spreading what they have eaten, the praire and the serengeti consist of wide spaces that can accommodate millions of animals. In addition you have to remembere that animals thrive on smells. and a male of some species that does not live in a herd can smell a female ready to mate from miles away, while we have lost that capacity when mating in what we call a civilised environment.

Also this society frowns on bad smells, which is why Jock and I keep ourselves clean in a manner acceptable to such a society. Our societies, by the way, have neither a prairie nor a serengeti but have to make do with relatively small cramped spaces where people practically live on top of each other. You are right though, that, like it or not, we are somehow still members of this society but Jock and I keep its use acceptable to us. In addition we could not use the streets as toilet and so are forced to keep clean in a manner that does not offend the people we live amongst. So we try to be as unobtrusive as possible without losing our dignity."

Jock who had not said anything up to this point and had sat quietly on his chair backwards, so that the back of the chair was in front of him. Presently Bugs was nudging him that all the Notters wanted to hear what he had to say about society at large. Jock, fiddling with the back rest said that his philosophy of life was simple but puzzling all the same and to this day he could not figure out why the human species is the way it is. He rose from his chair:

„Bearing in mind that tortoises can live up to one hundred and more years and snakes over their life times have several skins they can shed when it suits them or when they feel they have outgrown the one they had, lizards can lose their tails and regrow them while chamelions can change colour, not to mention fish who can glow in the water, nature is a marvel to be sure, yet a human, apart from his brain is stuck in a rut and only has, if lucky, eighty to a hundred years, and if unlucky a lot less than that.

But as to life itself I have since my twenties never had any cause to think differently to how I think now. My philosopohy is that most men and women in our society are active from the ages of twenty to seventy, a span of some fifty years. But every twenty years there is a new generation of people that are maturing while their parents grow older. These young people may follow in the footsteps of their fathers, or they may rebel against their own upbringing and want to do things differently, even it it means doing it the hard way and learning from their own mistakes. Personallay I salute the latter because in the end you have a better class of human if he himself has gone through the mill.

In Victorian Times society remained static during the queen's reign, basically because people were all cast in the same mould, plus the technology was not there. Even so, I think the human race has been short changed in Life's Stakes. Think about it: a baby has only the *potential* of making something of itself; there is no guarantee as he depends largely on the milieu into which it is born.

For the first ten years an infant comes under parental scrutiny, is taught right from wrong and fashioned, as it were, into a ‚useful‘ human that would fit into the mores of the society of the day. After the age of ten, girl or boy begins to notice that there is a world outside the cocoon but, if the parents have other ideas, boy/girl will be harnessed into learning something that society of the day calls ‚useful‘ – that of earning a crust in later life, paying taxes and making sure both sexes too are in a position to pay their dues. But, that *society* that fashions the human into a ‚useful‘ citizen is an *artificial* construct and as such it needs people to do its bidding. It does not like outsiders or the very members of its club to think differently. It exhorts parents to raise children to fit into its mould; become members of its club that follow a precisely laid down order. And that order has changed very little over the millenia: a bit of tweaking here and there as to what is acceptable, but nothing major that I can perceive.

True, society no longer hangs unfortunates caught with stealing a loaf of bread, but that does not mean it has become a fairer society. The unfortunates on the breadline who have to steal to put food onto their table are indeed still with us and will always be. Members, the monetaried class of this society are basically only concerned with earning good money for themselves and the unskilled lot who help them make their money earn only what owners of large factories can get away with paying them. It means that poverty will never go away. People are lulled into a fals sense of security because they fondly believe that now the Welfare State is extant poverty has disappeared. It hasn't. It is still alive and well and surviving whatever we do to try to eradicate it.

What has happened is that some recipients of this largesse have managed to find ways of milking it successfully while the less brash make do with what they are given, which is paltry considering how some members can live more than comfortably off the public purse.

In many ways the Welfare State has been a curse. It was established by well-meaning people who thought that helping the poor would eradicate poverty, but it hasn't; all it has done is making quite a few people realise that working is an *option* which they can take up or leave. What makes people want to work is pride in their achievement: taking responsibility for their lives and the families they have created while there are some that think that if the State throws money at them they would be fools to reject that.

It is the same with hospitals. The NHS is free at the point of delivery and Aneurin Bevan fondly believed that because poor people could not be persuaded to go to a doctor when they were unwell, would rather than die quietly. So he thought that within his lifetime the free hospitals would be self sufficient, meaning the sick could now see a doctor and get treated free of charge, and everything would be tickety-boo.

He never factored in the human element which is that when something is free, people of all stripes will demand it as their *right,* to have for free operations of every sort, cosmetic ones too. The NHS will always be overstretched as there will always be new technologies being invented that enhance life but are not necessary to stay alive. Facelifts, breast reductions and increases come to mind. But all these are now expected to be had for free because they are available, so people demand them. The thinking is why should they pay for something that can be had for free.

As to society: what is curious though is that it has successfully persuaded all and sundry that it is desirous to belong to it, even striving hard to be accepted into this artifice and its members trying hard not to fall out of its rigidly laid down frame. Success is deemed to be called that, when sons and daughters grow up in that mould, have jobs that pay a wage so they can pay society's dues.

Like Bugs, I have decided to exclude myself because I recognised it for what it is: a rigidly laid down form. I recognise too that for me, that society is very picky; it does not like individuals like Bugs and myself – we are square pegs in round holes and we are frowned upon, because we are ex-members who have decided to go their separate ways because that life suits us better. Bugs and I come across every day people whose faces narrow and as they walk past our pitch and some even advise we should stop what we are doing and get a job instead. We smile and carry on and tell them ‚such is life‘.

Dee remonstrated with him over the paltry payments of the workers:

„The thing is, Jock, I am all for workers getting paid the proper rate and I know in many cases they are not, although there are notable exceptions, but I think one has to consider that, yes, the factory owner is for profit, but on the other hand, the worker goes home after his shift without much caring whether the boss has made any profit that day. He is only concerned that his job is still there in the morning. The boss however has to hunch over his books to see if he has made enough to pay his workers when their payment day is due. For him is is a twenty-four hour job. It never leaves him and while for some people profit is a dirty word - some even refuse to work because they say they are being exploited - without any profit the factory would not exist and neither would the jobs. The profits pay for the outgoings, the overheads, and that includes the paypackets of the workers. Ellie and I get paid well enough by our boss Grant, but even so, we rely on the extra tips the customers give us for serving them promptly. Incidentally we share the tips we get.

Speaking from experience, my father was a printer and ran his own printing outfit. It was small but he employed five workers. The outfit did small run stuff with two printing machines, Heidelbergs I believe they were, and the maximum run he would take on was a run of around five thousand. My father paid his workers the going rate and while they were loyal to him and liked the work. Although the rooms they worked in were cramped, they went home to their families in the happy position to know that the job was still there for them in the morning. Moreover they had pride in their work. Other than that they had no cares but to spend their free time with their families. My father, however, every night after supper would retire to a small room he called his office, hunched over order books, constantly concerned that the book of orders was full enough to guarantee he could meet the outgoings of which a large amount were the wages for his workers. He came last in the payment stakes. My mother got used to serving meals, often from leftovers when there was not enough money from father because after paying the workers there was nothing left for that week.

Father died of a heart attack at the young age of fifty-seven and there were debts and Mother paid those off with the sale of the printing machines. There was nothing left after that. Mother grieved over father and eighteen months later she went the same way. So Jock, where are your fat profits of factory owners who paid their workers peanuts so they could live better? No doubt there are such owners who run big companies but there are smaller ones as well and not all of them qualify for your opprobrium of fatness and profits at the expense of the workers".

Grant who listened to Dee's speech felt sorry for the plight of her parents, yet was quietly pleased that he was held by the girls to be a good boss that paid them a decent salary. As for Jock he merely accorded Dee the right to speak her mind and all he did was to nod approval in her direction.

Chapter 10

Jock

Joachim Brenn was born into modest circumstances in England. His father had been a bin collector for the council and his mother a cleaner for three different establishments. Joachim's grandfather was born in Algeria but had come to France after 1962. Being born in that part of Africa, the French people called such people ‚*pieds noirs*'

It was a complicated business, being born in Africa and yet being European. Algeria is the largest country in Africa, extending southward deep into the heart of the Sahara, the most forbidding desert that constitutes more than four-fifths of the country's area. The contemporary Algerian novelist Assia Djebar has called her country *A Dream of Sand.*

For a bit of history Algeria was an integral part of the *Maghreb* and the *Arab* peoples. The decline of the Ottomans was followed by a brief period of independence that ended when France launched a war of conquest in 1830. By 1847 the French had largely suppressed Algerian resistance to the invasion and the following year made Algeria a *département* of France. French colonists modernized Algeria's agricultural and commercial economy but lived apart from the Algerian majority, enjoying social and economic privileges extended to few non-Europeans. Ethnic resentment, fueled by revolutionary politics introduced by Algerians who had lived and studied in France, led to a widespread nationalist movement in the mid-20th century.

The country has sought to regain its Arab and Islamic heritage. At the same time, the development of oil and natural gas and other mineral deposits in the Algerian interior brought new wealth to the country and prompted a rise in the standard of living.

Nevertheless, after 1962 when the Algerian peoples had been granted French Nationality, a sizeable portion of Algeria, consisting of various religious faiths, Jews, Christians, Muslims, had come to France. Although these people were now French Citizens, the actual French called them *pieds noirs*, because they had one foot in Africa and one foot in France. Berber, Arab and Islamic cultures had existed long before that but the mass outflow from Algeria to France contributed to the fall of the French Fourth Republic.

Although these Algerian peoples had now French Citizenship, they were still looked upon as second class citizens. For one thing they were not white but neither were they black. The situation for Joachim's grandfather and his family was not brilliant and he thought he could do better in England. He never talked about his erstwhile homeland, yet insisted that the family spoke French at home. Joachim's mother was actually French born so the language was no problem. Neither was English. Father had learnt on the job so to speak and mother was well enough educated to have learned English at school.

Joachim had inherited mediterranean looks, dark eyes which flashed when he was angry, which was not very often, and blue-black hair whch sat in waves on his head and made a little roof over his forehead because it was so thick. At school he was unusually bright and his teachers loved him.

Joachim, while the family had no money, had a good start in learning. So, quite how he ended up as a vagrant, calling himself *Jock and* sitting beside Bugs outside New Covent Garden, had less to do with his father's early death and mother's grief over the death of her husband, than that of societal acceptance and understanding. Joachim came increasingly to feel a square peg in a round hole. As far as he could see Society at large only understood money and those people who had been lucky enough to make their fortune. If a person did well and had money society did not look too closely of how that money was made, only that it belonged to that person and the more they had, the more it showed in the houses they had, the cars they drove and the largesse in tips they dispensed in restaurants.

Bright though he was, Joachim had a massive chip on his shoulder but being bright could not help him recognise that and get over it. While maths, advanced maths, physics and chemistry posed no problem to him and his teachers were in awe of what the boy could ingest by way of learning, his parents had no understanding of their boy's brain power and did not especially think it was anything to be proud of. But his teachers felt that he was made for higher education yet Joachim was more interested in getting to grips with algorithms and computers. He did well in that medium and earned a respectable amount of money, but he did not like what it did to him.

In his early twenties he had the flash cars, the house, the marriage and all the trappings that went with a well-to-do man. He got married and his wife was happy to spend what he earned. Quite early into their marriage there were big differences. His wife liked money and it bothered him that she liked it so much. „I want to be rich" and also famous" she told him, very rich, because I have seen that society does not like poor people and famous people are celebrated and adored. Money, dear Joachim, is power, fame too I reckon".

„What do you want power for", he countered, „you have enough power being married to me and you have to admit you have a totally free hand, I do not try to control you, all I want from you is to love me as I love you. Moreover I think you have got it completely wrong wanting to be famous. What is that for? I have understood from an early age that when you are anonymous, nobody knows you and you can walk down the street without being accosted; you are an *observer* then of all kinds of things. But when you are famous you become *the observed.* Do you really want that? Every nutter in the world professes to know you and either loves you or resents you in equal measure."

But his wife held that she did not mean power in their marriage. She meant power in society and fame too if it came to that, because that society always looks down on powerless people because they have no clout and what she wanted was clout in society and with fame also came respect. As for the nutters she would have minders to deal with them.

„ Power and Fame, my dear, bends society to the will of those who hold that, is what I say".

For his part, the more Joachim earned the more his wife liked it but the less he liked it and not unlike Bugs who he had yet to meet, decided at some point that the life that this Society had mapped out for him was not for him. The family had followed the Christian faith, were catholic and father made little Joachim go to church every Sunday. Joachim loved Church, more so when the priest who held mass came down the aisles waving the incense container around, Joachim had loved the smell, the whole mass to come to think of it.

The differences in how each viewed life did for that marriage as well and the turning point came when his wife decided that being married to Joachim was being shackled and she could do much better with someone who thought like she did. To begin with she blamed him for not being able to get her pregnant so they could have children and this escalated to other things, money in particular and the resultant lack in power and, inevitably, one day when he came back from work, had found the house empty of everything, carpets, furniture, wardrobes. There was not one stick left except walls, floors and ceilings where his voice echoed back a hollow tone. Wifey had left to find greener pastures. Joachim had loved his wife and could not understand why she had left him in pursuit of money and this an arbitrary power and he found it hard to have been dumped because his world view differed from hers. In spite of the arguments over money he had never especially felt that the lack of it from her point of view had a bearing on their love, so when she deserted him he had been dumbfounded as he had not seen it coming.

Joachim did have friends and they all told him he would get over it, that he was still good looking and only in his thirties and sometimes wives did things like that, husbands too, come to think of it. He should get over it and find another wife who might understand him better. Joachim did not want another wife, he stilll wanted the one that just left him for he loved her despite the differences money concerns. At the same time he did not want to chase after her to get her to see that her ideas about society and money were wrong. What he wanted was for her to come back to tell him she loved him still and wanted to be with him. There was of course scant chance of that, so Joachim felt that if he could not have this one he would have no other. It is supposed that at this point he changed his life and became Jock. He felt that if his wife did not come back and her idea of society as he knew it did not love him, he would not love it back either and so he bowed out.

He had been buying some vegetables at Covent Gardens when right by the entrance there was a man sitting on the floor talking to passers-by. There was something about the man on the ground that had appealed to Jock and after this purchases he came out of the hall and sat beside him to ask him his take on Life. At that moment, as he sat down and introduced himself to Bugs, he said that his name was Jock. The man on the floor was Arthur Thompson, better known as Bugs and soon the two of them found their common language, French. A new friendship was born and they started doing everything together. The were indeed members of cardboard city which was a slot under the underpass of a motorway, to escape rain and snow and on the main, even whey they were on their travels their possessions as well as the card board boxes which were old fashioned TV boxes, big enough to sleep in, were left alone. Other members of their stripe knew them, liked them and decided it would not do to steal from them, so they were largely left alone.

Chapter 11

Max

It has been quite a few years since Marcus had become Woody and it had also been a while since he had decided that sufficient time had gone by for him to risk going home to visit his father and at the same time get introduced to his new step-mother. Damatina, who called herself Tina, had married his father, the patriarch of the family Easterwood. It was Bert who had told Woody who was astounded, both at the news and how fate operated.Thinking about it he thought it quite hilarious that his mate Bert's wife had become his own step-mother.

When Amethyst first came across him at the Pumphouse Theater and had called him Marcus, he had told her to keep a low tone as nobody knew him as Marcus, but only as Woody. She had told him then that their father had married again but here Woody was one step ahead as he had had it from Bert first.

When Bert still shared 66 Bertram Close with him, then a squat, which he, Bert, had actually found and had invited Woody to share the digs provided he promised to share what goodies he had come across on his daily travels. Woody did his share and little by litte the house without amenities, 66 Bertram Close, became a cosy abode with lots of furniture, all gathered for free from skips. It was what people had thrown out. In time the house had become quite crowded. No longer did the pair, Bert and Woody, have to sit on the floor before the chimney, before a roaring fire, maintained with pieces of broken down furniture. How long ago it all was.

*****

The years had flown by, little Max who was adopted into the family Easterwood was not little anymore. He was now eighteen. The last couple of years he had shot up and had become a lanky six footer. Tina had to pinch herself sometimes, looking at him, that it was not the demised Pelly that had come back to life, so alike him was Max. He wore his hair afro style; because it was so curly, he just ran a rough brush through it and left it like that. The colour of it was yet another thing. Tina could not decide what colour it was. In a certain light it looked a russet red, but at other times it was definitely a deep chestnut brown, to go with the unfathomable colour of his very dark eyes. He was the spitting image of Pelly, her brother who had met such an untimely end.

Now here was Max and Tina and Brendan loved him like their son. He still talked about nana Akki and gramps Liffet because they had formed parts of his early childhood and he still wrote letters to them, but over time they had become fewer though he still wrote for Easter, Christmas and their birthdays, which he never forgot. But as a teenager he now had the priorities of a young man who was beginning to discover life. He also had a secret which he was more than keen to keep to himself. He, like his father before him, had started to use drugs. It had all started with that packet of cigarettes he had found on the pavement and, together with Ozzy had secretly smoked its contents. But while Ozzy had decided that smoking was not for him, Max had taken to it. Then at college somebody offered him a spliff and it went from there. He knew it was illegal, moreover knew that it had been drugs that had killed his father and his mother too and that it was a downright dangerous road to travel on but Max had no intention of letting drugs rule his life; it was just a pastime he enjoyed, though one it was surely best to keep under his hat. He was careful not to smoke at home as the smoke and the smell hung about clothes and he wanted to give the appearance of being a regular kid.

When he was fifteen Tina had told him that he had been adopted and that he was the only child of her younger brother Pelly who had died of a drug overdose and that his mother had met the same end alongside whom however she had called *Puck*. Tina instilled in her son that drug use was wrong on every level and Max had agreed. That was three years ago but since then things had changed and Max had taken up this pernicious habit, not spliffs, but serious drugs like cocaine, yet he still did not think that it ruled his life, though it became expensive and was using up most of his pocket money. That money, in the form of an allowance set by Papa, was generous as in the family Easterwood there was no shortage. Tina and Brendan were indulgent parents and never thought to ask what their son did with the money and outwardly there were no tell-tale signs so his parents were none the wiser.

Also, as yet Max only smoked the stuff; he had refrained from injections as he was afraid of the needle. But he fondly believed that as long as he did not start to inject any drugs he would be safe from addiction. In that he was to be proved woefully wrong. Neither of his real parents ever injected and yet they were serious drug users and death had claimed both of them because of it. It was also the case that both his parents had progressed to 'freebasing' a more dangerous way of ingesting coke and as yet Max knew nothing about that part of drug use.

He still kept up with writing to nana Akki and gramps Liffet and was minded, in every letter to them to stress that he still had the little snake and that he still very much liked it and would look after it and taking care it would never be lost. He also told them that that snake was now hanging from a silver chain around his neck, so it was close to his chest.

Now eighteen and by law an adult, he had not lost his interest in drawing and the sketchpad went with him everywhere. It was that which lulled his Mama into a false sense of security. When she kept seeing her son with his sketchpad under his arm she assumed that nurturing his talent meant he had no time for stupid things, like drug taking.

Drug taking was always still foremost in Tina's mind and and she was always on the look-out for signs that Max could have inherited that dangerous trait.

*****

Max kept up with his correspondence to his gramps Liffet and nana Akki and clung to his childhood names for them and in all the letters to them he referred to them as such. Both of them had accepted that and in their return correspondence they signed themselves as gramps Liffet and nana Akki too. They had not fostered another child since his departure to England, because nana Akki in one of her letters had said that no child could replace him. There was of course still Shayne, her daughter, begotten with Longhorn, but it was her and Longhorn's secret and they still had never talked about it and Lightfoot also, in all the years he was married to Akwase, had never been made wise to it either. But Akwase remembered keenly and every time Shayne's birthday came she lit a candle. Lightfoot was always puzzled about this wife's lighting of the candle as it came along at the same time every year, but Akwase just smiled and said her mother had always done it and she merely carried on the tradition.

It seemed to have satisfied her husband for he just accepted it, in the way he accepted a few things about his wife, which he put down to their common heritage as members of the Shawnee. In some ways this had made Max feel important too because he had been special to them, but now he was growing up he regarded himself fully part of the family Easterwood.

112

Much had changed in the Easterwood household too. While Brendan had made the promises he had made when he had married Lindsey but not kept his word, he made promises to Tina who became his second wife, and he did keep his word. The Easterwoods were weatlty beyond imagination but to Brendan the kudos that came with the wealth had begun to pale. It was now more important to him to be a good dad to Max, then to add yet more millions to those the family already had. He no longer went to his high-rise every day, but was happy to spend time with the boy who was an eager listener to his stories about people's greed.

Tina had been right about Max's talents of drawing. Since that colour sketch of his foster-carers house which he had called *Shavany*, he had become a talented draughtsman. Wherever Max went the sketch pad went with him too. Some time after that 'Shavany' sketch, he was introduced to his older brother Marcus, who, since the first tentative visit to his family home, had had warm feelings about his new step-mother, so much so that he had become a frequent visitor to the house. And since his marriage to Stephanie, she came too.

It might have yet come right with Max and his drug habit had he not met Ysenda. Max had gone into a shop though he could later not say why he had entered the shop and was at a loss to figure out what he was doing there. He stood there undecided when his Ray-Ban-covered eyes lighted on a girl that was in the process of handing over some money for chocolates. She paid and made for the door at the same time as Max too had decided to leave. But two people could not go through that door simultaneously, so Max stood back to let the girl out first. Outside she threw him a winning smile and told him her name: Ysenda Burrows. Max said it was an unusual name but it sounded nice and said his name was Max Easterwood. The name seemed to mean nothing to her and instead she said that she had, at school, tried to get her name over the line, but her peers had looked incredulous so she said that Ysi would do. The next hurdle at school was that calling herself Ysi was soon translated onto *easy* and to prevent such a label she said her name was pronounced *Ysi* like the name of the goddess *Isis* but without the s at the end which was readily accepted. And so she was Ysi for the rest of the schooldays. But now, telling Max her full name, she realised that it was still a problem, so, in a resigned kind of manner she said to him that Ysi was really ok, she had got used to be called that.

In the way that drug addicts seem to recognise each other even when they had never met before, she said in a quiet voice that her dealer *Paul* was just in the next street, that she lived close by and if he liked they could go to him to get sorted. Had made no objection and so they went there. On the way she volunteered that she always used Paul since he had reliable gear and she did not have to worry about overdosing on stuff. Max had nodded and so this unholy relationship had started.

What Max needed in his time of life was someone who might have persuaded him that taking drugs was a bad move and he should get off that. Shayne might have done that but she viewed Max like she viewed a brother and as such did not have any influence over him. She had perceived though that he was smoking something unwholesome when she had found a suspicious looking cellophane packet that had fallen out of his pocket. She had told him then in a general way that some in the Shawnee tribe used magic mushrooms but she had never tried it and also had no intention of doing so. She told him that she liked the world the way it was; she did not need rose coloured glassed to imagine a world that did not exist. Talking like that to Max, the latter had nodded and said that he never forgot that his real mother and father had died of a drug overdose but he himself had no intention of going the same way. Shayne had left it at that but Max had sounded unconvincing.

In contrast Ysi said no such thing but simply supposed he was like her and what they needed now was her dealer who could help them get sorted. After that she also told him in a matter of fact way, as if it was the most normal thing in the world that she lived nearby in Cranberry Road and if he wanted they could go to her place and have a good time.

*****

The good time they had together was such that Max did not return home that night and when he ambled in the next morning and Tina had asked quietly where he had been, he just said that he had stayed with one of his mates and together they caught up with studies because he did not wish to fall behind.

Tina readily accepted that, was even glad to be told so because to her it meant he took his studies seriously enough not to want to fall behind. And with that explanation he flew to his room, went to sleep and did not emerge again until supper time.

When he did emerge to appear at the dinner table – it would have looked odd to miss the house routine – he was bleary-eyed and hung-over. Wearing his shades in order to prevent his ever watchful Mama from questioning him too closely, he was surprised that neither parent mentioned his looks. They had fondly assumed that Max had been in an all-nighter with a mate, studying in order to pass the nessessary exams.

At dinner, apart from Mama and Papa and Shayne were also Ozzy and Michelle, the latter keen to enter into a conversation about life in general. While Michelle seemed no longer the woman ready to ditch all men and get back to a matriarchial society, she was far too observant a girl. Max's view was that she would have noticed in a trice his hung-over over state. And so he sat somewhat taciturn at the dinner table and disappeared to his room just as soon as dinner was

115

declared finished, with the excuse that he still had work to do for his exam which loomed in two weeks time. Max was following the same medical course as his cousin Ozzy, the intention being that he, Max, would be a doctor, who would later specialise to become a surgeon, while Ozzy had fewer ambitions and thought that being a doctor would was good enough. Briefly Max had thought of becoming a vet, but then decided that to be a surgeon was more worthwhile.

Chapter 12

Woody divulges his secret

It was not until Marcus, who was still known as Woody outside his family, had married his Stephanie a while back that he had eventually decided it was time to show his wife his painting room. Steph, as he called her, had always wondered what was behind the locked room but had accepted her husband's promise that one day she would see the room unlocked and the mysteries behind that door revealed. Up to that time she had accepted that her husband's income came from his job at the Pumphouse Theatre. She realised of course that that job paid a pittance, but she had a comfortable income from her mother, from the takings of Maisie's Den, the vegetarian cafe now run by other people, and she was not unhappy about complementing Woody's meagre earnings with her own. But Woody was unhappy about that and told his wife that it was a husband's job to keep his wife, not a wife's job to keep her husband, but Steph's take on life was that one shared with the loved one what one had. Woody merely acquiesced but hinted to Steph that he hoped that one day he could prove to her his worth. Steph had smiled and said she was looking forward to that day, but in the meantime they had to live and she had money and what was the hassle?

When she was first taken to Woody's parental home, where he was known as Marcus, she had been amazed, both about the location of the house and also the expensive furnishings inside. But having found Marcus's parents down to earth and making her welcome she had in moments assumed that what her husband meant that one day he would show her that he had been worth being married to, because, he would benefit from the will of his parents.

On one of the visits to his erstwhile home, he had been introduced to Max, who had managed to make Marcus aware that he was good at sketching. Prompted by him, the boy went up to his room to fetch his sketch book and plonked in on Marcus's lap, so he could pass judgement. The boy then pointed to a row of pictures on the wall, all signed *estro* with the remark that it was his dearest wish to be as good as that 'bloke' who had painted those pictures.

Marcus was quite taken with Max's sketches, both in colour and in pencil and told him he had real talent and should continue in this vein until one day a light would go off in his head and he would start painting what was inside his head, rather than what was before him in nature. He invited the boy over to his house and together they would paint.

And so it had begun. Max said he was eager to see his house and would come soon. On the way home Woody had been quiet and had wondered what Max would think about his house as it was nothing like his parents' house in either looks from the outside, nor the furnishings.

After Bert had departed to 3 Millpond Close and Woody had occupied 66 Bertram Close by himself, the furniture in the house was mostly retrieved from skips when the pair had lived together and was still much the same though Bert had moved out and Steph had moved in. But in the short time that she had married Woody, aka Marcus, Steph had made a nice home of the house. Here and there things were quietly renewed. The carpet with the threadbare bit which was hidden under the table where nobody could see it, was replaced with a large wool carpet that Steph had bought in a sale, but had been new. In addition the chipped crockery was replaced with new gear and a range of glassware came into the house that came from a department store rather than a skip.

After the purchase of the glassware her husband had told Steph that they had enough stuff to make living comfortable and that was enough of luxury. He had no intention of emulating his parents.

The day then came that Marcus opened up that locked room. Max had phoned to say that he would like to visit the following day. Marcus took the opportunity to finally let Steph in on his very closely guarded secret. And when Steph first entered that secret paint room, she did not understand what he was trying to tell her. All she saw was easeals and boards against the wall, painting side unseen. She looked at Marcus and said

"It appears to be your paint room, and all I see is boxes of paints and boards and easels. You need not have kept that from me and my question is, why did you?

Marcus whom Steph still called Woody, because that's how she knew him when she was, along with her mother, serving the Notters in the backroom of the cafe, said nothing but turned all the boards from the wall towards her, so she could see the pictures. Steph looked at the signatures and all of them, those that he had considered finished, were signed *estro*. And since Steph still did not understand the meaning of the signature Woody explained it all to her.

"You see, darling, I kept that room closed because of the secret behind it. I am not what I seem. The lighting job at the pumphouse theatre is a smoke screen to hide my real work wich is painting".

In round about ways he explained his departure these many years ago from the Easterwood family because his father's life then had been very differerent. He told her that he wanted none of the riches his father coveted but wanted to make his own life. It had not been easy because he had decided that tramping the roads was better, though it was not. He told her that he had found quite soon that cardboard city had not been for him and that was when he met Bert and through him he had become a *Notter*.

"I had enrolled at Slade and Kalman Erikson, the art tutor there, who is no longer in life, said that my work was outstanding, but if I did not want to be known to the public I would have to hide in plain sight and that meant taking on a job, any job, which would have the result that it made me legitimate. And so I became the lighting man of the Pumphouse Theatre. It paid a pittance but it was a job, while my real job is producing these little works.

Unfortunately I have to tell you that I am a very rich man. I did not mean to become rich, especially not a well known person which is why my father never knew about me. The pictures you have seen hanging up in their living room are all mine, but nobody actually knows it's me, except you now do. None of the Notters are aware of that either, but Bert has known the whole time. His family is actually even richer than mine, a Brookman having married a Halbard, but he got sick of that circus as well and bowed out.

It was Bert who had found this squat when he asked me to share it with him. I did and there was nothing in it, just bare floorboards and it was Bert to introduced me to his system of *havenottery,* finding stuff for free and taking it home. To earn some money for himself he did his routine *'Burlington Bertie'* there and he was a hoot with the public. In his free time he was *my agent,* getting my unknown work displayed in the window of *Grogman's Art Gallery* because I did not want anyone to get to know that I was the painter of these pictures.

As for the squat, little by little it got furnished, through Berts' system of *havenottery*, meaning the retrieval of stuff other people threw out. I believed in that system. It is actually recycling and when you think about it people really have too much money when they throw perfectly usuable stuff out because maybe the colour of the carpet does not go with the wallpaper anymore. My family of course never even looked in a skip, never mind taking anything out of one. Everything my family had was the best and most expensive that money could buy but I did not want it. I genuinely never hankered after those riches, because to me it proved nothing; what was important could not be bought with money. I did not know that though when I bowed out of the system, but somehow I knew that this kind of life did not satisfy me. There had to be better. I started with tramping the streets because I felt that there was more honesty. I had to learn a street truism though which is that given half the chance the people on the lowest level of existence wanted very much the kind of life which I had so carelessly discarded.

I met the *Notters* who were all there because Fate had thrown them onto the scrap heap. They had to learn that life still was not over for them; they would learn that through a play would you believe. With the play they learnt that respect which they all still craved could be obtained again if they worked at it. Yet for me it is Bugs and his friend Jock who earn most of my respect because they remained true to their beliefs, refusing point black to be dragged into a society they despised."

*****

While Woody had been talking Steph had stayed silent and kept staring at him as his story unfolded. She had had no idea about her husband's riches and when he had finally finished his story and let her have a word, all she managed to say: "Well, I never! You certainly have fooled me and my mother and everyone else, the Notters included".

Woody interjected.

"You see in a way that pleases me, because you have married me for what I call the right reasons, for love. You certainly did not marry me for money, because as far as you knew I had none, but that small job that paid peanuts, but I loved it and love it still and I still don't want anyone to know about my painting stuff, or the fact that my painting signature is *estro*. By the way 'estro' is the end of the word 'Maestro';

Bert insisted I was a maestro because, he said, I seem to have answers for everything.

Coming back to the paintings, in a way though I feel a fraud because I am not poor while society pities me for my peanut-income when I have access to riches. I have come to terms with that now because it is not having the money I resent, but being a *known* personality even, god forbid, a celebrity; I will do everything I possibly can to avoid being that.

Max will come and visit us tomorrow and I shall tell him nothing, but will remove all the boards to the back room, so all he will see is some paint boxes and a couple of easels folded against the wall and together we will sketch. I shall show him how to paint because clearly the boy has talent and it needs to be promoted.

My father and Tina know nothing about my work and I had to bite my tongue when Tina explained to me how she had bought four paintings from a small shop in Vauxhall, Grogman's, and Dad had asked my sister to find out who the painter of them was. It was a shock hearing that because when I had left the family, my father had only been interested in old Masters and those only in order to see their auction prices go into the stratosphere, when he bought one or two pieces then sold them a few years later, having made a handsome profit even after the commissions and taxes were paid. Learning now that dad is genuinely interested in art rather than the profit it might bring if he hung onto it for a bit, that is certainy a shock, but a pleasant one. Tina is evidently good for him. But I still have not had the courage to tell them that I am the painter of those little works that hang on the living room wall.

Dad was always scrupulous in paying his share to the exchecker, but then the family had so much money, no taxes or commisions would even dent any bank balances. And he was quite benevolent too. He gave lots to charities. When first he did that he was pleased to bathe in the glory as the zeros after the figures were read out, but by and by, he had come to the conclusion that it was not necessary to keep a salon to show off what a good bloke you had been to give so much away every year for these so-called good causes. He recognised that it was not so much the good causes that had mattered to him but the burnishing of his own image. But as he got older, especially after Tina had come into his life he changed somewhat. He still gives money to charities, but it is anonymously now, rather than sit on committees being slapped on the back about the millions he had given.

My father had changed a lot through having married Tina and I will eventually tell him that *estro* is me. Eventually, but still not now and the only one who knows now is you."

As for Tina she had not minded not being called mother. She was happy to be called Tina. She felt that being step-mother was good enough; neither Marcus nor Amethyst needed another mother. They had had one and she died, so Tina did not feel she was a replacement but rather hoped the siblings would see in her a friend and in that she had succeeded.

Chapter 13

Time moves on

Max was now technically an adult and Tina, whom he called Mama, told him that every day he looked more and more like his birth dad. In other ways Max was very likeable and was always prepared to lend a helping hand if such were needed. He still wrote, if not very often, to gramps Liffet and nana Akki, telling hem what he was doing Although he now knew that gramps Liffet was Lightfoot and nana Akki was Akwase, he saw no reason to call them any different to when he had been little. Indeed letters from gramps that came back were also signed Liffet and when Akki put her name on the bottom of Liffet's letters, she signed as Akki as well.

Meanwhile Max's sketches had become true pieces of art. He knew he was adopted because Tina talked about Max's Dad and she regretted that Max never knew him or his mum for that matter, but Pelham/Pelly and Tina's had grown up together, Tina being the older sister by some five years. She had a fondness for her brother she did not have for Myra, since she had never known her.

Tina had been the first person to learn of her brother's unhappiness at home and when she noticed the first tell-tell sign of his drug taking, she had been aghast and had tried her hardest to talk him out of it. Not that Tina knew anything about drugs, but it was Pelly who had told her in confidence that he was taking 'stuff'. "What kind of stuff?" his sister wanted to know.

"You know, stuff, but it's only lightweight stuff, like grass, you know, but you know what, taking it makes me feel better and I can take Mother's snooty ways better too. I find it laughable but, seriously, quite tragic, in the way she is in awe of money and her stupid but rich friends. I can't stand any of them but Mother revels in her being top dog and presides over all her swooning cronies. Father just sits there and smiles and lets her get on with it. Deep down he is just as bad because he covets money and his name. Halbard, what the hell is that? To me it is just a name, but to their hangers-on, it is the next name to God, whoever he may be. I smoke grass because it makes me feel happy and in that state I can take my family."

Tina said that from what she had read about what he says is stuff, everybody says it leads to heavier stuff and eventual addiction and he should beware, that far from it being light, it seems dangerous to her. But her brother would not listen and so it had proved: by the time he was nineteen he had graduated from taking grass, to cocaine. It was then that even his mother began to notice. Pelly who was always to be had for a bit of mischief told his mother that he was taking drugs. At first she did not believe him but then told her daughter who confirmed it. Pandemonium. A drug taking son in the family! They could not have that and so she had got her husband to agree that their son should live away from home. Since money was no object to the Halbards, a flat in a swish apartment block in Knightsbridge was found and purchased and Pelly was more than happy to live there all by himself, where he could do what he wanted. And did. And also came to grief.

Tina often talked to Max about his Dad and the way she talked about him made Max feel sad he never knew him either as a father or as a man. Tina had told Max that he was adopted and that his dad died along with his mum but she did not tell him that it had been his grandmother, Pelly's mother who insisted he should not come into contact with any of the family's friends when he was high and unpredictable, which is why they had bought him the flat. Tina had left that bit out, though she was truthful in every other respect.

Gramps and nana still remembered fondly their little Max who was never slow to tell them that he was taking good care of the snake.

*****

But what of the other woman that was his nana as well, Fenella Gettevan? Max still called that one nana Finelly even though at his age he knew perfectly well to pronounce her name but for him she remained nana Finelli. One thing stayed the same too: he did not like nana Finelly any better than he had when she had sent him small parcels of presents for which he still remembered having to say thank you, even if he did not like them. And still he continued to dislike anything she had sent.

For for the last two years, even these disliked parcels had stayed out. Fenella had simply found that her grandson was old enough and did not need presents any more. The real reason was that she was too tightfisted to pay for any gift or for postage from America to England, even though she was still by any reckoning a rich woman. Her take on everything to do with money was that it was always better off in her pocket than anyone else's. She never wrote to Max, so considering she had initially lamented the loss of her grandchild in order to garner sympathy and a large dollop of cash to compensate for the loss, it turned out that she had not, after all, lamented his loss all that much.

Tina did not encourage Max to write to Mrs Fenella Davey Gettevan. Here she felt that since that woman never wrote to Max, the latter had no reason to write to her either. She did not tell Max that though, because she felt that it was wrong to discriminate. Fenella was a blood relative but saying outright that her son need not write to her would put the wrong idea into her son's head: that it was all right to send letters to a foster carer but writing to what was after all his grandmother on his mother's side could be disregarded. That Fenella never wrote anyhow did not make it any easier,

126

but saying it was one thing and thinking it and quietly promoting that she did not care for the woman was something she could voice to her son.

Chapter 14

Amethyst has concerns

Amethyst's had decided to revert to her birthname. The change from being called Amy she realised would not in the long run make that much difference. For one thing, her children, Ozzy and Minnie – nicknames of Oskar and Margaretha, their birth names – called her *Mother*, while husband Konrad called her darling, or sweetheart. So, the decision to change to her full name was neither here nor there. As for Marcus who had always called his sister Amy, he would have to get used Amethyst. If not, well, he was her brother and exceptions had to be made. She remembered after some years of fruitless searching for him she had found him hale and hearty fiddling with the lighting over at the Pumphouse Theatre, when she and Konrad went to see the 'The Beggars Opera' which had had such rave reviews in the press. She had called him Marcus whereupon he said to keep her voice down as everybody there only knew him as Woody.

She had managed to talk to him after the show, down in the bar, telling him that their father had got married again and had been giving her the job of finding her brother. She had urged Marcus to mend fences and go and see their father. The latter had wanted to know about a painter who, despite earnest searching of who he might be, had produced nil results. Amethyst smiled when she recalled her brother's face, one of sheer astonishment that Father might be interested in a painter nobody had heard of. He had reminded his sister that their father was only ever interested in the buying of old Masters and making a profit selling them at the auctions months or years later. She had told him that their father had changed and the reeason for that must have had to do with the new wife, their step-mother Damatina whom everyone called Tina. The marriage had completely changed father. Marcus had promised that in that case he would visit soon. And so he had and since that first visit quite a time had passed too.

Amthyst allowed that her children were growing up. Oskar was now 17, nearly eighteen and Margaretha 16 months behind. When they were born she had told her husband that they would be called what it said on the birth certificate, but however good her intentions, as they started to crawl they acquired nicknames, of the sort Amethyst said would never happen in a month of Sundays. But it did. The family called Oskar the minnow *Ozzy* and and Margaretha answered to the name of Minnie, not Maggie, or Mags to be sure or any derivatives of them, but Minnie. Occasionally family friends reminded her of her steely resolve that her children should have the names they were registered with, but Amethyst just said that they were called what they were called because they looked like what they were called.

The children had arrived in the world in relatively short succession. Initially Amethyst and Konrad thought that the distance between their births should be three years, but fate had decreed otherwise. Her marriage was strong and Konrad was an indulgent husband, so she had chosen well in marrying him. She had told him that once when he had countered:

„On the contrary, my darling, it is I who have chosen well in marrying you." Ah, Konrad, such a love. She loved him dearly and their marriage was founded on solid mutual respect. So she supposed that all things told both had chosen well in marrying each other.

Yet Konrad had a secret he was very careful to keep to himself and so far he kept it well. His character was such that he could differentiate between work, people at his work place and home life. And his secret was that is secretary;

Christine Merton had become his mistress. She had been working for him for seven or eight years and for the first half nothing personal had intruded to hint at a possible future relationship of a personal nature. The secretary's middle name was Ursula She had married Mr Merton but after two years of marriage he had the misfortune to die of an unspecified illness and after mourning for him for two years, she had fallen for her boss, Konrad McReady. The latter had not paid her any attention but working together nevertheless brought them into close proximity with each oth some. After four years of working for him he had playfully started to call her *Chum* and she had liked that, because it was an amalgamation of her names but also denoted something a little bit more personal. Forever after he would call her *Chum* and in her capacity of secretary she was more like a PA. In other words, she was wholly reliable and Konrad entrusted her with many private things as well. And sometimes he loaded her up with work that he thought that perhaps he should engage another hand to help her.

Chum swatted such notions swiftly away, telling him that she could well manage on her own. The truth was she did not want another female in close proximity to her boss when she herself had notions about him. How the affair had began and had endured for over three years. On occasion Chum would lightly suggest that it had gone on long enough, that he should divorce his wife and marry her, but this, for Konrad, was a bridge too far and he would change the subject, merely telling her that it would not be easy as he had two children and divorced parents were never good for children's equilibrium. So the affair carried on and it became a bit of a habit; they would take tea across the road at the Savoy, where, like as not, they would then retire to a room upstairs that Konrad seemed to have on tap on a regular basis.

Nevertheless, Konrad always came home for supper and Tina never suspected anything and fondly believed that her husband was of the most attentive sort; to all who would listen she would say how successful the union was and how she could not imagine having married anyone else.

*****

While Amethyst fondly believed that her husband was faithful to her - she certainly was faithful to him - a different wife might have suspected the existence of a mistress a lot sooner, but Amethyst suspected not a thing and was instead concerned about Ozzy She could not put a finger on what was so concerning about her adolescent son, but it seemed to her that there was something altogether not one hundred percent as it should be. He had for the last year formed a close attachment to Max, which Amethyst and also Konrad promoted. Max, to them was a child with a thoroughly open heart, a teenager now, that had accepted wholeheartedly Tina as his Mama und Brendan as his Papa. He was a little older than Ozzy but the two were firm friends. He also was still sending odd letters across the Atlantic to gramps Liffet and nana Akki. The couple were precious to him. And sometimes he included a sketch of himself and that of his family so his erstwhile foster carers had an idea of how he developed. Indeed letters from Liffet and Akki came back with fulsome praise and Liffet always wanted to know if he still had the silver snake. To that question Max would add that he would never let go of it and stressed again that he had it now on a silver chain around his neck, so it was close to him always. And everybody who knew Max also knew of this silver snake that had come off living on his jumpers and was now hanging on a chain around his neck.

Amethyst liked seeing Max and Ozzy knocking about the place. Usually they were just bantering on the balcony and playing games, after teasing each other with one or other of the footballers either of them favoured. However, in the last couple of month it had seemed to Amethyst that the two

131

of them had become somewhat secretive. She could not figure it out. On the one hand she was unconcerned, because both boys were now teenagers who in certain situations spoke a language quite alien to grown-ups. Occasionally Konrad might have a word with Ozzy about the untidiness of his room, at which point the youngster would look at his shoes and mumble something incoherent to his father. After enquiring to be more explicit as father could not understand what he was telling him, the language became more incoherent still, while the staring at his shoes intensified. Whether this was a ploy or just how teenagers behaved with their parents, Konrad could not discover and after a while became aware of the incongruousness of the situation and would say: „Ah well, be away with you", after which the staring of shoes stopped and the boy hastened away. Konrad then would find Amethyst to tell her that he for one could no longer understand children and he was sure that in his days he had not mumbled to his father in quite that manner. Amethyst would shrug her shoulders as if to say, well what can you do.

*****

Ozzy and Max as young people were quite different. Perhaps it was because they were different that their friendship grew close. Ozzy had none of the talent for drawing which defined Max; Ozzy's talent lay in the fact that he seemed to have a sixth sense when something was not quite right in his family. And he, long before his mother, had realised that there was something about his father that was secret. To be sure Konrad was always his affable self when he was home, but Ozzy sensed that there was something – in the last months at least – that was different. It was also this sensitivity when he told his pal Max that he had decided that smoking was not for him. Max by then had decided differently; he had decided that smoking was very much what he liked to do, but not at home. Nobody in his family smoked

132

and smoking left a scent like perfume, easily detectable and he wanted to keep the secret for himself for now.

*****

While Amethyst was trying to figure out what might be concerning about their son and he and Max whispering stuff together out of earshot of everyone, she eventually realised that there was a different problem concerning her husband. He had carelessly left a suit on the chair in their bedroom with the remark that it needed dry-cleaning and would she be a darling and take it to the shop. Amethyst said she would, kissed her husband who flew out of the door saying he loved her immensly. Amethyst smiled, sat at the kitchen table and poured herself a cup of coffee. The suit could wait. She tried to figure out what work she had to do until her husband came back and found that not a lot was on the agenda. So she took the suit and collected a ticket for it. It would be ready later in the day. When she collected it at around four in the afternoon, the assistant at the shop gave her the suit and a fifty pound note together with a little yellow post-it-note. Both items were left in the top pocket of the suit. Amethyst paid and took the suit home. She never checked pockets of her husband; that was his job and if he left stuff in there, that was his lookout. The family was not short of cash. Konrad was the CEO of his own company which was doing well and Brendan still gave his daughter a monthly allowance which left them off quite well. So fifty quid left in a suit was neither here nor there, though Amethyst thought it was nevertheless honest of the assistant to have owned up that she had found the money in the pocket. Konrad would never have missed it as he was a bit careless about money. „why bother about money when I have you", he would say. So she decided not to mention the money to him, but that little yellow post-it-note gave her to think. On the note was in Konrad's creless hand-writing ‚*Chum, remember, 4.10 at the Savoy as usual.* It was the ‚as

133

usual' bit that had made her think. She dismissed it, yet later she thought about the note again and what the word ‚*Chum'* meant or who that might be. Then she dismissed that again, having decided that Chum was one of her husband's clients, had to be. Konrad often met clients in all sorts of places, and the ‚as usual' had a regular ring, so it had to be one of his regualar customers. Yet she remembered hearing the name and was trying to remember in what context this *Chum* person had come up. Nothing clicked in her brain that would lead to the recognition of the name. She knew her husband though: Konrad, while always polite was not noted to be familiar with people and Chum was definitely, according to this yellow chit, quite familiar to him. The note had no date on it so it could have been an old note carelessly stuck in the top pocket, except that her husband did nothing that could be termed careless.

Amethyst thought about their marriage. She had nothing to complain about. Konrad was thoughtful and when not pushing work was happy to be at home. And yet, and yet. It would not leave her alone and so for the first time in her married life she thought she would check it out. It was too late to do anything about anything today as by the time she made it to the Savoy it would be too late. But tomorrow she would check it out, just to be sure. She felt bad about checking up on her husband but on the other hand it was not every day that a post-it-note with the intriguing wording *as usual,* was returned from an assistant at the dry-cleaners. She decided not to mention either the money or the note to Konrad, but tomorrow she would gain certainty.

When Konrad came home at the usual time and they had had dinner together she only mentioned that she had cause to wonder about Oskar and Max who had been bantering about the house after school. Konrad dismissed it and said they weere just teenagers and he for one was happy that the boys were allowed to be themselves, even though they were speaking in uncomprehensible tongues when tackled about their shortcomings. He did notice during the evening that his wife seemed to be not quite herself, that she was somehow distracted, that there was a restlessness about her, but when he asked if anything was the matter, she just said she was concerned about Max and their son.

„Is that all it is", laughed Konrad, in which case I wish to put your mind at rest; I think you concern yourself unnecessarily. Let them be, it will all be fine". And with that they turned out the lights and went up to bed.

*****

Having got her children off to school, Amethyst sat down at her kitchen table nursing a coffee and thought about things. Today was a new day and she was not at all convinced she should follow yesterday's plan and go to the Savoy. She felt singularly uneasy checking up on her husband. He had never given her the slightest doubt there could be another woman in their marriage. So why now? Amethyst suspected somehow that the note was about a woman, client or otherwise and it would not leave her brain alone. She had to have certainty.

The trains were packed even though it was in early in the afternoon. She thought she should have taken a taxi. A young man offered her a seat for the first journey, but then she had to change and in the last train she stood, hanging onto one of the handles that were hanging from the ceiling. At Charing Cross she got out and had to walk the rest of the way. She told herself that she should definitely have taken a taxi, it was stupid having to walk along the Strand. It was a long walk and twice already she had wanted to turn around and go home. It felt so alien, to check up on a husband who had been a model father and helpmeet. It seemed plain wrong, just because of a silly yellow note that said 4.10 at the Savoy *as usual*. Amethyst walked on. It was ,the usual' that bothered her and she wanted to find out.

135

Furtively she entered the Savoy which was empty of people. The doorman had let her enter because she said she was looking for someone who was expecting her. She did not want to be seen so she stayed out of eye contact with any waiter who might have wanted to lead her to a table. So she stood there by the wall and scanned the place. It was dark and it took her a while to adjust her eyes to the sombre decor of the hotel. Making herself all but invisible she saw at the far end of the room a table with two people sitting there, holding hands. Amethyst''s heart missed a couple of beats as she recognised the man as being Konrad. So it was true after all. Her husband was cheating on her. For all she knew he had been doing that for a long time and she knew nothing about it, had fondly believed his lies, when he came home a little later than usual and now in the darkness of the Savoy she now had a reality check. Should she go up to the two people at the table and declare her presence – should she, instead, mention it to him tonight, or should she say nothing and see what might transpire?.

Amethystdecided on retreat unseen and headed out of the door, then fled down the street and hailed a taxi. She could not face the trains again. She had seen enough and now had certainty about her husband and another woman, though she had no idea who she was as she had not recognised her face but knew it was not anyone of their acquaintance, which at least was a realief, though only a small one.

*****

Oskar, Amethyst and Konrad's eldest was in the late stges of teenage and at nearly six feet almost as tall as his cousin Max. They were best friends and Max still had, when he was talking animatedly about something, a slight American burr. Max, Amethyst accepted, had become an accomplished artist and she wondered where he had got it from. Of course he was not a natural son of the Easterwoods so if one was looking into the heritage one would have to know about his birth parents. Max though was a blood relative of Tina's who, in fact was his aunt. Tina had never made a secret of the fact that her brother died of an overdose because he had been a drug addict. Max's mother too had died with him and she had been an addict as well. What Amethyst's other concern was, apart from that about her husband, was that the hope that Max would not succumb to the same pernicious habit and, worse luck, would take their son with him too.

It was the case that Oskar thought highly of Max and the two of them were frequently hanging out together and everywhere Max went, his sketch pad went with him. He had several heads sketched of Ozzy's features and Amethyst had looked at them and thought the likeness of her son quite astonishingly good. Oh, yes, most certainly, Max had talent wherever he had it from and it was a beautiful gift and she hoped that that talent would save him from going down the same way as his parents had.

Musing in this manner Amerthyst realised she was beginning to seee gremlins in everthing and told herself now to get a grip. True, she did see her husband in the Savoy with an unnamed woman, holding hands, but that did not translate as yet in him having an affair. And neither did it mean that both Ozzy and Max were up to no good. She had discovered though that the two of them did smoke secretly. She discovered that inadvertently when she found a fag end in among Ozzy's books when she tried to clean out his bag of the detritus teenagers were collecting in their bags, bits of lunch, empty wrappers, that sort of stuff and then there it was, among the books, a fag end. Again, it did not mean of course that Ozzy was smoking; just that there was a fag end. But somehow Amethyst knew, just knew that Ozzy smoked secretly and she implicated Max along with it.

Her hitherto skyblue worryless existance had thrown up black clouds; gremlins or no gremlins. Life had thrown obstacles in her way and she was required to deal with them. But how? Confronting her son was not her way and in ordinary times she would have told Konrad to see what he made of the situation. Only, she did not find any courage at the present to confront her husband with the fag-end business of her son; she would also have to blurt out that she knew he was conducting an affair behind her back. She was not ready to do either and so, she said nothing, but wowed to observeboth: matters of her son's fag end and Konrad's supposed affair, to see what might transpire in the process to give her more certainty of either.

Chapter 15

Konrad Is Caught Out

Amethyst's suspicions about her son's secret smoking, was not unfounded. It was Max who had found, so he claimed a lot later, a full packet of cigarettes on his way home from college. Ordinarily he usually went home with Ozzy and his sister; when he bent down to pick up something on the pavement, Minnie had wanted to know what it was and had admonished him:

"Mother always warns against picking up stuff from the pavement as nothing good could be found there but bacteria". Max had countered that it was all poppycock, that sometimes people lost things and other people would find it and it was surely finders keepers. Minnie still wanted to know what it was that he thought was so precious that he had to 'find it and keep' but then her brother chipped in and, coming to Max's aid, took the packet of cigarettes from Max's hand and put it in his pocked. To Minnie he said he would race her to the next post, which to his sister was always proof that the boys were up to something. However, she agreed about being raced, because usually she won as she was faster. And so it was that the siblings raced and indeed Minnie had won hands-down. For Ozzy it meant that she had forgotten about wanting to know what it was that Max had picked up off the pavement and was now languishing in his pocket.

When Max had taunted his pal with the cigarettes that he had found, but were now in Ozzy's pocket, the latter had looked at the packet which was full and said that it was a bad habit to start that, but Max had said that since it cost nothing they might as well share in the smoke to see what it was that people who did smoke found so fascinating about it. And so it was that the youngsters had their first cigarette and there was a fair deal of coughing and spluttering and they did not even finish that first cigarette. Ozzy would decide later that smoking was definitely not for him, but Max kept trying and found the smoking was after a bit much less as nauseous.

Ozzy's mother was thus concerned about her son, but she did not want to interfere in her son's friendship with Max, whom she liked, and so perhaps, had she intervened and alerted Tina, Max's smoking might not have led to a drug habit later.

When it eventually became obvious what Max was up to it was at first assumed that because Max's real parents had died of a drug overdose, it might have been in Max's genes and it was on the cards that Max would go the same way. But Amethyst who had other concerns had taken her eye off the ball. Her concerns were about her husband and her marriage and for the moment that trumped everything else, so Max's habit was slowly forming and nobody was any the wiser.

*****

Max had started the pernicious habit of smoking. Amethyst suspected it but had no proof except that his clothes started to smell of stale tobacco whenever Max was visiting. Accusing her son bluntly drew a blank also because he vehemently denied everything to do with smoking. Since his mother had other concerns, that of her husband being unfaithful to her and she now having proof, she did not know how to broach the subject. Ozzy perceived that there was something not quite right but he decided to say nothing; he felt it had not been his place to say anything, so he just became the silent observer. He could see that something

140

serious about his parents was in the offing and he grew taciturn over it but still said nothing.

In any event Konrad was always his usual affectionate self towards his wife and in the end she doubted herself that she had actually seen him and this woman at the Savoy, holding hands. She wanted to persuade herself that perhaps it had been a dream. It did not work. Amethyst was a down to earth woman not given to dreaming impossible things and so, one evening, after supper she came out with the following:

"You know darling, you should be more careful when you leave clothes to be taken to the dry cleaners, for the other day you left a fifty pound note in the top pocket. And only because the assistant cleaning lady was honest and gave it back to me on collection did I realise you had been careless. You know I never check pockets, so it is up to you to make sure the suits are empty of possessions."

Amethyst watched his face after her little speech, but her husband betrayed nothing. He just nodded his head and said he supposed that fifty quid would buy a poorly paid person a few things and it was nice to know that there were still people in the world who valued honesty more than greed. Having now broached the subject, Amethyst did not want to leave it at that, so she carried on:

"The thing is, that was not all you left in the top pocket; along with the money you left a post-it-note that said 'Chum, 4.10 at the Savoy as usual'. What was that for?"

Amethyst watched her husband's face more closely now to gauge his reaction.

"Did I leave that as well? I must be getting old. The note was probably for Christine, the secretary to remind her that I hold meetings at the Savoy rather than the office".

Amethyst persisted. "Well, it is not as simple as that, darling, for I could not make out who Chum was, so I went to the Savoy and saw you with Christine at the table in the far corner of the hotel, *holding hands*. I am not stupid and want to know how long you have been having an affair with your secretary?"

Konrad stared at his wife. Clearly he had not expected to be put on the spot in this fashion. But now the secret was out and he had to explain himself and that to him was far from easy. It was the case that he still loved his wife, but life was complex and he found himself in an unenviable position of loving two women, something that he knew Amethyst would not be able to understand, much less tolerate.

So there was the dilemma but Konrad knew it was time to put his cards on the table. And Konrad was at a loss how to do this. He loved his wife, but he had got roped into an affair with his secretary and it had gone on for quite a time. Occasionally his secretary made noises about his leaving his family, but that was a road he did not want to go down on; he loved Amethyst and could not see himself getting a divorce. At the same time, he knew that he was stringing Chum along and that was less than fair. Chum for her part knew that this was difficult for her lover and she let herself be swept up with her lover's enthusiasm of love making and it was easier to be folded in her lover's arms than confront reality.

Chapter 16

Fenalla's discovery

Fenella Gettevan had taken stock and concluded her life was unsatisfactory.Very unsatisfactory. She was lumbered with an unsatisfactory husband and, to top it all, had an unsatisfactory balance sheet and a miserable life. The latter she put down to the first two, Karl, and her inadequate balance sheet. Life with Karl had not improved. She kept telling him that she failed to understand how his marriage to Mary-Jane had lasted so long when he was such a miserable husband. Karl in turn said that life with her was no picnic either and he regretted ever having left Mary-Jane and his children. Fenella could not leave it at that and sneered that his ex-wife could not have been that brilliant in every way since he found time to conduct a clandestine nine year affair with her daughter. Karl's answer to that was to leave the room. And so the rows continued.

By any standard Fenella was quite rich and there were many people who would look at her balance sheet and conclude that its bearer had certainly nothing to complain about. But to Fenella what she had was not enough and she bcmoaned the fact that her income stream, the proceeds of her slipping and falling in stores and malls, had dried up. Naturally it was the fault of Karl that it had, him and that ghastly man, Bob Wagtail who dared to say that if she continued with her action it would be vigorously defended as he had video evidence. That had nailed everything for Fenella for she knew that that avenue of moneymaking would be lost to her as more and more stores had cameras installed, chiefly to deter shoplifters and she had been caught in that same net, more was the pity.

But Fenella never could accept that what she had done was actually fraudulent. To justify her actions she told Karl that she was not the only one who followed up on an opportunity; she had merely seen a gap in the market and filled it. Had not been there a forerunner at the beginning of the 20th century, involving the world wide brand name of Coca Cola? All that hallaballoo then over whether it was right that a soft drink should actually contain cocaine when it was sold even to children. But the cocaine content had not been the half of it. The problem there had lain in the bottling of the drink. Returnable bottles arrived at bottling plants with slugs, roaches, mice, even cigarette butts and slime and unmentionable creatures of the undergrowth. The trouble was that early rinsing machinery could not remove these 'foreign things' and so they became part of the refreshing and delicious drink sold to the public.

The foreign things contained in the bottles along with the drink made excellent newspaper copy, but the important thing was that bottlers tended to – like in Fenella's case – settle out of court for sizeable sums in order to avoid adverse publicity and expensive lawsuits they would have to defend. Naturally it attracted quite quickly fraudulent claims; once it had attracted publicity there were many people seeking redress and it was even found that one woman who threatened litigation had been paid the same hush money *twice* as she moved around the country filing lawsuits.

So, Fenella felt she was not the only one who followed up on a gap in the market; she was not even a famous one, but since that income stream had now dried up she had surely grounds to want to replace her loss with another winning formula. However much Fenella blamed third parties, the fact was that she needed a replacement and she had racked her brain to get an equivalent one without having to do much work. She had tried but had as yet to come up with anything tangeable, not to say workable.

One time, in a small cafe she had had some cake to go with her coffee and found a small sliver of glass in the cake. Making a fuss over it at the counter, the girl looked crestfallen and said she would have to consult management. Making a fuss was of course Fenella's forte but rant as she did, the manager of the cafe merely said that none of the products were made on the premises, everything was bought in and she would have to complain to the manufacturer. However, here Fenella was on sure ground as she knew the law. She told them that her 'contract' was with the cafe and she would sue the cafe; what the shop did with it was their affair. In that of course Fenella was entirely within her rights. So, the cafe accepted liability and said they would forward the cake and piece of glass found in it to the manufacturer. They would let her know in due course.

Of course, once home, she harangued Karl about how terrible it was to eat some cake then find glass in it, what was the world coming to. Karl told her that she had done right to say that the onus was on the cafe to put things right. If the manufacturer was at fault it would be the cafe that had to deal with it.

But, if Fenella hoped that her income stream would be put back on line with this, she was mistaken. The cafe did come back to her to say that the manufacturer refused to accept liability by stating that the glass was not from their product: nevertheless without accepting liability they sent a cheque for one hundred dollars and a huge new cake free of charge. Fenealla accepted with bad grace. The cheque for the small amount of money was never going to improve her balance sheet and neither was the cake. Karl, moreover, had done a bit of research into the matter and had found that the cafe was just a small shop, did not belong to a chain, and if she continued with a lawsuit the cafe would simply shut shop and go bankrupt and she would in any case get zilch. For once Fenealla accepted that verdict but for her it was back to the drawing board. She needed something a lot meatier than finding a piece of glass in a cake and winning a cake and a derisory amount of money. She also realised that using blackmail to get a sufficient amount of money out of Longhorn over at Connecticut would be a long shot. She had tried it though as Fenella's mantra as always was not to leave any stone unturned.

She had turned up at Longhorn's casino and had demanded to speak to him. Longhorn did and it took quite a while into Fenella's talk for Longhorn to realise which way the wind was blowing. Even before Fenella could enlighten Longhorn that she knew he had a daughter whose name was Shayne and who was being brought up not by her rightful mother, but by his sister Birri, Longhorn had cut her off in mid flow and before Fenella had had a chance to blurt out the secret. Longhorn did not want to know but told her bluntly that if she was asking for money to keep anything quiet, she had come to the wrong place. He then told her that there was perhaps plenty of money to be made at his casino but she would have to place a bet first then pray to the gods that her bet would come good.

Fenella was not into betting. She never laid out money where it was doubtful that a return cold be gained and so the meeting broke up and Fenella stalked out in bad grace again. Longhorn's secret was consigned to history, while she still had to discover something that would bring her a sizeable income without having to much work for it. Better still one that did not involve the legal practice; something she could do quietly and on her own without anyone knowing about it.

However, for now she was at square one and no nearer to any new wheeze that could translate into a new income stream. Meantime Karl as a husband was as unsatisfactory as ever. Not that Karl felt much different about his wife. He had long since regretted having divorced Mary-Jane, though she had divorced *him* once Fenella had put her wise about her husband's affair with her daughter for nine long years. The long suffering Mary-Jane finally thought that her husband was a louse while at the same time wondering why she had never tumbled to these 'clients' out of state that took him away for weekends. For her part, discovering that Fenella had actually married her ex-husband she assumed correctly that Fenella had been duplicitous in order to get the divorce and knowing that eventuallysoftened her attitude towards her ex-husband.

However it was, Karl missed the tranquillity he had had with his ex-wife and he too missed the children. He felt he should have been a lot stronger in resisting Fenella's constant pressing for divorce in order to marry her. He should also have listened better to his partner James when he had told her one time that Fenella was canny, but, boy, would he pity any man who was married to her. Instead of listening to reason he was now shackled to a woman in an unsatisfactory marriage. Yes, to Karl, without a doubt being married to Fenella was worse than what he had imagined to be married to Myra with her drug habit. He found now, that having promised marriage to Myra in a future that, as far as he was concerned, would never come, he was now married to her mother for real and there seemed to be no way out of that. Talk about jumping fromt the frying pan into the fire with Myra; having married Fenella was jumping feet first into hell.

*****

Fenella sat in her bed and brooded. She was fed up with everything. She still had half a million dollars in the bank and it was not enough for her. She simply bemoaned the fact that her lovely income stream from her fraudulent slip and fall venture had come to a premature end. She had racked her brain but try as she might nothing comparable by way of a money spinner came to her head. The glass in the cake and the threatened lawsuit turned out to be a fiasco, as was the intended blackmailing of Longhorn. She was losing her

147

touch. Moreover, her marriage was another fiasco, being tied to the most boring man in the universe. And her daughter Myra thought the world of him and even had hopes of marrying him. Well, she, Fenella did marry him and she could state definitely that she could never understand how his ex-wife, Mary-Jane could even have two children with such a bore.

Thinking about her husband and how unsatisfactory he was made her get out of bed and start tidying the drawer, Karl's as well. He of course had left hours ago for his office downtown which he ran with his partner. Fenella thought wrily that the partnership had now one client less. Rooting around in the drawers she came across a large file with a buff cover. It was Karl's. Idly she looked through it and suddenly had a light bulb moment. What she had in her hands was her husband's life insurance policy for one million dollars. In the event of his death he had decreed that his ex-wife and his children were to be beneficiaries. Or not if she could prevent it.

Fenella now suddenly had a plan; carefully she put that file back into the drawer the way she found it and closed it. She would broach the subject gingerly when the time was right, which could not be soon enough. What she had in mind was for Karl, in the event of his untimely death, to make the million dollar policy over to her; after all she was his wife now and she had every intention to make him acknowledge that. For the next two days she stopped haranguing Karl about being unsatisfactory in every way and was even nice to him. Karl for his part was suspicious about Fenella being so nice to him and realised that something was in the offing, but he could not fathom what that might be.

Two weeks went by and Karl was beginning to think that his wife had at last seen reason and had finally accepted that he was a sufficiently good husband, when one night, after dinner, in dulcet tones she began to talk about the end of Life. Karl had never had any idea how much his wife was worth financially; he had never seen a bank statement but if he had he would have been astonished to see just how much she had in the bank. Of course he had helped her to riches with the slip and fall lawsuits but he never gave it much thought as to what she did with the proceeds. When Myra was still alive he was under the impression that Fenella had given her daughter a generous allowance which made it easy for her to obtain all these silver-foiled drugs that eventually lead to her demise.

Fenella was not actually suggesting now to Karl that either of them should die, only that precautions should be taken in case *he* did. Because Fenella had been so nice to him, Karl had let slip that he had an insurance policy in the event of his death of which Mary-Jane and the kids would be the beneficiaries. Fenella feigned ignorance and professed to be astonished at hearing that.

"But what about me?" she inquired of Karl: "what about if you should die, it means that if Mary-Jane and the children will get the proceeds of your policy you are leaving me high and dry with nothing to fall back on. I don't think that this is entirely fair, do you?"

Karl told her he had never even thought about that, but now that she was bringing it up he would have to think about it. The problem was, he said, the legal partnership was not bringing now the proceeds with her out of the picture and he had a lot less liquidity and he needed to think very carefully how to spend his income. The children still went to an expensive school and he had promised his ex-wife that in that respect, as far as the children were concerned there would be no change. He also had to make to Mary-Jane monthly alimony payments and those sums were further eating into his available cash.

Fenella was unimpressed and told her husband that it was surely time his ex-wife faced reality and sent their children to a normal school which was free. Karl shook his head miserably and said he could not change that because it was what had been agreed at the divorce stage and any new renegotiations would have to be sanctioned by a court of law. His ex-wife would never agree to change from fee-paying schools to state schools without kicking up a tremendous fuss.

"Well, I understand all that, but at the same time it seems to me unfair that you are putting your family first and me last and I do have a solution and that is that at the very least, if you can't renegotiate the terms of your divorce, you could make your insurance policy over to me, so that at least if something horrible were to happen to you, and I God forbid,would not have to go into the streets with the begging bowl."

However it was, Fenella got Karl to sign over the policy to her and less than two weeks after the hapless Karl had done so, Feneall went back to tell him that while Albert, her first husband had been unsatisfactory too, he had been a shining light compared to what he, Karl was and she rued the day she had the misfortune to marry him and could not, for the life of her see what the hell, Myra had seen in him.

Chapter 17

Shayne

Time too had moved on for Shayne who was now a young woman of nearly 20. She was a beautiful specimen of womanhood, some four inches short of six feet, with raven black hair whch she kept short and a natural skin complexion with a hue that pointed to her tribe, Shawnee, a slight tint into the red. There were quite a few suitors interested in courting the young woman, but Shayne had so far shown no interest in the opposite sex. Bigfoot, her father had said that he would never interfere in her private affairs and as to some boyfriend she would produce one, he was sure, in good time, when she was ready.

Neither Bigfoot nor Birri, had ever enlightened her as to her true parentage and so Shayne was in ignorance that actually Akwase was her real mother and Longhorn the father and that Birri had insisted that since the baby was born out of wedlock, it should be she the parent who would bring her up.

Birri was still married to Bigfoot but over the years they had grown distant. The reason for that did not lay with Birri but with Bigfoot himself. As Suni, Birri's sister, had foretold all these long years ago that Shayne would be her only child and Birri had flown into a rage for being told that, it had nonetheless come true. Now Birri did not mind so much. Motherhood had proved harder than she had imagined but for Bigfoot who had wanted a large family he firmly thought that failure to do so lay with him. He was under the impressen that since he himself was a hulk of a man, he would have no trouble in producing offspring and he could not understand that several years into the marriage Shayne was the only child in that family. In the first few years of non production he had shrugged it off, but as time went by and Birri did not become pregnant, it started to gnaw on him. It never occurred to him that the fault might lie with Birri, that she was barren; he just accepted that it was he who was at fault but over time he grew bitter over it. Birri, who had never relished sex with him did not seem to mind his increasing reluctance to be intimate with his wife.

While Birri and Shayne, did not get along, the latter was very close to Suni, the youngest in the quartet, so when there was a row, which was frequent, she would flee to Suni to seek clarification. And it was on one such occasion it was also Suni who enlightened Shayne as to her true parentage, after which a lot became clear to Shayne as to why she and her adoptive mother did not get along. But Suni said it would be foolhardy to tell either Akwase or Birri that she knew. After all, the latter had kept it a secret even from her husband and it was surely best to let sleeping dogs lie. Suni also advised that it was not in Shayne's best interest to let Birri know that she knew. It was for her ears only and it was a secret that it was also best for Shayne to keep to herself.

After their afternoon chat which was now several weeks in the past, Suni had closed the door on Shayne and had watched her walk down the garden path. Whenever Suni had an idea formulated in her mind she saw no reason not to execute it at the earliest. And so the following day she had gone over to her sister in law, Akwase. It was never Suni's idea to beat about the bush, but was always blunt in her requests. And so this time as well. She had been invited by her sister-in-law to come and sit down on their comfortable sofa and, having pushed a drink into her hands, Suni came out with it. She wanted the address of Max's adoptive parents in England. Akwase who new her sister in law well and knew she would never ask a question without a motive in her brain, looked a bit puzzled.

"Why would you want that?" she asked Suni and the latter said that Shayne wanted to go and spend some time getting to know Max. Her studies at college were finished and she had time on her hands. She was not getting along too well with her mother and it seemed a good idea for the girl to get away for a while. Absence makes the heart grow fonder as the saying goes. Akwase was a bit puzzled about that because, while Max had been in regular correspondence with her and Lightfoot and still called them nana Akki and gramps Liffet, it seemed a bit odd to her that Shayne wanted to visit Max. Suni told her that she needed the address because she wanted to write to the Easterwoods to receive an invitation for Shayne to go and stay with them for a bit. Akwase had accepted that explanation and could see no further reason to refuse her sister-in-law and so she had gone into what passed as her husband's office to fetch the address. Suni said that nobody had even a photo of the boy and since he was five when any of them had last clapped eyes on him, he would by now have turned into a young man ready for the world. It seemed only right and proper that one had a closer idea of his character and Shayne was the girl to do it. They seemed close enough in age to get along. Akwese said that it was true that there weere no photographs since Max had been taken to England but he had sent a few sketches of himself over time so she and Lightfoot could see how he was developing. To her mind he had turned into a very goodlooking lad.

However it was Akwase put Max's address into Suni's hand who then departed. She would write the letter to Mrs Damatina Easterwood and she was confident that the family would issue the required invitation in due course.

The letter duly written it was not long before indeed the hoped for invitation came to Suni. The latter had thought of asking for this invitation to be sent to Shayne but then realised that her sister would not see it as a breach of privacy to open her daughter's letter and so she thought it would be prudent to have the invitation come to her and let Shayne explain it to Birri in good time. There would be ructions but she would be on hand to coach Shayne through the worst of it.

*****

True to her inclination Suni did not delay in sending her letter to the Family Easterwood which asked if it were convenient for her niece Shayne, to come to England in her gap year and make acquaintance with Max whom, alas she had never met but had heard a lot about him. If they could recommend a nice bed and breakfast place where she could stay, so as to be not too far away from them, her niece would be grateful. The letter duly sent Suni was astonished to receive a letter back almost by return. Also not long after Shayne would come tumbling through her doors to seek 'sanctuary' in Suni's house after a tiff with her father, too trivial to mention, but when pressed, she had missed dinner and her father had been unhappy about that and had upbraided her.

Suni showed her the letter from Damatina Easterwood who had written the following:

Dear Suni,

It was so very nice to hear from Max's erstwhile family and my husband, and I and Max would be more than happy to offer a room in our house to Shayne, for her to stay as long as she needs to. I have spoken to Max who was over the moon to hear from Shayne and even more 'over the moon' to read that Shayne had been wanting to make his acquaintance for many years now, but felt only now able to come to England because she had finsihed her studies and was a bit at a loose end until college started the following year. We would not know here in the vicinity a suitable b&b for Shayne but feel that a room in our house would be the better resolution. In short the three of us would be more than happy to accommodate the young woman to come and stay in our home. We look forward to have final

154

date of arrival when we would collect her from the airport, assuming that she would come by plane.

In anticipation of this rare visit, we remain,
cordially
Damatina ,Tina' Easterwood.

Shayne read the letter and it was her turn to be astonished. She was asmazed that unbeknown to her Suni had written to the Easterwoods and even more amazed that that family, which now included the elusive Max, would entertain having a woman, of whom they knew nothing, in their own house. She had not expected that, but Suni was at hand to explain that although she knew the Easterwoods to be extremely rich, they were entirely human. That they were rich Suni had been told by Fenella, who had lamented that it was surely beyond the pale that a rich family like the Easterwoods would not compensate her for the loss of her very dear grandson, and to cap it all, her own daughter had died in questionable circumstances and yet Mrs Easterwood had replied to her entreaties for money in a perfunctory matter, but leaving her in no doubt that no money was forthcoming, while reminding her that he was her brother too and she had felt it was only right and proper that his offspring should be reared by the family rather than having to make do with foster carers because the dead woman's mother could not be bothered to care for the boy.

Suni had said nothing to Fenella. She had decided to keep her own counsel, that being the better part of valour. She too had not liked the grasping Fenella all that much but saw no reason to be nasty to her since she too had lost her daughter, however she felt about also having lost her grandson.

Chapter 18

The Journey to England

The Day of Shayne's departure had come. Birri was ambivalent about her daughter going over the water to a family she had never met but knew about since it was Max's home and had been for many year now. That Shayne had instructions from Suni, that of bringing back the silver snake with the emerald green eyes she knew nothing because Suni had not thought to enlighten her about that. As to losing her daughter for a bit she did not really mind, for her it was a chore less to have to cook for, one mouth less to feed and catering for Bigfoot would be easy; he was not into food and for him, as long as he had something before him on a plate he was happy enough. But Bigfoot minded that his daughter was leaving and for such a long time too it seemed to him; he was fond of the girl who was always in a positive mood unlike his wife where he never knew which foot out of bed would mean she was in a good or bad mood for the whole day.

However, for Shayne's sake he was happy that she experienced the world. She was young and the only advice he had to give her was not to lose the Shawnee ways, to remember that she was first and foremost a Shawnee.

In spite of it all there had been quite a bit of argy-bargy about her mode of going. Bigfoot had wanted her to stay on terra firma which meant going by ship. Shayne had pointed out to her father that there was no terra firma going by boat as it sailed on water and one could drown just as easily if a ship capsized, as one could die if the plane fell out of the sky. Bigfoot could see that but it still seemed incongruous to him that a big machine, weighing many tons, carrying hunreds of people could be sustained only with speed and air under its wings. To be sure birds could fly effortlessly, but by comparison they were weightless, their feathers water and windproof and it was a different thing altogether. Shayne however persisted and so Bigfoot had been minded to buy her the flight ticket. At the airport everyone of her family was there, though Birri had professed a fersome headache and had stayed behind, but Suni had come and Lightfoot and Akwase too, even Longhorn and Okonde with their children in tow and it had been quite an emotional farewell from her family who all wished her Godspeed with tears in their eyes and reminders that she should not forget them but write about her experience in the air.

And so Shayne had taken her seat in the aeroplane and had watched with not a little trepidation how the plane had taken off, felt the bump as it took into the air and watched through the window how terra firma disappeared with some speed. How the houses and street lights got tinier and soon she could see nothing but clouds, then the plane rose above the clouds and she had glorious sunshine. She had been a little fearful about what her father had said about big machines like that having a habit of falling out of the sky for no reason at all; it seemed to him standing to reason that they did, seeing how heavy they were compared to the bird.

But when the big plane was in the clouds and people in their seats loosened their belts and the stewardess came round offering food, it wa a different feeling altogether and she relaxed too. Before her was a tiny screen that charted the plane's route across the Atlantic and then she watched a film too. The journey across the Atlantic was in other ways a quite uneventful and the plane had landed safely. Having gone through passport control, and retrieved her suitcase, she was met by Tina and Brendan Easterwood, her hosts who had sent her the invitation to stay with them. The letter had said she could stay with them for as long as she liked; they had not wanted to hear about her suggestion of staying in a hostel, hotel or other such establishment; that they had more than enough rooms to accommodate her and since she was practically family, what was the problem?

It had been Tina and Brendan who had welcomed her, but Max had not come to the airport. Tina had told her that Max had a prior engagement but he would see her later. And with that Shayne had been taken to Tina and Brendan's swish home and she had marvelled at the luxury of their furniture. She had never seen anything like it. Her room too, at the top of the house was beautifully and richly furnished, all satin and leather and the actual room was far bigger than anything she had at home. She had been told by Tina to make herself at home, there was plenty of time till teatime and there was no need for her to think she had to make conversation. It would all happen in good time. That it had been a long journey and she needed to get used to being in a different country now. With that she was left alone.

Shayne had looked out of the window and saw grass and trees and beautifully manicured lawns. So that was England then. It was really no different from America. It was a town house that she was residing in now and through the massive windows whe could seen people walking along the perimeter of the wall that defined the property. The people walking by seemed the same. They walked the same way as they did in America and as yet she could see no difference in the two countries bar the fact that they might speak slightly differently to how they spoke at home, though it would be a type of English, with a different accent, which is how she had been taught at school.

That the family was rich she could easily imagine from her surroundings. Outside the lawns were beautifully manicured and at the far side she could see a large swimming pool with deck chairs all around one side. She would try that pool for she could swim like a fish. But for now she looked forward to meeting the much talked about Max and remembered that Suni, her auntie, had pressed her not ot forget to bring back that enamelled snake. Ah, that snake! To take that back was very much in the future. First she had to meet and get to know him and for now she was in no hurry to relieve him of it, having only just arrived, it could all wait. All in good time, she said to herself, as she laid on her large bed with the silk covers and promptly fell asleep. It had been a very long day.

*****

Shayne was woken by the near silent entry of the maid who had come in to close the curtains and look at the sleeper. Her mistress had asked not to wake her, that she would wake up in good time when her body clock told her to and there was lots of time for everything else. Teatime had been missed and so had been dinner time, for now it was dark outside and the wrist watch on her left hand told her it was eight in the evening. Shayne was horrified and as the maid was still standing there, undecided as to what to do since the new guest had woken up, Shayne asked her her name. She said her name was Mary and with that the maid decided that it was time to leave.

*****

When Max was told two months before Shayne's arrival that a member of the Shawnee family, a young woman called Shayne had been invited by the family for a stay at their house, Max had been intrigued. He was still in correspondence with gramps Liffet and he in his letters to Max had kept the latter informed of all that was happening with the Shawnee people. But neither gramps nor nana had ever mentioned a girl with the name of Shayne, nor that she was the daughter of Birri and Bigfoot Teakwood. Not that Max would have recognised Shayne's parents, as gramps Liffet had never spoken in detail about his sister. Gramps Liffet in every letter had only ever written that he hoped that his erstwhile charge who was growing up in England would not forget the Shawnee and indeed in every reply that Max had sent to him in return he said he would never forget the tribe and that also he was still in possession of that sliver of silver, the green eyed mamba and he would always take care of that.

So when he was told that a Shawnee daughter was making an appearance for a period, possibly six months or even a year, he had been intrigued as to what she might look like. When it came to the arrival date, Tina had asked Max to come with them to the airport but Max had said that he could not make that date as he had lessons that day. So he had got out of meeting the girl at the airport. That had been a fib. Max had no lessons that day and he could easily have gone to the airport. But he did not want to. He had his reasons, one of which was that by now Max was smoking regularly and they were not cigarettes he was smoking but snorting cocaine. He thought that Shayne in all likelyhood might be a woman of the world and would see immediately that Max was a drug user and he wanted to prevent being found out in this way. Mama, or indeed Papa had been in ignorance as yet over his drug use. Mama who had lost her brother to that pernicious habit was quite vigilant but Max was always a step ahead of her. For one thing he never took the drug into the house, nor made use of it there, but he hid it in the cellar in a place that no one in the family would look when they or one of the staff would go down to fetch a required bottle of wine for consumption upstairs.

However, Max knew in the way that drug users are wary of being found out, that his eyes might be the give-away, started wearing sun shades indoors. When he first started with that, Tina had said to him

„What's with the shades"? but Max had been ready for that and had told his Mama that of late his eyes had been tiring when sketching and he had walked into an opticians who told him that he should avoid eye strain by wearing light coloured sun shades. Tina had accepted that and as to the amount of money he spent on buying ‚coke' his pocket money was on the generous side and Brendan for one never asked what he did with the money. He felt that Max was now a young man and if he took a girl out it would be Max who would be picking up the tab in a restaurant.

It would have been a lot less trouble had one or other parent been a little more suspicious as to why their son was suddenly wearing sun shades indoors as well as outdoors, which was of course to prevent detection of eye dilation or querying what Max did with his money every month.

Especially Tina who had harangued her own mother over the way she had dealt with her son by buying him a flat in Knightsbridge in order to keep him out of the way of snooty friends asking awkward questions might have been justified in looking at Max more closely. Tina had told her mother that that she would never have got her brother out of the way and unsupervised into a flat, no matter how swish. Indeed, she had insisted that the flat in Knightsbridg after Pelly's death be sold since it was unlikely that anyone else in her family would ever require to live there for any reason. She herself would never allow Max to live on his own even though she had as yet no idea about Pelly's habit having been transferred to his son too. And so, under ther noses of his parents Max's drug use took hold while its user insisted that he would never get addicted. The only one who knew about it but decided to keep quiet was his friend and cousin, Ozzy.

Oskar had decided quite early on, after smoking the forbidden cigarettes that had been an unexpected find on the pavement on the way from school, that smoking was not for him. He told Max it would lead to addiction since there was something that cigarette companies put into the paper in which the cigarette was wrapped – saltpetre – it was precisely so that the smoker would get addicted and therefore become a regular client of a brand of cigarette whatever it would be. Max of course had said that only stupid and weak people would become addicted that people with a mind of their own had a will to say enough was enough and keep to an occasional smoke out of fun.

That of course was not the case and Max indeed progressed from cigarettes to marijuana, then hashish and finally this led to his buying cocaine and getting to know dealers who were happy to count him as a regular client. Max however refrained from telling any of the dealers where he lived and always made sure that he appointed a time and a place wherever so he could receive the package himself. He also made sure he always used known dealers to make sure that he always received the same quality and strength. So Max became addicted despite his strength of character to say *no* and slowly he also became withdrawn and at times sullen and nobody in his family could put a finger on it as to Max's mood swings.

Outwardly he was still the same, still sketched and often saw Woody, whom he called Marcus, where the two of them would sit and sketch a variety of different subjects, but Max was careful that he was always wearing his sun shades and Marcus, after the first query as to why he needed those, accepted that he had eye strain and his optician had advised that sun shades avoided that. Marcus,who had never had eye strain of any sort, accepted that people were different. Max too, unlike Marcus, had light coloured eyes while his were dark brown, so the latter readily accepted that light coloured eyes were possibly more susceptible to eye strain, so he too too had no inkling that Max was now a coke-addict. Having let Stephanie into his secret room and told her that he was the originator of the *estro* paintings, he had felt that it was time that his parents knew too, so one day he went to his ols home and told father who had simply not wanted to believe that his son was so very brilliant to have painted the pictures on his wall. Eventually he had accepted that this was so but Marcus had extracted the promise from dad that this was a secret and had to stay in the family, for he did not want to be widely known by any public.

As to Shayne's arrival at the Easterwood home Max's worry was his drug use being found out. He had no idea what this girl would be like nor what to expect of this new guest and so, he decided, it was best to be careful which included not being present at the airport to greet the girl.

When he did meet Shayne two days later he was pleasantly surprised how natural a young woman Shayne was. Max had talked to several girls from college and they all, without exceptions, had let him know that they would never let a boy get the better of them. Most professed to be ardent feminists and, indeed, never stopped telling him that women's rights trumped those of men's and the girl with whom he shared class, Michelle, even told him that within fifty years or so, science would be sufficiently advanced that women could produce babies without the help of a man.

„What it amounts to is basically, that *woman* has the womb, her most important asset, and man would be superfluous. In fact it was probably best not to produce boys in the first place. Women could live without them, no question", she said only to launch into harangue about ancient history.

„In pre-historic times it had in any case been a matriarchial society, where women ruled but, since science had not yet invented a system by which woman could have babies without the help of a man, it still needed men to help create a baby and so a man, nominated as King, was used for the purpose of procreation but then he had to die afterwards. This system prevailed for a time but then the so called king complained and said it was unfair he should have to die after producing progeny and so women relented and let him live a litte longer, but he still had to die before the baby was born. So Kings complained a bit more and then emotions got involved by which these Kings no longer died because the child bearers fell in love with them and so a King lived with the female with whom he produced an offspring and then, nobody knew how it happened but it slowly became a patriarchial society, unfortunately in my view, whereby it was *woman* who was now subservient to *man*. And look where it got us. Wars and destruction all caused by men in their bid for dominance; that would never have happened had it remained a matriarchial society.

But of course it was not just humans where it would be possible to have babies without the involvement of men. In the animal world quite a few species are this way, viz Komodo dragons who have evolved to reproduce both sexually and parthenogenetically because they mainly live isolated in the wild and become violent when approached. However, when the Komodo female dragon clones her own eggs, the resultant emerging babies are all of the male variety more's the pity I say.By contrast scientists have proved that the lowliest of the low, the aphids could produce offspring by the thousand without any help of males, and what they reproduce are all females which in my view is all to the good.

As to humans, we women have now realised that we have the womb which is more powerful than a man's penis. Eventually science will advance to such a degree that it is possible to produce babies without the help of any man. After all the Virgin Mary did and I for one   look forward to having *my* babies with no man in sight. As far as I am concerned men or boys such as you will be history in my lifetime and, moreover, we women will be quite happy with our own sex. If animals can do it and indeed have been doing this for millenia it will be possible soon for humans to do likewise".

Max had listened out of politeness but much of what Michelle had been saying went over his head. He never believed that women were happy on their own. But all the while the girl had been talking Max had been looking at her mouth that went up and own and widened and narrowed, as she spewed her bile in Max's direction. He stood there, enduring this girl's ear bashing, with his arms hanging by his sides, staring at her, but saying not a word. But quietly he knew what he knew. After all there were only two sexes in the world and he could not see why they could not live peacefully with each other. He thought of his Mama and Papa. They had no problem with being who they were and he could see no reason why he – in time with the right girl - could not emulate his parents happiness. With that in mind, he turned on his heels and went out of earshot. There was some more bile she shouted to his back, but Max no longer heard, nor took in what Michelle had said.

Instead, he was thinking about Shayne; she was, sexwise, one of their number but thankfully, from talks he and she had over time she did not think in that way. She was a girl and was happy in her own skin. Max liked the girl. They would get on he knew, but of his secret he would tell her nothing. He was also determined that she should see in him a regular member of the male species and this somehow excluded imparting to her his habit. In the event it would not turn out exactly how Max had planned it but for now he was happy with the girl who had come into the house, courtesy of his Mama and Papa and also for now he was content and also quite confident that he could keep his secret hidden from the world he inhabited.

The two of them had had many talks and once she had alluded to that silver snake he now wore on a silver chain around his neck and when Max had shown her the tattoo on his upper left arm she had wanted to know why he had a tattoo when he had the snake. Max had told her that when gramps Liffet gave him that snake he had told him that the gift was not just to remember him by, but also that this little sliver of silver was to keep him safe. He had always been in mortal fear of losing it and so he had the tattoo done by way of double indemnity, to be kept safe.

Chapter 19

Konrad's Dilemma

Konrad and Amerthyst's marriage was of the kind where both parties went about things in a civilised manner and even awkward stuff was dealt that way. Although one could not say that having an affair was just something awkward up for discussion, yet that too was dealt in a civilised manner. Nobody shouted, no harsh words were spoken but Amethyst sent her husband to the spare toom to sort himself out. Konrad did not like to be in the spare room. He wanted to be in the marital bed with his wife, for to him nothing had changed in the way he loved his wife. But even he could see that the situation was intolerable to Amethyst and so he agreed to be in the spare room while he decided what to do. And that was a dilemma for him. While his and Chum's consummation of their love was carried out in the Savoy, Konrad was dubious as to how this would pan out if they were to live together as a couple on a permanent basis. They had no social life together, because Konrad's time away from work was taken up with his family while Chum was languishing in a flat by herself but had family of her own, a mother and a sister. Father had died some years previously.

She was close to her sister and had opened up to her about the affair with her boss, Konrad. Sister Mariella had told Chum bluntly that Konrad wanted it both ways, such as being secure in his marriage and watching his children grow, while having a bit of extra on the side with her. Chum of course had agreed and told Mariella that she had made noises about coming clean with Amethyst and putting their love on a regular footing. She had told Konrad that she was tiring of the Savoy and the room upstairs. That room upstairs was impersonal and what she wanted was to live with her lover as man and wife and for that he had to divorce his wife and marry her.

Konrad knew that Chum was right, that he should do the decent thing and either close down the affair with her or the marriage with Amethyst. And that was his dilemma. He did not really want to lose Chum but neither could he contremplate divorce from from his wife. He knew that he was not fair to either woman; both were entitled to expect a full relationship, to the exclusion of anyone else. He had been in the spare room for a while and realised he could not carry on like that. So Konrad moved out.

When he told Amethyst that he was moving out, she thought, for better or for worse, her husband had decided to call time on their marriage but she raised no objection to his moving out. She watched him pack some of his clothes into a suitcase, then he kissed her on the forehead and said that it was best for everyone while he decided the future of his family. Then he was gone. Amethyst watched him through the window get into his car and head out of the drive way. She assumed that this was the end of her marriage which she had told to who all who would listen that hers was the happiest of marriages. Now, as she stood at the window watching the tail lights of her husband's car head out of the drive she turned from the window and went about her business. Her children had gone off to school so she could delay telling them, so for now she sat down on the kitchen table, having loaded the wasching machine, watching it turn, making herself a coup of tea, then wept bitter tears. How the hell did it get to this stage, from an innocuous little scrap of yellow paper with a bit of a scribble about four o'clock and Savoy, to the break up of her marriage?

Amethyst was inconsolable but after crying into her beverage for half an hour, she took stock and decided that for the sake of her children she had to carry on. Her children were no longer small, they were adolescents and would soon go out into the world and make their own mistakes; she would no longer have to help them out of any mess of their own making; there would then just be her. Ok, but for now the children were still in her house and until the time that they left that they would have to be told that their father had found new love and had left the house. The washing machine had finished its cycle and she stood up to unload it. There were still chores to be completed like in any household.

*****

If Chum now thought that Konrad's moving out of the spare room into a service flat would mean that he was now free to put their clandestine relationship on a regualar and proper footing, she was mistaken in that. Konrad had no thoughts of rushing from one relationship into another. For one thing he still loved his wife and could not contemplate a divorce. He also loved his children and wanted to see them grow into full adults. Marriage, he knew was not a bed of roses even if the going was good and his and Amethyst's marriage had been very good. So what happened? The weakness of the flesh, he concluded wrily. He had not been looking for an affair. For him Amethyst was more than enough woman. Sex was very good as well and he had certainly no complaints.

Chum had been his secretary for near on four years when one Christmas there had been this office party and although he had in mind to go home and leave the employees to get on with it, he was somehow roped into it and after a few glasses of champagne he found himself in his office with just himself and Chum and one thing led to another and it led to the regular spot in the afternoons in the Savoy. He had felt guilty but had also decided that this affair was his alone to solve and solve it he meant to but it just carried on for near on three years or more now. In one respect he liked the fact that there were now two women in his life, but in another respect he found that satisfying two women, one of them in

168

clandestine ways, quite stressful. Part of him longed for the simple ways of his marriage where he could just come home from work and there was Amethyst and his noisy kids and everything was peaceful and simple. Then Chum happened and everything became complicated.

Yes, he looked forward to the times in that room upstairs with Chum; she excited him in ways that were new to him – it was different to what he had in his marriage – and for a while he thought he could fashion the two relationships to his liking. This turned out to be erroneous too as both women had expectations different to what he had imagined. As to his wife he understood that she would have no understanding of an affair with another woman and would certainly never tolerate that and, in truth, he could never expect her to either, so he had decided to keep his affair under his hat and carry on as before as this seemed to be the easier option.

To be caught out in the way that he was had put him on the spot. Stupid of him to leave an innocuous little post-it note to Chum in the top pocket of his suit. But in another way perhaps he was meant to be found out in the way that he was, because now it was decision time and clearly he could not carry in in the manner that he had hitherto. But now he was in a service flat and did not like it, while Chum was quietly pressing him to come and live with her, but he was unwilling to do that. What did he know about Chum that would be different if indeed he would live with her. Amethyst was more than enough wife for him and in truth he did not need another. The truth was staring him in the face; he really did have to call time on the affair with Chum and go back to his wife and ask for her forgiveness. That is what he had to do, but doing it was another thing. It was best left for another day. His mind was made up but as yet he did not have the courage to tell Chum that their affair would have to come to an end. He anticipated the tears and the unhappiness and he did not look forward to that. However it was his soup and he had to eat it.

There, in his lonely service flat he realised just how much he missed Amethyst and the children and for him that was the deciding factor. He could not contemplate living with Chum and starting a new life with another women. He wanted Amethyst and his old life back.

That was the decision Konrad made to himself. The reality would be different but he had to find that out later, much later. He called Amethyst but the call was not answered. She was probably out. It irked him but at the same time why should she stay in and cry over the absence of an errant husband.

Chapter 20

Fenella Is Not Happy

Fenella now had Karl's life insurance policy made over to her. It was for a substantial sum, but the trouble for Fenella was that it could only be cashed on death of the policy holder and not even Fenella stooped this low to plot her husband's death, though he had not improved of being unsatisfactory. Fenella needed money, or at least, what she had in the bank was insufficient to be rich, as she saw it.

While she accepted unhappily that her income stream through slipping and falling in stores had had its day, it was still only logic that dictated to her that this was so, her brain still could not accept this fact. It had been such a lovely income stream for doing very little for it, bar bearing a few bruises, that she just could not take in that for her that avenue was closed, but she was about to find out.

When Fenella was miserable she usually got over it by treating herself to something. Usually it was an item of clothing. Fenella was in her fifties but still an attractive woman, with slim hips and legs and she knew how to present herself to bet advantage. This time she thought she would treat herself to a new suit. She had seen one in the mall and so got herself there in her Lincoln Continental. The mall belonged to WallMart and for people with huge cars there was, for a fee of course, a man at hand who would park it for her. She went into one of the outlets and later she could not say how, she ended up on the floor, on her backside. She had slipped on a bit of wet floor. This time it was for real. She had not seen it and before she knew it landed on the floor, Her brain was perplexed; for years she had scrutinised floors for the slightest of imprerfection to slip and fall, and here, with her mind of a new suit, not watching where she was going, ended up on its marble floors. Fenella may have been perplexed for a few seconds, but after that brain kicked in and she started to moan and make a fuss.

The store had a First Aid Station and within seconds, there were a man and a lady in First Aid Uniform, standing over her with concerned expressions on their faces. The way Fenella moaned the pair thought she had broken something but soon realised their error. So they helped her to a chair and attended her. They could not see any injuried, nor broken bones, so they offered her a cup of coffee and left to fetch that. But Fenella thought that she would make the most out of her unplanned situation and continued with her moaning. The coffee came and she drank that, all the while complaining that her whole body hurt. Fenella forgot about the suit and after a suitable time got up from her chair, summoned her car and drove home.

Losing no time to ring her husband, she explained to him what had happened and that she would definitely sue the store. Karl, listening to his wife, was more dubious and tried to explain to her that WallMart was not a good store to sue, since they had successfully sued various of its chains for the customary sum of $100,000 and had indeed been successful. This new thing to Karl seemed a bridge too far. It was provocation writ large. But Fenella was adamant. In her head she was already richer by a nice round sum of $100,000 and this was an opportunity she was in no way prepared to lose.

Karl realised it was pointless persuading his wife to let go of her endeavour merely said on the phone that they would discuss matters in the evening when he got home. They did discuss matters in the evening but all that produced was a fierce argument because Fenella would not listen to any argument that detracted her from increasing her bank balance in this way. To placate his wife, Karl agreed to fire off the fist salvo to the store to indicate that his client would sue, that she had sustained both mental and physical injury and the best way to alleviate both, was to pay compensation, fixed at $100,000. Karl had been in a huddle with his partner James and James had been dubious of its success. So had Karl, but the kind of 'what can you do' look suggested that they would go forward with the claim. Answer was swift; it arrived at the law firm in an oblong grey envelope and the contents of the letter within was anything but encouraging:

'We have received your claim and let you know that it is disputed. We accept liability in a limited way, since our First Aid Team had attended your client and had found that there were no broken bones and also no other injuries that our Team could detect. We accept that your client had a mishap in our store and hope sincerely that she had recovered. As to your claim of $100,000 to settle the issue, it seems to us very excessive. You may be aware that we have CCTV in all our stores and indeed, your client's fall was captured on one of the cameras. While we try not to minimise people's injuries it seems that the sum you mention more than merely excessive. Looking through our records it was discovered that you have made claimes against several of our stores in our chain and have been successfully paid out. This was before we had CCTV and we gave you for your client the benefit of the doubt. With the installation of this technology we are now in a position to evaluate every claim and we have found that, while we accept that this country may be the most litigious in the western world, it is not the case that outrageous sums of money need to be paid in compensation for the smallest of mishaps..

We view your client's claim excessive because of the smallness of injuries sustained. We therefore suggest a far smaller sum, to settle the issue, that of $500 for hurt feelings and ssuming you accept that we consider the matter closed. Should you, for your client insist on such a large compensation for such a small incident, we let you know that any action would be rigorously defended'.

It is impossible to describe what happened when Karl had to tell his wife that the maximum her genuine fall in the store had amounted to a good will cheque of only $500, which, when fees were taken out of it, left a net amount of $400. Suffice it to say that Fenella went wild and accused her husband and her partner of gross incompetence, while secretly conceding that this last action, though genuine, had proved to her once and for all that this line of fraudulent income stream was now forever in the past. Fenella took to her bed for the next two days and Karl had to go to a restautant to get his meals. He was not unduly sorry for that; he would do anything to get out of a disgruntled wife's remonstrations as to how unsatisfactory a husband he was.

Chapter 21

Dexter from Texas

Konrad was still in his service flat contemplating his next step which was to return to his wife and children and call it a day with Chum. He was undecided but still fondly believed that the decision to go either way was his to make. It had been over six months now that Konrad had moved out of the spare room and Amethyst had stopped crying over his leaving her for at least the last two months. She was getting used to living by herself and the children. As for Oskar and Margaretha they were now into their late teens and no longer needed to be cared for as if they were still babies. Oskar, was in medical school and Margaretha was training to become a chartered accountant. Neither sibling wanted their mother to still call them by ther nick names. They insisted they were practically grown up and wanted her to refer to them to what it said on their birth certificates. For Amethyst this was a bit of getting used to but she tried to accommodate them. After all her brother and also her family had called her Amy and she too no longer wanted her family to use that name. She had been christened Amethyst and that is what she wanted to be known as, so it was not unreasonable that her children were now young people and wanted to be known by their proper names.

Oskar occasionally asked if Father was coming back, to which Amethyst said she had no idea but would let Fate decide. She had been honest with her children and had told them that their father had tired of their marriage and had found somebody new. Oskar knew immediately that it would be father's secretary whom he had caught sight of when he went to his office. He agreed she was good looking in a sort of way but he for one had not been impressed and could not understand how his dad could throw over a perfectly happy marriage to go with 'that' woman. Margaretha had no opinion bar the one that all men were the same; they expected women to be in agreement with everything they did, while wives and mothers and girlfriends had to be paragons of virtue to please menfolk. She for one would not be following in that mould; she would dictate what went down, no question. Oskar had looked at his sister quizzically and asked if she was going the same way like Michelle who had harangued Max for at least ten minutes, telling him that men would become obsolete within her life time. Margaretha told him she would not go that far, for she liked the fact that there were boys and girls in the world and she would hate it if all of them were only women. Sie said:

"You would *see* a change then. That Michelle did not know what she was talking about. If it ever came about that men would become obsolete and there were really only one sex in the world, you would find that the women would take over the roles of the men and start wars and destruction just like the men had done over the millennia. Some of my sex would lose their femininity and become warriors with big muscles. And if there were only women in the world they would become the bitches that some of them are already and the only balance *now* is that the two sexes are different enough to establish some sort of harmony. In fact I remember one of our teachers telling us about the female hyena. The teacher said that the female had developed amazing muscles because she had to fight over the food in order to feed her young. And so she had become more aggressive than the male hyena and also bigger.

There you have it. If this happens quite naturally with animals, it would be the same with humans. That Michelle has been reading all the wrong books, has or is consorting with all the wrong girls to come to that kind of conclusion. I can assure you dear brother, it will never happen that there will be only women in the world. Your sex will still be needed and not just for producing babies, but for harmony and balance too. That is what I say".

"Well said", ventured her brother and continued: "Actually, I think you are right in that because Michelle who proclaims to be such an ardent feminist and man hater has been making eyes at me. I was flattered of course, but at the same time did not trust it; I know better than take it seriously. For all I know she is fully intent to make a fool out of me just because she thinks she can and so I am very wary about these 'eyes'. She had tried to get me alone to talk to me but I did not trust it and walked away, leaving her standing there, looking surprised".

Having spoken, Oskar stood up from the breakfast table and Amethyst who had listened to her children's little speech was quietly smiling to herself. Oh yes, her children were certainly young people now. How time has flown. Only recently she had given birth to them, it seemed to her; they had had a hands-on father and now they were all grown up and nearly ready to make it in the world. On the whole she felt she and Konrad too had not made too bad a fist of raising them and for the most part, the part where they needed both parents, he had been there for them all. Now he was gone and she was getting used to being a family without Konrad. Soon the young people will have gone and she will be left on her own. Would she have her husband back? She did not know at this stage but the tears had stopped.

Oskar and Margaretha had finished their breakfast and were leaving the house. It was Spring and outside the windows on the north side of the house the cherry blossoms were in full bloom on the trees. Their flowering would not last long, a few days at most before the street became a patterned carpet of fallen blossom, but while it lasted it was magical and she would try and walk down that street to enjoy the spectacle. With that she remembered that she needed to do some shopping, meat too and the latter she never bought in the supermarket, for that she always went to a butcher who specialised in meat.

A woman shopper in Waitrose had told her that there was really only one butcher worth visiting and that butcher was in Notting Hill and it was called *Lidgate*. It was actually a very famous butcher shop and simply everybody who was anybody was buying their specialist meat there. It was truly a family buthers, in its fifth decade – a son each time taking over the business from his father Nigella Lawson recommended it and so did the famous TV chef Gordon Ramsay. Charles Lidgate had founded C Lidgate as far back as 1850 at 110 Holland Park Avenue. Danny Lidgate took over from his father David who inherited the business in 1979 when his father died and so it passed from a father to a son. Following the 2013 meat adulteration scandal, sales on pies and minced beef were reported to have increased. Indeed, if more names were needed to drive home the excellence of that shop, Richard Branson was said to be a favourite of it too. The products on sale also included meat from the Highgrove Estate, owned by Prince Charles, Their scotch eggs made in-house and in-house made were also its tasty Cumberland sausages.

Since the shop had so much to recommend itself it had to be something worth looking into. Amethyst had time on her hands and decided she would go there for her meat. She got ready and looking at the glorious spring weather had decided on a powder blue outfit that would be just the thing. She would not need a coat, it was warm and sunny outside. And with a last look into the bedroom mirror, she went downstairs, locked the door and headed out of the house.

*****

Amethyst hailed a cab and went to Holland Park. The cab stopped outside the butcher shop and she could see that indeed it was a very popular shop as there was a long queue that snaked along the pavement. She got out, paid her fare and slotted herself behind the last person, a man in a light coloured herringbone coat, gleaming shoes and tailored trousers. 'Elegant' Amethyst thought as she stood behind him. The queue went forward only slowly and the man in front of her turned to her, saying he had not expected it to take so long. Amerthyst commiserated with him and told him that for her it was the first time to the shop and she did not know what to expect but thought too the queue was a long one. Behind her more people started to form a longer queue and they were nowhere near the window. Amethyst started to feel cold and thought she should have done what the man in front had done, don a coat. But it was too late now. The man in front turned out to be American by his accent and he noticed that she was cold, so he took his coat off and hung it over her shoulders.

"You know", he said, "Spring weather can be deceptive. I have only been in your country a week but have noticed that you have a very unreliable weather system. I live in the Southern States of the USA, Texas, and Spring there is heaps more reliable". Amethyst laughed. The man talked funny, but she liked his face and graciously accepted the borrowed coat.

While they were waiting to enter the shop – the queue had shortened so there were only three more people before the window, the rest had entered the shop and were being served. The man introduced himself as Dexter Shelling, resident of Austin, in Texas. She in turn told him that her name was Amethyst McReady and she resided in Kensington. "Is that far from here?" Dexter wanted to know and she told him that it was just a taxi ride away and with that the two of them managed to enter the shop and complete their purchases.

Coming out of the shop she took the man's coat off and handed it back to him, but he said that since they had been so long in a queue they should finish off with him inviting her to a coffee. He had learnt of a place behind this thoroughfare, in a side street and it had been his intention to visit the place, but he thought it would be so much more sociable if it was not just him, but would she object to being invited to join him? Amethyst could not think of any objection, so agreed and the two of them walked to the little cafe. There Dexter introduced himself formally and said that actually he did reside in Austin in Texas but that was only because, for personal reason, he frequented his own ranch once a week only as he had to deal with paying his people and make sure the ranch was run properly. For that he had two very reliable seconds in command. He also said that he had a wife and two children but they lived largely at the ranch, while he resided mostly in Austin.

To make polite conversation Amethyst asked him if it was a very large ranch and Dexter said he was no longer sure but thought that his *Highview ranch* was around the 40,000 acre mark. "Wow, that is big" said Amethyst.

"I suppose so, but I have found a while back now that money or property don't mean a great deal anymore; I have come to see that there are things that money cannot buy such as personal happiness and in that department fate has not dealt me a fair hand. I have always understood that we make our own choices; I sure made mine and have been prepared to live with those choices, but living with them on a long term basis is a lot harder. Act in haste, repent at leisure. Is that not the saying? It certainly is true enough in my case, but I have to play with the cards that I have drawn. It is just that over time they have become a burden, worse than I expected, yet I see no way to overturn that burden".

Amethyst liked the man and what he was saying and in her present state of mind, she found Dexter, on the face of it, very affable and easy to talk to. When they had finished their coffee, Dexter told her he was staying at the Dorchester for another week as he had business of a personal nature in London but after that he would be flying back to Austin. Would it be possible to invite her to dinner at his hotel?

Overseas that hostelry had an especially famous reputation and he certainly could vouch for the quality of the food he had been eating this past week and on the basis of that could at least recommend it.

Amethyst accepted and at that point had no reason to query anything that Dexter told her. A more astute listener would have questioned why a man like Dexter who stayed in a hotel would be making a meat purchase at Lidgates, since there were no cooking facilities in his rooms, and a man with 40,000 acres of land in Texas would not reside in a hotel that *did* have cooking facilities. A man like that would be pampered wherever he went for he had the wherewithal to pay for it. It was also doubtful that he would hand the meat – it was prime steak of the porterhouse quality – over to the chef at the hotel to cook it for him. By his reckoning the food at the hotel was first class and what meat he would have found on his plate would have been without question, excellent, so there would never be the need to get the chef at the Dorchester to cook him a steak from Lidgates.

That was what an astute observer might have asked, but Amethyst, though no longer crying over the departed husband, but still missing him, asked no such question, yet briefly wondered instead what personal business he could have in London, since he was, he said, born and bread in Texas and had a ranch there. It *had* seemed a little odd to her that a man, staying in an upmarket hotel, was standing in a queue for the purchase of high quality meat from a high quality family butcher, meat that he had no facility to cook. Perhaps it was a present for someone. That had occurred to her, but since the man had seemed affable, not to say entertaining while buying her a cup of coffee, she dismissed those thoughts.

For now Amethyst was happy to accept the man's dinner date and on parting he told her that he would send a cab round to her home to collect her two days from now. She had happily given him her address and Dexter had made no reference to the location of her home, since as an American he had no idea what was a good area and what was not. They parted on very friendly terms and Amethyst went back in another taxi with a spring in her step. Life looked a little brighter than when she had got out of her house.

*****

Amethyst's errant husband had not been to the house since he moved out. It was not that she had forbidden him to come and see the children – it had been his decision. He had told her on the telephone that he found it too painful to come to what had been his home and until he had sorted his personal life out, it would not be fair on her or him to turn up at the house. As for the children, he had suggested, and she had gone along with it, that they should meet in town with him at a specific place and he would then spend the day with them.

Neither Oskar, nor Margaretha had minded about the arrangement. But they had found it strange to see their father in unfamiliar surroundings. Father had explained things to them and Oskar for one could see that his coming to the house would be awkward, so they were waiting for him at *Maisie's Den*, the vegetarian cafe that was now run by different people. Greeting their father was to the children not strange as they had known him to be their Dad since they were babies, it was only the surroundings that was a little strange, but they felt they could get used to it.

As Konrad came through the door and greeted the youngsters, they lost no time in telling him that Mother had a new boyfriend with the unlikely name of Dexter. Konrad betrayed no feeling about this news to his children, but inwardly he winced. Hitherto he had fondly imagined that the decision to come back to the house as a full husband, having dispensed with Chum, was his to make, only to find now that there was a new equation he had never taken into consideration; that his wife was capable of meeting someone else and moreover might replace him. The news threw a spanner into his way of thinking but to the children he just nodded his head and said that perhaps it had alway been on the card that their mother would eventually meet somebody else. Both sibilings had been introduced to Chum and also had lost no time in telling their mother that they could not understand Father, since they considered that woman to be nowhere near as good looking as their mother. The latter smiled wrily; ugly or attractive, it made not much difference since clearly her husband had decided that he needed, after years of marriage and almost grown children, more diversity in his life.

It had been nearly a year now since that ominous yellow chit had been the culprit the unravelling of the marriage. Oskar had told his mother that he had mentioned to his father that she had a new boyfriend, but Amethyst, at being told that, had pulled a face and told her son, that he was hardly a boyfriend. It was true Dexter had been to the house, had been introduced to both her children and they had found him quite funny. They had liked him, and by her lights that was ok, but *boyfriend* – he most certainly did not qualify for that yet and, in truth, she had not really thought about whether or not he could replace her husband in the lovestakes.

She had loved her husband and was in some ways still in love with him, even though he and she were now – what was the term – estranged, but Dexter as a boyfriend, that was altogether different and she was not sure that she wanted a new entanglement. How clear-cut everything was when one was young. To Oskar it was very clear that Dexter was a boyfriend. Come to the house a couple of times and, hey presto, one was asked when the wedding would be. In any case, boyfriend or no boyfriend, Amethyst decided that she would never marry again. For now that was not even possible as she still was a married woman – a woman with a husband, even though he was not living with her anymore, but was still a husband whichever way one looked at it.

Amethyst thought about Dexter. He was polite to a fault and had not made any kind of advances on her and she appreciated that.

Chapter 22

Shayne knows Max's secret

Dinnertime at the Easterwood House. Everybody was present. Max sat beside Shayne and Marcus and Amethyst sat next to each other at the top end. Max however was astonished to see Michelle sitting next to Oskar. The very girl who had harangued him last time he had seen her, about how men would be obsolete in her life time and that babies would be born without any help from the male species. Oh yes, he remembered very well and now she was sitting next to Oskar. By the look of it they were on very friendly terms. Oskar had told him that she had been making eyes at him and he had dismissed the idea because he had thought that it was to make a fool of him. And now it seems she had been successful in her endeavours. Enough anyway to get invited to the Easterwood dinner table. Max wondered briefly what had changed her mind; he would collar Oskar at the next opportunity, though not now.

Brendan was at the far end, sitting at the short side of the table and next to his left was Tina, occupying the first seat along the long side of the rosewood table. It was a special occasion that the whole family, extended or otherwise, had come together by way of invitation sent out by Tina. The special occasion was the fourth anniversary of Brendan and Tina's marriage. Both felt it needed to be celebrated and Brendan felt that for the occasion the whole of his family had to be present. And so they were. The dining room table sat 12 people and present at the moment were ten family members who were served dinner by one of the maids. Oskar and Margaretha had come as well. Together with Max and Shayne they were now young grown ups; while nobody was looking they had become young adults. Tina was surveying the family and noted with satisfaction that they were all quite good looking.

Shayne had been staying at the house now for nearly eight months. She only had another four months left before she had to get back to America again and was not looking forward to that event. She had got to know the family Easterwood very well. When she had first arrived she had been dubious about the overstuffed armchairs, the expensive rugs that carpeted the floors and the rosewood dining table. All this had been very new and different to what she had been used to at home, where everything was a lot less salubrious, not to say plain. She may have been dubious about the decor which certainly screamed money but she had, over time found that this was only the decor. The family itself was quite down to earth and certainly approachable.

It bothered Shayne however, as she sat next to Max, that neither Brendan nor Tina had any idea about their son's cocaine addiction. It bothered her greatly. Shayne had some knowledge about drugs, not the cocaine sort but that her grandfather, Rooter had indulged with gusto in magic mashrooms. He used to partake in that indulgence, so her aunt Suni had said, because it relaxed him when he had a particularly knotty problem to solve.

Magic mushrooms, she knew all about those. Suni, her auntie, had said that after a heavy indulgence her father would have a kind of hangover as he came down from them. But he swore by them and her aunt said he never actually became addicted, for he knew how to control it. The existence of the mushroom's magic potions were prehistoric and as long as six thousand years ago it had been used in religious rituals. It was also used by the Aztecs. But the Spanish believed the mushroom allowed the Aztecs and others to communicate with devils. Despite this history the use of them has persisted even in remote areas. How it was discovered by the Shawnee Suni could not say, but what she could say with certainty was that her father had believed in the use of them as a calming influence.

Max's using of cocaine was altogether different and could in no way be compared to the magic mushrooms of her grandfather and it bothered her that nobody in his family had ever tumbled to the fact that Max was addicted to the stuff. Tina's brother had died alongside Max's mother and although Max's mother had been a few years older, his father, Pelham, the illustrious Puck, had only reached twenty-two when he died. To Shayne such an age was no way to exit the world due to an overdose of a pernicious drug.

Shayne felt that Max's mother should have insisted that her son remove his sunshades, for the dilated eyes would have told her what was the matter with her son. Alas she had accepted what Max had told her; that he had seen an optician, who had performed an eye test and had told him that basically all was well, that there was nothing wrong with his eyes, it was eye-strain due to his predilection for sketching and that wearing sun shades would eliminate the problem. That was what Max had told his Mama and it had been a lie. Max had not visited any optician but had bought the expensive sun shades from an upmarkeet shop. He opted to wear them to eliminate having to field questions about the state of his eyes and the nearest thing to hand was the invention of an optician and having undergone an eye test. This was readily believed and indeed he had got away with that so far.

Food at the Easterwoods dinner table for the ten people that sat there that night was plentiful, though, considering the wealth of the family, quite plain. Melon pieces and serrano ham was served on wooden plates and the main dinner consisted of croquet potatoes, runner beans and pork medallions with a white wine and cream source served separately in little silver chalices. For dessert there was the option of a cheese platter or a calorific pavlova gateau and the way the family tucked heartily into everything, the cheese platter disappeared along with the pavlova and when the plates were taken away, all of them had been cleared.

While Oskar was chatting to his grandfather, Brendan, Max took the opportunity to rib Michelle about what had changed her mind about men and their obsolescence in future procreation. If he thought that Michelle would be embarassed about being collared in this fashion, Max was mistaken, for Michelle was nonchalant about it all and said that she had grown up a bit since their college days and the reason why she thought the way she did was because some of the girls at college had been ardent feminists and she had got sucked into their way of thinking. Meanwhile of course she realised only too well that in order to keep the balance of the human species it needed two sexes and to think that one of them, the male one, should be obsolete was of course total nonsense. Oskar was now her boyfriend and they got along fine. With that she hoped that Max was doing well and decided to get involved in the conversation Oskar had with Brendan.

Max thought it was time that he left. He was in urgent need of a fix. Shayne was the only one who had perceived as to why Max was absenting himself and she was resolved to look for an opportunity to have a quiet word with Tina about it. She did not consider that to be snitching: she considered it as being of help to Max before he might go the same way as his father. Seeking to have words about that with Tina, she looked the better bet to be drawn into a confidence rather than Brendan. Shayne felt that if anyone could help Max it would be Tina. How to tackle it though was the problem. She did not quite know how to broach the subject and looked for an opportunity. That presented it quicker than she thought when they had found themselves in the kitchen where two women were concentrated in loading two dishwashers with all the dishes. Perceiving Shayne wanted to talk, Tina motioned her to the adjoining breakfast room, to the round table with the red gingham cover and chairs with cushions of the same material. Tina sat down and motioned Sheyne to to the same.

Without any further preamble Shayne asked if she had ever queried why Max was wearing sun shades even indoors. Tina said she had quizzed him over that and he had said that an optician, after an eye test had suggested he should wear sun shades to avoid eye-strain. Shayne looked at Tina evenly and said:

„It's rubbish, that, you must know. Ask him to take his Ray-Bans off and then look into his eyes. I have thought long and hard before I came to you with that, although I have known for some time. But you have been a wonderful family to me, have treated me like one of your own and I am very grateful for that. We – I am a Shawnee – still have a jaundiced view of White Man, and probably will always have, because it was White Man who invaded our country, taken it over and banished us to the margins. I cannot forget about that but realise that it was hundreds of years ago and you yourself can certainly not be held responsible.

I did not want to be a snitch, but I have been told that Max's physical parents had both died of a drug overdose at a very young age, and from where I am sitting Max is going the same way. That is why I thought that I would come to you and tell you. The sun shades are there so as to avoid your noticing that his eyes arc dilated owing to cocaine addiction".

Here Shayne stopped to let Tina take in what she had just been told, The news for Tina was dreadful. She had had no idea, as Max had kept everything ulta secretive and she now scolded herself to have been so stupid when she should have been more vigilant. She had simply accepted what Max had told her and she should not have done. Had she not taken her own mother to task because she had let her son rot in a Knightsbridge flat because she did not want him to come into contact with her snooty friends, to whom she would have had to explain things? And now this girl was telling her that Max, Pelly's son was going the same way. Tina looked at Shayne and said weakly:

„Are you sure? How do you know?" Shayne told her about her grandfather Rooters' partaking of the magic mushroom.

„He too got addicted though he would not have it, but said that he only took it when he had problems and that was one way of staying calm. Unfortunately the magic mushroom is nothing like the modern cocaine and everybody who takes it thinks it is managable, when it is not. It is usually with cigarettes that any addiction starts., Everybody thinks that they can control it then find that the first packet might last a week, but already the second and third last half as long and after a bit one finds one has to buy them by the packet in order to smoke one in a single day and sometimes that it not enough.

I love Max dearly, just like a brother, he is so very sweet, but I have discovered his secret and he does not know that I know. But cocaine is a pernicious habit which can and will lead to death just as it has with your brother."

Shayne stopped talking and watched Tina's eyes welling up. Then Tina got up and said she needed space to think about it all, but she was very grateful to Shayne for having had the courage to talk to her; it meant a lot to her. And with that Tina left the room and went upstairs.

*****

Tina never asked her son to take off his sun shades, because she did not have to. Deep down she had known, had known instinctively that Shayne was right about Max's addiction. Tina was shocked, yet not surprised, but was infinitely sad. Despite their loving care of Max he had become a *junkie*. She thought about her mother and how she had harangued her about letting her son rot in his

Knightsbridge flat because her snooty friends were more important to her than the well being of Pelly. And now Max was going the same way. Perhaps it was in his genes after all because both his father and his mother had been addicts. As for Myra, over time she had understood why, with a mother like that, she had become addicted, Pelly too and all the wealth in the world did not shield him from that. But for all Tina's ruminations she had no intention of letting Max go the way of his father. Something needed to be done about it and soon.

Certainly, Brendan had told her that Marcus had wanted nothing to do with wealth, thought that wealth was a corrupting influence, especially on children. Yet he was not raised with a view that money grew on trees, but he could see that there was an abundance of money which could and did buy people who were only too willing to do work for which they were handsomely rewarded. After all they had families too and what they earned put food onto the table and made living just that bit easier.

But that was the workers. Marcus could see that one had only to flash the cash and people would come running. He had wanted nothing of that and had wanted to experience the other side of a coin: extreme penury. That was why he left the family. Tina could see that: she was a Halbard and she too came to see money as a corrupting influence. Amethyst, Brendan's daughter was different. While not indifferent to money because she knew its value, nevertheless had never coveted people because of any riches which was why she had her feet firmly on the ground. For her it was family that counted.

When she married Konrad, he had his own business and to him it made little difference that she came from a very wealthy family. He kept telling her that he made enough money for the two of them and in any case, it was a husband's job to bring home enough bacon that his wife did not have to go out to work unless she wanted to. And so they had married and Amethyst had been happy to stay at home and produce two children in fairly quick succession. The marriage had been successful, yet not successful enough for Konrad to stay the course and had to find in his secretary a willing diversion.

Tina was thinking about all of this, the family she had married into and her own family as well, and now Max. Tina did not want to interfere but could see that Amethyst got on with things, Konrad left and now she met this new man Dexter, a Texan. However rich both families were their children – and that had included Marcus as well as Amethyst and now Max – were not raised thinking that money was nothing; on the contrary, they were raised to know that money had to be worked for, to be earned.

Meanwhile there was now Max and he had, despite their loving care, became a drug addict. So he had taken after his real parents after all; it had been in his genes the whole time. Tina wondered if he had taken the same path if she and Brendan had left him with Lightfoot and Akwase. Would becoming a Shawnee have made any difference to the outcome? She did not know the answer to that, but what she did know was they she would not persuade Brendan to buy an expensive flat for their adopted son to keep him out of the way. She would deal with it in whatever way she could and for the moment this would be rehabilitation. But before that could happen she and Brendan would have to talk to Max and let him know that his secret was out and he was on the same way as his actual parents were which was the way to distruction. She would tell him that in no uncertain terms.

Chapter 23

Ysenda

In the way that drug addicts not only seem to recognise each other even though they had never met, they also seem to be drawn to each other like magnets. When Max stood in that little shop, undecided as to what he was doing there, the only other person in that shop was a young girl who handed over some money for chocolates that she had purchased. Max had looked at her fascinated. She was striking rather than beautiful with dark brown hair scraped carelessly back over her crown, finishing up there as an untidy birdsnest. She wore grey jeans stuck in brown cowboy boots that were very scuffed and had obviously seen better days. She had on a grey jeans jacket with tassels at the sleeves and on the front the zipper had several missing cogs. In order not to come over as rude, he had stood in the shop looking at the shelves behind the counter wondering what he should or could buy now. Deciding to get out of the shop without buying anything, he was doing so at the same time as the girl. Good manners let the girl go first and she did, but once outside she threw him a winning smile and said quietly apropos of nothing that she lived nearby, that her name was Ysenda Borrows and that her dealer *Paul* was only a couple of streets away, and if he liked they could go there and get sorted.

Max had nodded, told her his own name and together they proceded to her dealer and indeed got sorted. On the way there she had told Max that while *Ysenda* was indeed her name, everybody called her *Ysi* as in Isis, the Goddess but without the s at the end, definitely not as in *easy*; the distinction was important to her. As to her last name,

Burrows was her late mother's name and which she was using. In turn Max told her that his family name was Easterwood, but the name meant nothing to her. She had observed however that the clothes the lad wore, unlike hers, did not come from a charity shop. Indeed Max was expensively attired. Black jeans, expensive footwear and a black leather bumfreezer jacket, not forgetting the Ray-Ban sun shades even though it was overcast. Noticing the lad's attire, her view was that a lad like that had to be still living at home. So after they got sorted she suggested that they retreat to her flat two streets away, Cranberry road, and Max had agreed.

It was a rather run-down flat, eighteen flights up in a housing block, no. 1847 Cranberry Court, Cranberry Road, the large number of the flat denoting that it was on the eighteenth floor. Helpfully, Ysi said that normally there were not one but two lifts but both were broken and she had letters to say it would be fixed, but so far that had not happened, so tenants were required to shin up the stairs to whatever floor they happened to live on.

Arriving in the flat Max could see that it had the look of being somewhat neglected. It was certainly very different from Max's home surroundings with its plush furniture, expensive Persian rugs not to mention original paintings hanging on every wall. While Max took in the surroundings of his new found friend, he had decided that the surroundings were unimportant to him. The flat actually was a bedsit and was sparsely furnished; bare essentials, a kitchen in the corner of the living room, which had a hob and a kettle, an oldfashioned water tap dispensing hot and cold water over a stone sink that had not been cleaned in a good while. The living room was also a bedroom with a roll-up bed to save space. There was no bathroom as such, but through a curtain there was a shower and a little sink and over that a mirror which was in bad need of a clean. In what passed as a living room cum bedroom featured a lonely bedside cabinet next to the roll-up bed that had on it a range of female things: half a pack of tampax, some face cream and a bracelet in some kind of metal plus many empty sweet wrappers, a small note pad and a couple of pens.

Max did not much mind about the state of the bedsit; but it was a large room and next to the bed, a little way away there was a small round table and two chairs. Max sat down in one of the chairs and Ysi sat down on the other. Being seated, both of them got down to snorting what they had purchased in the way of having got 'sorted'. Over in one corner was a built in record player, part of a walnut cabinet, the only decent piece of furniture in the flat. It was of a modern type. On top of the cabinet were two LPs. One of them was titled *Fleetwood Mac* and the other one *Canned Heat*. Ysi explained to him that Canned Heat was her favourite album, that she was rather old fashioned in her taste of music, did not like heavy metal stuff and really preferred the sounds of the 'sixtys She told him that

1. „Canned Heat had originally been a blues band. Formed in 1965 it was an American band and was so named because of *Sterno, an ethanol/methanol* cooking fuel that junkie people drank when they could not afford alcohol and the results of their drinking this stuff was often fatal. Ysi pulled a face about people drinking cooking fuel but said that she liked the sounds the band made. Max said she seemed to know a lot about music but Ysi said 'not really' - it was what she had read on the sleeve of the record and otherwise she just bought what she could afford and what she liked. After that the two youngsters stayed silent while they were snorting the powerful stuff. In time both became somewhat hazy and Ysi rolled out her bed and both lay down side by side fully clothed and fell asleep.

*****

It was dark outside when both awoke at the same time and Max realised that he should be getting home as he would be missed at dinner. Still somewhat befuddled he stood up, took his Ray-Bans off the floor and told Ysi that he would have to leave. She was still lying down and just nodded and turned over. At the door Max turned round and Ysi said some back soon, you know where I live. Max nodded and with that he disappeared throught he door and down the stairs. Eighteen floors down.

When he appeared back home, dinner had ended but a plate had been put aside for him on a warming device. There was nobody in the dining room. He was rather hungry and devoured the food left out for him, then looked into the living room through the open door. Seeing Mama and Papa seated in their armchairs he did not feel like having to explain himself to his parents and so took the stairs and went up to his room. He was suddenly very tired and all he wanted to do was to sleep off the remains of the drugs. He thought of his new found friend, Ysi. He had liked her and he would certainly pay her a visit quite soon, then with that thought he undressed and got into bed.

He did not hear Mama coming in to check up on him and had gone out again when she found her son asleep in his bed. She now knew what it was with him, since Shayne had enlightened her and she was concerned – very concerned - and elected to have words with him the next day. She thought about Pelly and what a waste it had been that he had died at such a young age, when life for him had barely even begun. She thought again of how she had berated her own mother about shutting him away so as not to have to field awkward questions; and now history was repeating itself. Where had she and Brendan gone wrong? They had lavished all possible care on Max, made him feel one of their own – well he was since she was his actual blood aunt really – and he was not lacking love. Yet still he had become an addict, just like her brother. One thing however she was sure about: there was no way she would let him die away from the family, in an apartment. What he needed was rehabilitation and she would start to make enquiries in the morning. Max would not die like Pelly did. With that termination Tina left Max's room and went downstairs into their sitting room, where she found Brendan, slumped in his armchair having dozed off. The television was blaring on about stuff of no interest and so she went to switch it off. Brendan woke and apologized for having dozed off.

"Never mind", said Tina, "we seem to have a problem with Max". And she related to him what Shayne had told her in the breakfast room.

"How serious is it, darling?" Brendan wanted to know and Tina told him that to her mind Max was heading the same way as Pelly had all these years ago.

"He has been trying to hide it from us by wearing his sunshades and I fell for it, as his explanation was that he had visited an optician who had told him it was eye strain. I fully believed him, but Shayne told me otherwise and I am quite concerned about it. I don't want to happen what happened to my brother and I don't want him to move into a flat away from our supervision even though we leave him a free hand – too free a hand, I would say, considering what he has been doing. And another thing is I think we give him far too much pocket money and never ask him what he does with it. It now turns out he is buying drugs with it and not ,marijuana either, but the hard stuff, cocaine. Shayne said she did not think that he was as yet injecting himself, because they had talked in general terms and he is afraid of needles, which is a small blessing, but it would not be long, to my mind before he gets introduced to that method as well, because drug addicts seem to find each other and get drawn to each other like magnets. It's how Pelly and that girl Myra, Fenella Gettevan's daughter, found each other. I think what we need here is to send him to rehab, but you need to talk to him first. He is very close to you and Marcus; maybe we should draft in

Marcus as well to help, I fear I am out of my depth and need a bit of help. I am quite upset about having had to be told what the matter is with our Max; I feel I have failed and should have noticed myself. I know it started with this packet of cigarettes he and Oskar had 'found' and then smoked it. Oskar had had the sense to see that smoking was bad and told Max he was on his own, but Max had taken it up, secretly under our noses, that is what upsets me most of all. We should have twigged long before now."

Brendan agreed that he should have an initial conversation with Max and if that did not help, he would enlist Marcus to see if he could do any better. Rehab seemed at this point to be the best option. It got late and Tina and Brendan retired to their bedroom.

*****

Max was in his bed sleeping off the remains of the stuff from Ysi's dealer. He had to admit that it was rather good stuff. Ysi had certainly been right about that. He switched on his table lamp and thought about the girl. He had been quite impressed. Although dressed in rather shabby clothes, she seemed articulate and had the air about having had a decent eduction. He would certainly see her again. As yet, physically nothing had happened while they lay side by side on her roll-up bed, being both out of it, and he still had a slight hang-over for it had been potent stuff, but Max elected to do the same again quite soon. Ysi did not have enough money on her to pay the dealer, so he had chipped in for her share as well, so that both of them had the same amount which they snorted in double quick time. As far as he was concerned it had been a brilliant day and also, as far as he was concerned he would fly through his studies as taking stuff like that made absolutely no difference to his alertness. In that he was proved to be wrong, but he had yet to find that out.

It was two days later when Max rang Ysi's bell. His father's conversation with him he had viewed with some disdain. He did not like to be questioned closely about what he considered his privacy. But when Brendan put it to him that he and Mama had found out that he was taking cocaine, he grew alarmed.

"And who told you that?" he wanted to know and Brendan did not want to say that they had it from Shayne as this would amount to snitching and they did not want to land her in it, so his father said that both he and Mama had noticed that his demeanour in general had changed. They had further suspected that to their mind it had to do with drugs". Brendan had looked at Max and had asked him to take his shades off, because he said that he no longer believed Max's excuse of eye strain. Max felt he was put on the spot but took off the shades in the hope that his pupils had returned to normal since he had not taken anything in the last two days. Indeed his eyes betrayed nothing.

"Satisfied now, Papa?" he said as he put the shades back on. "It really is eye strain and sketching is very important to me, so I don't want to ruin my eyes doing what I love doing. And it is an issue. After all *Edgar Degas* in later life had significant loss of vision through cataract and retinal disease and I have no intention of going the same way".

Brendan thought his son's answer was a bit too prepared but at the same time he was pleased that Tina's concern about Max's supposed drug use was actually a bit dramatic, so with that in mind, his conversation with his son had ended and Max departed. The latter was rather pleased with himself; he had thought that he had handled himself rather well. He was keen now to get out of the house and to 1847 Cranberry Court, to the 18th floor of a certain Yesenda Shelling. He had a few questions to ask.

*****

Ysenda answered the intercom as Max rang the bell and he mounted the stairs to her door. Ysi smiled as she let him into the flat; she wore the same outfit but instead of the cowboy boots she had a pair of white trainers on her feet, which just like the boots too had seen better days judging by their colour.

"It's good of you to come and at the right time too, as I have just returned from Paul, who sold me this", and she held out her hand in which were two little packets in silver foil. "How much did you pay for that?" Max asked and Ysi said that it did not matter, to leave it for now. She had got paid that morning by the 'Social' and was therefore in the money. Max said he wanted nothing like that for free, but she brushed him aside and said "we shall snort that and see how it goes" and with that she plonked herself on one of the two chairs at the table and motioned Max to do the same. And so, the two young people sat at the table and hovered what Ysi had bought up into their noses. Then they sat back waiting for the drug to take effect.

While waiting for this Max told Ysi that he had got a grilling from his Papa who had suspicions of his doing drugs but he had managed to swat that aside by saying that he had no intention of going blind like *Degas* which was why he wore these shades and somehow he had managed to convince him that his suspicions and that of Mama were completely unfounded. After which he disappeared out of their eyesight.

Ysi said that from where she was sitting and bearing in mind the expensive clothes he was wearing she had the impression that he still lived at home and either had extensive funds with which to renew his wardrobe, or his parents bought stuff for him.

Max elected to tell his new found friend his life story:

"I was born in England, out of wedlock". Here he paused and looked at Ysi, then said, "actually my real father is a toilet seat". Here Ysi laughed and said as far as she knew toilet seats were inanimate objects, no matter how close to the private areas and could never effect a pregnancy, much less produce a baby.

Max said: "I know that and I don't think my mother was serious about that. My mother was American and while in America, she had conducted a clandestine affair for quite few years with my grandmother's attorney. Then she came to England and while here had sent letters proclaiming undying love and faithfulness, while at the same time carrying on with somebody else, my real father whom she called Puck. So when she got pregnant she had to explain herself somehow as the baby - me – she turned up with in America could not have been conceived by the attorney. He of course did not believe her story about the toilet seat and neither did my grandmother, but since nobody could prove anything they had to believe what they had been told. My grandmother could not be bothered to look after me and mother had not much of an idea about motherhood either, so I was fostered out to Connecticut, to foster carers, gramps Liffet and nana Akki, real names Lightfoot and Akwase, Shawnee people, who had every intention of bringing me up in the Shawnee tradition.

Lightfoot, whom I still call gramps Liffet had given me this silver snake to remember him by and said that as long as I believed the little snake would keep me safe. I have always, through the years, been in fear of losing it and have therefore had a tattoo made on my upper arm, just in case."

Ysi who had noticed the chain around his neck after he had taken his jacket off but had not seen the snake which had been hidden among the folds of his sweat shirt. Now he produced it.

"My", she said, "it sure is a wonderful thing. Where did it come from?"

Max said that at first he had kept it in a box, but later had bought a silver chain and for many years now it had been hanging round his neck. The tattoo was double indemnity so to speak.

Ysi took up the conversation: "You know, it is funny, us coming together like this, like meeting in that little shop, because I feel that fate had thrown us together. We have much in common you and I, for I was born in America to a proper father and mother and I was admired; by all accounts I was cute. My parents adored me but then, my mother died in childbirth, taking my baby brother with her and father was bereft. I was then about six years old. But he was good looking and soon a posse of women came looking for him with a view to replacing mother, both in affection and love and marriage. One woman in particular was of the persuasive kind and she became his girl friend. She had two boys and said that her husband had died and she could not make ends meet and my father had taken pity on her. Personally I think she was after his money. Women have an unerring instinct about a man with means and think of myriad ways to get into his heart. Well she, *Meryl*, managed it and father married her, chiefly he said, to to give the boys both a father and a home.

Dad had chosen wrong. No sooner was the gold band on her finger she became demanding and love flew out of the window. It was apparent quite soon that I was in the way and she persuaded my father that I would be better off in a boarding school. Dad was reluctant but she won and I was sent to Exeter in New Hampshire, where I was singularly unhappy. I was missing my Momma but now I was also missing my daddy who had been a good daddy and I was miserable at that school. I felt I was left there. To begin with I saw my father and his new bride in the holidays, but Meryl then somehow made sure I stayed there over holidays as well. When I was eight or nine I began to run away but was brought back each time. I had told dad that I did not like the school and that the teachers were horrible so he took me out of there and put me with another boarding shool, Oldfields in Maryland which was a girls boarding school. I did like it there but still missed daddy, but the teachers were nice and I learnt a lot. When I was fifteen I figured I had learnt enough and sneaked out and made my way to England on a cargo ship. I no longer remember why I chose England but think it was because the cargo ship was going there and the captain had felt sorry for me and let me ride with him. I could not go back home again because Meryl was not interested in having me there; all she cared about was to give her two boys a good home, but I think she wanted a rich home, which was why she got my father to marry her.

This flat is not much but I came by it by nefarious means and as long as the rent is paid – by the council – I am ok as long as I stay out of trouble. I have stayed out and I am my own boss now. I am not sorry about the boarding schools in Maryland for I learnt a lot and the teachers were relly kind and I was taught about art and literature, so I have had a good grounding.

The one thing that sticks in my brain and I still remember is being taught about the octopus, Its funny the sort of stuff one retains in one's brain. But I remember the business about the octopus because it is actually quite interesting. At first I did not believe what Mrs Cane had told us, but I looked it up in the school's extensive library and she had taught us right. It said in there that the octopus is a mollusc without a shell, otherwise the same as slugs and snails, but apparently it has brains. There are, I think she said some 300 species and each are different. The one she was talking about was a predator; its eight arms surround a mouth with a powerful beak and they get their prey using their poisonous saliva. It stated in the book that a blue-ringed octopus's bite can be fatal to humans. However, they don't live for very long, I think something like six years only; the male dies just a few months after mating and the female after the eggs have hatched. So, all in all, I would not want to be an octopus, brains or no brains.

Max concurred and said "I can only add a little thing of my own that I had learnt in lessons, and that is that I have learnt that earth worms, of which there are some 3,000 different types about, some of them a yard long and also very fat, about an inch thick, can *sing, really sing*, so loud that humans can hear them. How they do it nobody knows, so it seems that even the lowly earthworm has brains we know nothing about".

Ysenda thought that was very funny earthworms who could sing. Regarding her drug use, she explained:

"I got into drugs at a party where I was offered a free line and I had taken to it like a duck to water. Now I spend all the money the social services are paying me on coke because I like it and now I share it with you. While she had told Max her life story, the drugs had started to take an effect and both lay on the roll-out bed and gave themselves up to drug-heaven. On the record player was *Canned Heat* playing '*Going UP The Country*.

Chapter 24

Tina's worries

If Brendan thought to have allayed Tina's fears about Max's drug taking, he had not been successful. After the conversation with Shayne in the breakfast room Tina had talked talk to her husband about their son. Brendan had told her that he did have words with Max and had actually asked him to take off his sun shades, which he had done without complaint and that he had looked into Max's eyes and they had been quite normal. He was ready to believe Max's assertion that he wore them to relieve eye strain, just as he claimed. Tina remained unconvinced. The conversation she had with Shayne had shaken her and she had fully believed the girl who said that she had actually one little sachet of silver foil when it had fallen out of his pocket. While she had never used drugs in her life, she knew what it was: it was not grass he smoked, but cocaine.

*****

The two young people were blissfully laying side by side on Ysi's roll-up bed, fully clothed and sleeping the effects of coke off. As yet no intimacy had taken place but that was about to change. Max was the first to wake and seeing Ysi was still aslee, he went across the floor to change the record. It was one of those players that when the record had finished it started again at the beginning, playing the same four or five songs that were on that side of the LP. The music had followed him into his sleep and he was fed up hearing the repetitive songs. He turned the record over, took off his jeans and went back under the sheets next to Ysi. Outside it had got dark and normlly Max would get up and say that he had to be home for dinner. Except that he did not say that, but instead undressed and got under the sheet. He was thinking how amazing it was what one retained from one's school days; Ysi had remembered the brains of the octopus and he had been fascinated too. He had had no idea. She was interesting, that girl and he realised that she had had a decent eduction. That must have been appearent in that sweet shop, he concluded since he, Max, would not be interested in a girl that was thick, drugs or no drugs.

Ysi was waking up now and somehow it was just a natural turn of things that the two young people had found each other in coupling to the strains of Canned Heat's first song on the other side on the LP: 'Same all Over' It turned out that the intimacy was the first for both of them and Ysi winced as she felt Max penetrating her, but did not ask him to stop. A thin line of blood formed on the sheet but Ysi said to pay it no mind, so they carried on. By the time the LP had finished and had started again, the young people had engaged in a second round. When they had both layed limply next to each other, spent, Ysi said by way of nuzzling up to him: "Now you are mine and mine alone. Does that worry you?" Max said it did not so they curled up in each other's arms and went back to sleep.

Max spent the night at Ysi's flat and did not turn up for class either. It was Friday night and when Max surfaced again and did say he had to go home and no doubt face the music, it was Sunday night. He had spent the whole of the weekend away from home for the first time in his life. A mood of defiance had come over him as he left Ysi's flat to say that whatever would happen he would be back the following evening. Ysi said that her flat was maybe run down and surely was but there was one thing to be said about it and that was that she was having to answer nobody but herself and that pleased her.

Max pulled a face and said that his posh surroundings meant nothing to him, he would far rather be holed up here and with those words he took his leave, clattered down the stairs and made his way home.

He may have said that his posh surroundings meant nothing to him, but that had been a bit of bravado for now, as he was nearing home, he was not so sure anymore. He loved his Mama and Papa and was well aware how lucky he had been to have been adopted by them. Even though he had never forgotten his foster carers he had had every advantage imaginable and both Tina and Brendan had encouraged him in every way over his sketching and drawings and he also liked Marcus who had made every effort to mentor him in the way of learning how to paint. Yes, he was fully aware of that, but he had fallen in love with Ysi – no doubt about that – and wanted to spend more time with her. His studies could wait, he was ahead anyhow. Telling his Mama that he had to stay late to catch up was an excuse so he could snort drugs in secret. Now he did not have to because he had found an ally who knew about it and wanted to do stuff with him. It was heaven sent in every way and he would spend many more days and evening with his new love.

He realised though that he could not take her home, not yet anyway, maybe in the future, he had to see, but for now, as he was nearing home he wondered how he could put it to Mama as to why he had been missing for two days. He could not say that he had been catching up on his studies, as this was now old hat and he would not be believed anyhow. In addition he did not like to lie to his parents, to Mama in particular. It was one thing to be secretive about something and not tell, but quite another to tell an outright lie and he was not preparted to do that. He had lied though about catching up with his studies and also about why he was wearing sun glasses, but Max reckoned these had only been small fib because he wanted to keep his secret. A big lie was something else and he had no stomach for that.

So Max had mixed feelings when he got home but was in luck. Papa was out and Mama too was nowhere to be seen. Asking the maid who let him in, as to where anyone was, she told him that Mama was out visiting somebody and Papa had not come back from his office in. Max thanked her and mounted the stairs to his bedroom. There is undressed and went straight to sleep. He would face the music tomorrow. That there would be music he was in no doubt, but for now, the untroubled sleep of youth had him in its grip and he slept soundly. In the morning, appearing to breakfast there was only Shayne in the breakfast room and she lost no time in asking him where he had been all this time. Max mumbled something incoherent and Shayne who suspected drug use, decided that silence was the better part of valour. Mama had not come down yet, nor had Papa and so Shayne and Max were the only ones in the breakfast room who ate silently but heartily.

*****

Tina was the first to appear in the breakfast room that morning and when she saw Shayne and Max silently eating their breakfasts, she sat next to Max and, indeed, demanded to know where he had been. She had opened the conversation with:

"Hello, stranger, nice to see your gracing us with a home visit. It is beginning to be a rare occurrence. Perhaps you could tell us where you had been hiding out these last two days?" Shayne looked up from her porridge to catch Tina's eyes. They were not smiling, so she decided to pay her porridge undue attention again. But, realising then she was surplus to requirement she finished her bowl and excused herself. So Tina and Max were left alone in the room. Tina lowered her voice, in order to sound more amiable and asked Max outright where he had been. Max shuffled the bacon and eggs around his plate but did not answer. Tina would not let it go. She said:

"I know your father has had a word with you about drug taking and you had told him that the reason you wear

208

the shades is because of eye strain. Papa bought it but I did not, chiefly, because my dear brother died and I think you are going the same way if you don't stop it. Drug use is an insidious business and users always think that it will never catch them. I have had many conversations with Pelly about drug use and he always said the same thing to me, that he knew what he was doing, that he was only doing it for recreation and that he was in no way addicted and could leave it any time he wanted. Only, at this point he did not want to. My parents had bought him a flat in Knightsbrige, very posh, as if this made a difference, since it is possible to die in a run-down flat just the same. I had castigated my mother about shutting her only son away simply so he would not be an embarrassment to her upmarket friends, but I have no intention of buying you a flat so you can hide away there but I think and Papa I think will back me up on that: you should go into rehab, and quite soon."

Max who had been pushing his food around the plate listening to what seem to him a diatribe from his Mama, now looked up in alarm:

"Mama, rehab!, What can you be thinking. It is true that I have dabbled in drugs, but I am far from being an addict, I merely use it now and again, when one of my friends has it. Rehab, indeed, who had heard of such a thing! And with that he stood up and said he had studies to do and he needed to devote himself to those, if he had any hope of passing. And with that he left Mama to her breakfast and headed out of the door and up the stairs to his room. Tina did not stop him but carried on with her breakfast of scrambled eggs on toast, but was deep in thought about Max and Pelly.

Poor Pelly, dead at such a young age and now Max going the same way. That this was the case, Tina had no doubt, but she was nonetheless consoled in the way Max denied that he was an addict and that he was only using it now and again, and somehow Tina wanted to believe him, even though her heart told her that she was naive in doing so.

After all, junkies and alcoholics are excellent salesmen in trying to convince normal people that they are just like them – normal. Tina knew that they hid their stashes in the most unlikely places, lampshades not excluded, simply to try not to get discovered.

Tina knew all that and by the time she had left the breakfast room, she had resolved to keep a closer eye on her son. She wanted to catch him in the act, so that he could no longer say or think that this entire business was in her mind, simply because her younger brother had died of an overdose many many years ago. That Max would have to go into rehab, of this Tina was still convinced, but she had so far no evidence to support her conviction to send him there. She would have to bide her time. That that time would come, she knew as well and she was only hoping that he would not go the same way as poor Pelly before her son could be cured of this insidious addiction.

Chapter 25

Amethyst invites Dexter

The dinner with Dexter at the Dorchester had gone well; Amethyst found the Texan quite companiable, so much so that she invited him for dinner to her home. She had told him that she was married, had two children, adolescents now, and that her husband had moved out sorting himself out whether or not he wanted his mistress or his wife. As far as she was concerned, she had had the perfect marriage until it had unravelled on a small yellow chit. She explained to Dexter how the drycleaners had found the fifty pound note stuck in the top pocket along with a post-it-note. The shop had been honest enough to return both money and that yellow chit, but it was the small piece of yellow paper that had proved the undoing of her marriage. Having related her story of woe to Dexter, he in turn told her:

"I have often thought that it is quite extraordinary how we have all these plans in our twenties and how they never work out the way we have planned when we get to middle age and beyond. I have inherited the ranch, *Highview* from my father. It was a much smaller ranch, about 20,000 acres, which by Texan standard is not that big. But Dad did not want it any bigger and said that for him it was big enough, that it brought him an adequante income. But I had starry eyes and wanted a much bigger ranch, so after his death I developed it to the present 40,000 acres. And did it bring me the kind of satisfaction I had dreamed about in my twenties? No sir, it did not.

I fell in love with a girl who had nothing but it did not matter, because I had more than enough for the two of us. We got married and were blissfully happy. This is the life, I thought when *Marigold* got pregnant and produced our daughter, *Lala-June*. I felt we could not go wrong. I doted on my little girl. Ideally we wanted four children and so I was over the moon when Marigold was pregnant again with our son. Alas, the boy was stillborn and Marigold died a week after. I was devastated and cursed god and the devil in equal measure. However, no sooner had Marigold been buried, that several o women, at different times, turned up at my ranch with varying reasons to look after me and the child. I have since learnt that a woman has an unfailing eye for a man with means that might afford her a life of luxury without having to do very much.

One girl in particular, *Meryl* turned up with two young boys. Meryl's husband died in an accident and her two little boys were fatherless and homeless. Call me naive, but I felt sorry for these little mites and felt they should both have a father and a home. So I married Meryl and considered myself lucky to have found happiness again. It was shortlived. Meryl did not take to my Lala-June but doted on her two boys while telling me that the name for my daughter was ridiculous, that she should have a more normal name. Her boys, mind you, were not called ordinary names but *Pablo* and *Miguel*. She defended the boys' names by saying that their father had been from Puerto Rico which is why they had Spanish names. Lala-June, being a ridiculous name or not, was definitely surplus to requirement. When she was seven I was persuaded to send her to boarding school. For my sins it was the best boarding school in America, Exeter, in New Hampshire. Seeing that she was neglected at home I felt that it was the best thing for her. It wasn't. She was deeply unhappy, missed her real Momma, could not get accepted by her step-mother and accused me of not loving my daughter anyhow. But I did love her, so much so that, since matters were what they were at home, I felt boarding school was the best thing for her. I went to see her many times and it broke my heart to see her so unhappy there. When she was ten, she ran away. They brought her back. Asked why she had run away she said that the teachers were horrible. I took her out of that school and put her into Oldfields, a girl school in Maryland and she liked it better there and told me that the teachers were very nice. She learnt well and was top of her class. I went to see her often but every time she still told me she missed her Momma and did not like her step-mother. When she was fifteen she vanished. Could not be found. I learnt later that she had managed to persuade the captain of a cargo ship to let her sail on that ship. I know she came to England, even knew she went to London but after that the trail went cold. Believe me, Amethyst I tried everything. I hired a private detective who could only confirm that she was in London. She had been in a hostel for a time, but had left and since then there had been no news.

My trip to London was to try to find her. If you wondered what I was doing standing outside Lidgates to buy a steak, I went there in the forlorn hope to meet someone who could help me in my quest to find her. Then I met you".

Amethyst said that it was quite a story and she was more than willing to help him find his daughter, although she had to admit that she was no detective. She told him that her father had tried to enlist her   - some years back now - to find her brother who also had gone his own way, saying he wanted nothing to do with wealth, that it was a corrupting influence. She had tried for quite a few years to find him and had been singularly unsuccessful. It was a chance thing when she eventually, after fruitless searches, did find him in the unlikeliest of all places, at a small theatre where he was fiddling with the lighting. So, no, she was no detective, but, all the same, was willing to do all she could to try and find his daughter.

And so the two people had finished dinner and Dexter felt it was time to leave. "By the way", Amethyst could not help asking, "what did you do with that steak you bought in Lidgates? I mean I can't see you going to the kitchen of the

Dorchester and insist it was being cooked for you. I imagine they would feel insulted, taking it to mean the meat they provided for their clientele was substandard."

Dexter smiled: "No you are almost right. I did go into the kitchen of the hotel but asked they chief cook to put it into their freezer. My intention was that if I did find my daughter, I would give it to her, or even cook it for her. I am actually quite a good cook and in Austin, where I reside, I do my own cooking, even though I could afford servants to do it for me. I like cooking and also do my own shopping because I am quite particular about what comes onto my humble table and onto my plate. Naturally I don't do any of the artistic landscaping of my food. I put it onto the plate and then it goes into my mouth with a glass of nice wine, while reading the papers. A bit of a bachelor existence I know but I prefer it that way. Once a week I have to brave it to the ranch where my wife and her two boys are quite rude to me. There is no warmth from my wife but I got used to it and it does not bother me much anymore. I let her live her life and spend my money, while I am happy in Austin. That is my life. I am not unhappy, but if I found Lala-June it would be as near perfect as I have a right to expect."

At the door, already in his coat Dexter said: "Look, I don't make any bones about it. I like you. I am a Texan and we are reasonably straight about matters and don't beat about the bush. I would like to think that we could be friends. I cannot offer you anything at present except friendship, since I am encumbered but feel that it is only right and proper to lay my cards on the table. I would like us to be friends. We have met in a queue in London which is a strange way of being introduced, but I was told that Lidgates always did have a queue because it was popular and one did meet people there. Well we have met, and I would like to think that we could be friends."

Amethyst told him she was happy to count him as her friend but said it was a shame that for now this friendship was shortlived since he was going back to the States. It was a bit difficult to conduct a friendship through the ether. Dexter said that he had another week at the hotel and could string it out yet another week, so if she was amenable there was still plenty of time to get to know each othe properly. And with that he planted a light kiss on Amethyst's cheek and headed out of the house. Amethyst had called a taxi and she watched him as he entered the cab and then he was gone.

She went back into the house and the dining room and surveyed the empty plates. The dishwasher could wait; she went into the sitting room, plonked herself down into an armchair and thought about her dining companion. Oh yes, she would definitely be his friend and, moreover, she would try to help him find his daughter. Lala-June! She had to agree with that Meryl woman, Lala-June was definitely an odd name to give a girl. Only in the Southern States in America would names like that appear. Never mind, she would try and help Dexter.

On a more serious level, in the way that he talked she realised that Dexter would want to take that friendship further. Was she prepared for that? She had not thought about him in that way. She was still married to Konrad, who, however now had another woman and had had one for nearly on 4 years. Four years and she had never known. He had come home from his work every night bright and breezy, had told her how much he loved her and their children and all the time had carried on under her nose as it were with his secretary. The deceit of it! No, she could not forget about that. She knew that her husband wanted to come home, but in the way that she knew him also knew that in truth he wanted to keep this Chum as well as his wife and children. A ménage a trois, but she was not going to have any of that.

*****

Max told Ysi that it was not the time yet to move out of his home and move in with her; he wanted to wait until he had graduated. Ysi did not really agree with that; she wanted Max all of the time with her and so she said:

"I suppose I have to go along with that, but bearing in mind that you spend almost all of the time here, then fret about what you will say to your Mama and Papa, as to where you might have been, it would be easier if you just stayed here and concentrated on your studies here with me, which would at least cut out the stress of having to think up new excuses every time as to why you are not at home.

Chapter 26

Max courts Ysi

In the next couple of days Max tried hard to dodge his parents. He was simply not in the mood to face the music over what he considered his private doings. Study wise he did fine and that at least was an area he could boast that he had been working hard in order to pass the exams. It would be one thing he felt that got him off the hook about drug taking and being absent. For absent he was. He no longer turned up for dinner at prescribed times and neither Tina nor Brendan had any opportunity to grill him. Max did do his studies and it was relatively easy for him. He was bright and he found no difficulty in following the course and the marks from his exams were respectable. They were not top notch, but they were respectable enough for his parents to be lulled into a false sense of security.

For the rest Max spent all of his spare time in Ysi's company at their dingy flat, listening to music and getting high. And still neither of the youngsters seemed ready to accept that they had become addicts in the true sense of its meaning. Their relationship was now physical and both Max and Ysi thought that their sex was the high point and together with their drug-taking had reached new heights of ecstasy. They had played out Canned Heat and it was now the turn of Fleetwood Mac where the preferred song was '*Man Of the World,* to the strains of which they let themselves go into a dreamlike state of drugs. Then they slept it off in each others' arms. For Max it was a new experience and with Ysi it fulfilled all his hopes and wishes and dreams.

Ysi had made repeated noises about Max coming to live with her, but Max was baulking at the suggestion. As

yet, he was not ready to leave home. He realised that his
adopted parents had given him always hope and
encouragement and he did not feel that it was right that he
should repay them this fashion, telling them that he was
moving out.

Chapter 27

Brendan is asked to help

Amethyst was quite persuaded by Dexter and his story of how he had come to marry Meryl. Amethyst could quite believe that there were women in this world whose paramount importance was to marry a rich man, simply in order to get a roof over their heads for them and their children. She did not blame that woman for having the ambition to marry 'up'. What she did mind was the way in which this was done, which was to worm themselves into the heart of a man with means, but then, having been successful, resented delivering on what they had promised, either by inference or in actual words and deeds. Amethyst always thought that honesty was an essential truth in a marriage. Poor Dexter. She felt for him. He had imagined to get a bit of a second happiness and ended up with a harpy who by design had reneged on her promise as a wife.

Not only that but that woman resented the child from his first marriage and finagled it so that the little girl was spirited out of the way. Dexter made no excuses for himself and had told Amethyst that he felt more than guilty for having acquiesced to his wife's demand and sent his Lala-June at the tender age of only seven to a boarding school, where she was far away and knew nobody. He could never forgive himself for that. But now he wanted to make amends and find his daughter. He knew she was in London. A private eye had confirmed as much but all searches had proved fruitless and his daughter remained unfound. He had been persuaded to present himself in a queue before the butcher shop because someone at the hotel had told him that his best chance was meeting a nice bunch of people there. It was an upmarket shop and often people knew stuff that was not common knowledge. Indeed, he met Amethyst there and he had liked her on sight, the way she had stood behind him in the cold spring weather where she had been freezing in her thin green wool outfit. So he lent her his coat and they had started chatting. In a way he was rather pleased that she had been estranged from her husband. He himself was married as well of course and to boot to a very unsatisfactory women, but, nevertheless he was pleased to find that Amethyst, if not free, at was least not in a fixedly married relationship. That he had asked her help in finding Lala-June had been by accident. He did not want to burden her with his problems, but she had turned out such a good listener that he felt he could tell her why he was here.

*****

Amethyst had been appalled and her natural instinct was to help. But how? She decided ro lobby her father, Brendan to help find this Lala-June. Brendan knew a wide circle of people, both friends and in business and he was bound to be able to have some idea as to how to proceed in the quest of finding Dexter's daughter. So her next step was to visit him and Tina and broach the subjet. Brendan was always happy to see his daughter and when she told him why she had visited Brendan was astonished. He was a bit dismayed that the business with Konrad had not yet been resolved, that she in turn was quite resolved in thinking of divorce. As yet the fact that she found Dexter to her liking and was falling in love with him, that was not something she was ready to divulge to anyone, not even admit it to herself. For now she told her father that she wanted to help this man who was a nice man and fate had dealt him a rotten hand.

Brendan, who knew about people more than anyone else was dubious. He remembered his first marriage and how he had been largely an absent father. He too had made amends and had agreed to Tina's wish to adopt Max and look

220

where that got them. As yet of course Max was still a work in progress but quietly he knew that his adopted son was heading down a very slippery slope. Of this he said nothing to Amethyst, his only solution was that he would put his best man onto it and he was somehow sure that eventually it would bring a desired result.

This is what he said to his daughter, but in himself he was far from sure. He had tried his very hardest to find Marcus and it was only a chance meeting to a theatre that his daughter had found him first. Plus the fact that this Dexter who by all account was not short of cash had also tried the best private eyes and they could not come up with finding his girl and he wondered why. To Amethyst he said he would give it his best shot, that he was sure that eventually something would have to turn up.

Dexter had stayed a further week in the Dorchester and in that time Amethyst had been in his company almost every single day, so much so that Oskar had given a low whistle through his teeth and said that any minute now he expected the announcement of wedding bells and that his mother would become Mrs Shelling. Amethyst had laughed and said that at least she could assure her son about the impossibility of that, since she was still married to his father and as far as she could see, these wedding bells would have to be a figment of his imagination for the foreseeable future since Dexter was also married and, moreover, lived in Austin, which as far as she was aware was in the Southern States of the USA and she had no inclination to decamp to there.

Reading about the state of Texas she knew that it was the second largest State in America, the first being Alaska which was bigger by about 60%, but it was big enough. She also had read somewhere that the most ignorant of people could be found in Texas since some people had not ever been out of that state and actually thought that Texas was the whole of America. Well, at least Dexter Shelling who also came from Texas was no ignoramus. She had been in his company for enough times to perceive that her new found friend was an educated man.

Oskar told her that, it seemed to him, for his mother to want to learn about the State of Texas showed that she had an interest in the man himself. Moreover, judging from the way she and Dexter had been seeing each other almost every day, to his mind it had progressed from friendship to something altogether different.

To Amethyst, her son stating this, it was a bit too close for comfort and so she told her son that he was way into a future she had not even factored in and he could rest assured that when she knew more, he would be the first to be told. And with that she indicated that she was in no mood to be quizzed further on the matter. Her last parting shot was that Dexter had this morning taken the long flight home.

*****

Dexter had been in Austin for the last two months, but sent weekly messages to Amethyst, each one getting more personal as time went by. Amethyst did not mind. She had allowed herself to fall in love with him and wasn't much bothered over the fact that she was still a married woman. She still thought about her errant husband who had now been away from their marital home for nearly a year. He had, of his own volition, refused to come to the house, so he had contact with Oskar and Margaritha at Maisie's Den. It appeared to be the cafe of choice, since it was easy to get to and it had become a kind of habit for Konrad to meet his children there. Oskar actually did not mind. He was in his second year of medical school and he understood the curriculum well. Konrad, whenever he saw him asked for progress and Oskar was happy to tell him that he was near enough top-dog – not quite, but nearly – and felt he would make a very good doctor.

222

On a personal level he was still seeing Michelle, so much so that he told his father that he now had a girl friend. He was nineteen, nearly twenty and Konrad thought that if he liked the girl, it was fine with him for a first relationship. Asking him point-blank if he was sleeping with her, Oskar looked to the floor and again gave incoherent mumblings, but Konrad persisted. Eventually, bright red in the face, he told his father that, yes, he was. On asking how mother was, he lost no time in telling him that Dexter had departed for Austin, America but they kept sending each other regularly messages and letters and he thought that it was now more serious than it had been a month or two back. Konrad had winced and had only told his son that mother deserved a bit of friendship after what he had put her through.

"Oh, its more than friendship, Dad", Margaretha chipped in. "I sneaked a look in her drawers and found loads of telegrams and letters and these are beginning to have the look of a personal nature." Father said that it was wrong to check other people's private mail and that in the end it was none of her business.

It was nevertheless true what Margaretha told her father. The relationship between Amethyst and Dexter had become more personal. He may have been in Austin, but to judge from the telegrams and letters he sent her, he clearly had intentions of making her his wife. Amethyst knew really that it was all heading this way and it meant for her that if she wanted it to go forward she would have to ask Konrad for a divorce. Dexter was straightforward in the way Americans are in such matters and told her that he would like to make her his wife, but he knew he had no right to expect any kind of commitment from her, since he was still married as well, but if she would indicate that she was willing to marry him, he would see to it that he too would divorce Meryl. Since he had means he would also see to it that she and her two boys would not have to suffer hardship.

On another level Dexter was rather sad that he still had not had the result he had wanted about finding his daughter but that he would never give up trying. A great wrong had been done to her and he felt it was his duty to put that right. One possibility was that, since all efforts to find were stubbornly unsuccessful, that she had changed her name. That might be one reason why so far nobody had found her and if she had changed her name it would be harder still for anyone to find her.

Amethyst told Dexter that she had lobbied her father to help as well and she could assure him that everybody was looking for her. And yes she had to agree with him that it was entirely possible that Lala-June used a different name in order to stay anonymous. That possibility had to be factored in.

*****

When Amethyst went home to her father and Tina he had shaken his head and told her that the best private eyes that he had employed had come up with nothing. It had occurred to him too that she may have changed her name in order not to be found; it was at least another possibility that had to be considered. He suggested that Lala-June might have come under the Social Services, so he would look there again. Amethyst then proceeded to tell Tina and Brendan that the relationship with Dexter Shelling had become serious and she had made up her mind to divorce Konrad. She felt that sufficient time had gone by for Konrad, had he wanted to, to make up his mind and since he had not, she would be making it up for him

224

Chapter 28

Ysenda and Max

Ysi and Max were now firmly together as a couple and Max could be found at Ysi's flat when he was not studying. He was now rarely at home and there was nothing that Tina or Brendan could do about it. As yet the two young people knew nothing about the world looking for Ysi, for it *was* indeed Lala-June who had changed her name to Ysenda, a name she had found in a newspaper, that having been a byline of some journalist and she had adopted it. Telling Max that everyone at school had called her Ysi was an untruth, because long before she had met Max she had used her real name of Lala-June Shelling. But once she had become Ysi, for Ysenda, she thought she would use her mother's maiden name for it sounded to her more convincing. The bit about having been called Ysi to distinguish from *easy* was pure fiction.

Her one abiding reason for the name change was that she did not wish to get found. But there was another reason and that had to do with the bedsit she had obtained. In order to make that abode hers, she had to have a British name. Nobody in this country was called Lala-June: it was altogether very American and to get the Social Services involved she had to have a British name, so she had invented the name Ysenda Borrows. .Although she did not know that her father was looking for her, she had assumed that her father had abandoned her in favour of Meryl and her two boys. She had simply been in the way and had no reason to think otherwise.

For Max Ysenda, or Ysi, as a person was a revelation. She was his first girlfriend and the more he saw of her the more he liked her. The fact that she was a coke-snorter as well was an added attraction. The more the pair of them smoked, the more they liked it and to the music of Ysi's two LPs they had great sex together while the music of one or the other took them into the great hights of oblivion. Ysi's dealer Paul had lived up to her estimation about being a reliable dealer. They had nothing to complain about; he really did supply high grade stuff without them ever having to worry about that it was cut with substandard chemicals, or indeed was pure enough for both of them to die of an overdose. Paul was very reliable. But as any addiction, being carried to the great height of oblivion, after a bit it did not satisfy and one early evening as both of them woke from their comatose state, badly in need of another fix, Ysi said, as if it was the most normal thing in the world:

"I think we should up the ante a little and try heroin, just for larks". Max was dubious about it. Opioids had come up for discussion at medical school, such as were given to patients after operations, to help them through the first days of post operative pain. Max knew that that stuff was highly addictive. Still, neither he nor Ysi thought of themselves as addicts and still fondly thought they could leave it whenever they pleased, only it was now just too delicious to do so while they thought of themselves as being masters of their own minds and bodies..

It was all a fallacy of course. They were by now no masters of anything, but followed their inclination when they needed a fix and their path to Paul was now a daily occurrence. That they needed a fix was imperative because on occasion when they had come down they had also experienced terrible hang-overs and being strung out; this could only be alleviated by having another fix. Ysi who only had money given to her by the Social Services was in no way equipped to pay for the ever spiralling cost of these innocuous looking packets of silver foil but Max, who eventually ended up paying for both of them did not mind.

He did not have to earn a living and his Papa handed him a generous amount of pocket money and never asked what he did with it. He would have been at a loss in any case to come up with a convincing story as to what he spent his money on.

*****

To explain at home what he did with his money would have been the easy part. Much harder was to have to explain his ever more frequent absences from home. Tina, and for that matter Brendan no longer believed that he was catching up on anything, but came to the conclusion – a correct one as it turned out – that he had found a girl friend and was staying with her. Max was now a young man and both Tina and Brendan also assumed that sex was involved. On the rare occasion that Max now turned up for dinner at home, Brendan told him outright that by his lights he had a girl friend and if his assumption was correct he felt that it was only right and proper for him to bring her home and introduce her to the family.

At dinner that night were Tina, Brendan, Max and Shayne. Brendan's words were still in the air and Shayne kept her eyes firmly on her dinner plate as if there was something interesting to see in the food. Max had looked Brendan straight in the eyes through his sun shades and said that yes he did have a girl friend but it was nothing very much fixed and until it was he did not think it was right to bring her home. Tina chipped in and said she did not agree with that statement and felt the family was sufficiently broad minded to accept that perhaps the relationship between him and the girl might not be so that wedding bells might chime in the near future, but even so, they would like to have a look at his choice of young woman.

"If you don't want to bring her home", Brendan ventured, can we at least have her name?" Max volunteered that her name was Ysenda, but she preferred to be called Ysi as in Isis the Goddess, but without the s at the end. Brendan again: "Ysenda! What a nice and unusual name. It is a shame she had abbreviated to Ysi for Ysenda had such a nice ring to it. "What is her family name?" Brendan enquired further and Max said it was Burrows. He felt that it was enough of information that he had told his family that night and having cleared the plate stood up and went up to his room.

At the end of the dinner with people still sitting on their dining room chairs, Tina said "well at least we have a name now and as for the other there is nothing we can do now but wait how matters develop" and with that she declared dinner over and rose from the chair. Brendan, and Shayne did likewise and repaired to the living room to see what might be of interest on the television that might take their fancy to watch.

Shayne who also joined them in the living room sat down in an armchair and was deep in thought. She was not interested to see what was on television; she thought about Max and his statement that he had a girl friend, moreover had volunteered her name. Shayne did not mind about the girl friend. She viewed Max as a brother and had no other designs on him. But what did bother her was his general demeanour. In her view Max had changed in a few weeks so much that she hardly recognised the Max on six months ago. She knew it was drugs that prevented him to bring this Ysenda home and she correctly assumed that the girl had to be on drugs too. It was unusual for only one party to be on drugs. Normally people would only consort with other people who were like them. In the way of her aunt Suni, she knew what she knew and it was nothing good as far as she could see.

*****

No further progress was made by either Brendan or Amethyst in their quest to help find Lala-June. Brendan had mused that since his very excellent contacts had failed to find the girl there was only one option left and that was that she had indeed changed her name because she did not want to be found. Brendan said that it required a whole new way of thinking matters out but to his mind it was the only theory that made sense to him. But what name would she use? That was the conundrum and he set himself the task of finding the girl because Brendan still wanted to be successful in whatever it was he undertook and in this case it was important to him because it was clearly helping his own daughter. The fact that she was putting her relationship with this Dexter from Texas onto a firmer footing, with the possible outcome, that of divorcing Konrad, meant that Dexter would eventually became husband number two.

Brendan thought about Konrad. He had been an excellent husband when their children were small but he agreed with Amethyst that life was short it was one's duty to grab happiness where it presented itself. He still felt bad when he thought about his first wife Lindsey and how he had let her so far down that she felt she had to take to drink and then die at an unseemly young age, all beause he did not keep his promise, 'to have and to hold, for better, for worse etc.'

Money of course had never been a problem in his household. In fact it was money that drove him apart, his insane vision of simply adding more millions to the ones the family had and how Marcus had bowed out and told him that high finance and the city were not for him. That he wanted to be an artist and that was not commensurate with what his father wanted, which was to make money.

Marcus could not see it and felt that the entire world of his so-called high finance was a sham. Sure, the world adored Brendan, because the world adores money and even more the ability to make it in such abundant ways. But it proved a hollow pursuit. And it was Tina who had showed him the way. He had been a lousy and absent father but he now had seen the light and he wanted to help his daughter find that man Dexter's girl because he too had to make amends for having sent his little girl away to please a voracious woman who only wanted security for herself in an easily achieved manner and a nice roof over the head of her two fatherless boys. Amethyst had told him the story and Brendan had sympathised. But he was in no way going to sit in judgment over another being, having been so misguided himself.

****

After, what was perceived by Ysi and Max to have been astonishing sex, they had gone to sleep and on waking they had a conversation. Ysi told Max:

"When I had gone to Paul the other day to collect my two packets of coke, I had to wait a while in the other room while he was servicing another client. It had been quick because I just wanted the coke which Paul had ready for me but on the way out I had met Paul's client on the stairs. 'What have you got?, he said and I had told him the 'usual', my coke. 'I let you into a secret he said, then told me to forget about the coke but try the heroin. I was dubious about it because I knew that heroin was serious stuff and I was not sure I wanted to go down that road, but this bloke assured me and said that people had the wrong impression about heroin. If taken correctly there was never a problem with it. People died of heroin addition because the did not know what they were doing or they had been given pure stuff and were told it had been cut.

He himself had taken heroin for the last two years and said I should try it because it was like nothing on earth. Once tried I would never again crave cocaine, this was far better stuff. It wraps you up in pure cotton wool and there is no hangover afterwards, something to be considered, I think. And the feeling, man, the feeling! Being in heaven does not even begin to describe it. You have just such a feeling of well-being that it gets rid of anything else you have been worrying about. There is just one thing you have to bear in mind. The dosage and the fact that once tried, you want to try it again, and again, because you feel you have wings. With

230

that he headed out of the door and into the traffic. What do you say to that, Max?"

Max was dubious. Heroin, well that was something else altogether. In medical school they had talked about heroin but not what it might do to an addict, in the curriculum it was about dosage. Normally the hospitals dispensed morphine in differently strong or weak doses, because it was so amazingly addictive all doctors had to be aware when they dispensed this highly dangerous, but effective drug and yes, in a sufficiently high dose it did cut out pain, but the medic had stressed that it was highly addictive and was to be given only in extreme circumstances to alleviate pain, so not to be dispensed lightly.

„You see Ysi, this bloke may well have been right about being wrapped in cotton wool and that it would give us an incredible feeling of well-being, but it is the addictive property I am worrying about. I feel we are ok with cocaine and I think we should not listen to people who tell us otherwise. That is what I think, we should tread with the utmost care".

However in the end Ysi won the day and a week later they two of them went to see Paul to sell them two packet of heroin. Paul had asked them if they were sure about that, because by his lights too this was serious stuff. Yes he did have clients who used it, but he warned that there was no doubt about it, that man had been wrong. Ingesting that stuff, heroin, would definitely lead to addiction. Moreover one could start off with very little but in the end one had to take more and more to get the same high as one did at the beginning. Both listened sagely but departed with two packets of heroin and both of them fondly believed that as long as they did not use any needles they would be safe from additiction. They would be proven woefully wrong in this.

It was true though what the man had said, they snorted it and indeed were wrapped in cotton wool and floated to the ceiling and beyond to the strains of *Pink*

Floyd's Dark Side of the Moon Max had bought the LP because he thought that listening to same music of Canned Heat and Fleetwood Mac was somewhat limiting and they needed to listen to something new. An so it was that both Ysi and Max had become heroin addict and were in complete denial over it. They still thought fondly that they could take it or leave it, only, since they had such a good time with it, they wanted to carry on with it. Paul, their dealer was only too happy to supply the stuff and for a while now it had been Max who had been paying for it as Ysi could not afford to buy that kind of supply repeatedly.

And little by litte Max did not go home anymore. He could not face looking at his Mama and his Papa and their quizzical faces and said without saying anything out loud: ,why are you doing this to us? Max did not want to tell them and so he stayed out. And at the same time he decided to drop his medical course too.

Chapter 29

Brendan has an idea.

Brendan sat in his chair thinking. In particular he was thinking about the wretched business of finding that Texan's daughter. While he did not think that he was the man to marry Amethyst, he took his daughter's word for it that he was a decent man. He had never met him but on balance he felt his daughter was a good enough judge of character to have feelings for this man, which he, Brendan fully accepted to be real. She was his daughter after all and her marriage to Konrad had lasted from the birth of his two children to their becoming adolescents. He also knew that fate sometimes throws lousy cards onto the table and one had to deal with it. He did not, in anyway blame Konrad for taking up with his secretary. He had been sure that it was fate that had thrown them together.

And now Amethyst was thinking of divorcing him. He did not blame he for that eitherr; the marriage had in his view outlived its usefulness and why should his daughter while she was still relatively young not find love again. After all he had too, even when he was not looking for it. As to the man's daughter, Lala-June – what a name -. He had asked one of his clients who did come from Alabama about what he considered an outlandish name and his client had assured him that down South they had names like that for girls. So Lala-June it was but she could not get found no matter how much money he spent on private eyes. The girl remained elusive. And now that had got to him. Brendan may no longer have been interested in multiplying his family fortune but he was still keen enough to want success once he was given a task. And this task was to find Lala-June. The only logical explanation to her disappearance would be if she had changed her name and if so, he would look at the matter from that point of view.

Brendan thought about the girl. By all accounts she had a good eduction and for all he knew she had a respectable job somewhere that paid a decent income so she could live in a decent apartment. Alternatively she had come under the aegis of the Social Services in whatever name she used in which case it might be harder or easer to trace her. He would start putting feelers out with the Social Services and see where it might lead to. When Tina came into the living room she had expected her husband to be dozing off behind a newspaper and was pleasantly surprised to fin him there staring at the ceiling.

„And what it so interesting on the ceiling for you to be so fascinated by that", she teased him and he held out his arm. „Just thinking about Amethyst' lover and that wretched girl Lala-June. I have asked my client who is from Alabama and he could assure me that down South they had names like that for their girls. Beats me. Lala-June. Never mind. We need to find her and I have come to the conclusion that she has changed her name and is holed up somewhere not too far from us and we have no idea. Tomorrow I will try a new tack. I am determined to find that girl for him. That wife of his seems a right harridan and he seems to have honest intentions for our daughter and I want to help her in this matter. Its funny, me thinking like that about a girl I have never met while we have this problem with Max. I see now that it is a problem as I have not see him for the whole of this week and I am sure he has shacked up with that Ysenda or Ysi as he calls her. I just hope you are wrong about him having become an addict. It is after all only Shayne who has thought so, we have had no real evidence to think that. Shayne might know a lot more, she is his age and they do talk together, though since that Ysenda has come into our

Max;'s orbit he has made himself scarce and is out of the door before I can have a conversation with him".

Tina agreed with her husband but because her brother died in that flat alongside Max's mother, she could not help thinkimg the worst that might happen with Max too. Much as she had been trying to warn him about drug use she was sure that Shayne had been right, that he had become addicted to cocaine and was in denial about it. The only consolation she had that the marks in his studies were still good which meant he still was present in classes but how much longer might he attend them? Brendan thought that her thoughts were altogether a bit black and he told her that it woul not do do speculate when they had no concrete evidence about either the girl, or his drug taking. And with that, Brendan got out of his char, kissed his wife and together they went upstairs to bed. It had got late.

*****

The following day Bredan left early for his office an said he had work to do and would not be back for dinner. She could if she wanted to leave a plate out for him. He would be back around ten in the evening. And with that he headed out of the door into his car and was gone.

However, the thought of this man Dexter's girl would not leave Brendan alone. She simply had to be found, his reputation, he felt, depended on her being foun. Yet so far, everything that had undertaken had proved to lead into a cul-de-sac. How was it, that a young girl could get lost in this way against all the money that he had – and he was spending his own money – considerable though that was, to employ the best brains in finding a young woman who had absconded from a boarding school in America and had vanished into the blue yonder. It just could not happen, yet it did.

Suddenly he had a brain wave. It was clear to him that that Lala-June had used her considerable ingenuity to vanish from the earth, by changing her name and persuading prevailing authorities that this was her name, whatever it was. Brendan thought about it. It was clear to him now that this young woman had not made something of herself, but had come under the umbrella of the Social System. Why, he thought that he could not say, but that would make perfect sense. If, he reasoned, she had found a high powered job to prove she could exist on her own in a strange land, she would not have wanted to change her name. She would have proudly presented herself in her real name, only to show the world that she had managed, inspite of her family's rejection, to make something of herself.

No, the only thing that made sense was to come to England, change her name and get the Social System involved. So that is where he had to start. But the Social Services were anything but helpful. When his private eye had called them they said that Data Protection prevented them to give him the help he needed and they were at a loss to see how the system could help him in his quest to find this young woman. So that was a dead end and Brendan knew he had to start from a different angle. First of all he had to get one of their number into his confidence and in this he was lucky. He would try by date of birth. Amethyst had told him the date of Lala-June's birth because she had asked Dexter who gave it to her readily. There had to be many people born on the same day, but if he could get a person, preferably a woman, as a woman could better be persuaded to help him than a man would.

He presented himself at a window in an ordinary Job Centre and told some jobworth there he was looking for a young woman, possibly on their list, who had come into an inheritance as her uncle had died and all efforts to find her had proved futile, yet he knew she existed.

Strangely enough this had the desired effect. The Social Services, ever on the look out to help the helpless and the down trodden were less willing to help people who had come into riches. And if it proved that one of their charges had become unexpectedly rich, the Social System saw no reason to help them further in that quest. That person at that Job Centre had been very helpful and wrote down a number on a white sheet of lined paper. Brendan said thank you, exited and got back into his chauffeur-driven Daimler. He was quite pleased with himself. It was a start. Mounting the stairs to the high rise, he even whistled a tune. Brendan was totally tone deaf and the tune, heard by one of his colleages made the colleague wince.

Brendan lost no time to get on the phone to ring the person written down on that sheet. It was indeed a woman and her name was *Fabienne Greystone*. He called her but the ansaphone said she was out but he could call back after 1500 hours. Brendan put the phone down and whistled another tune that made the same colleage wince more, but Brendan smiled at him. He felt things were finally going the right way.

Chapter 30

Dexter puts his house in order.

While Brendan was racking his brain as to what possible names Lala-June could have used in order to stay both invisible and also anonymous, he had figured, it was more likely that she drew the dole, than had a well paid job. He had based that on the evidence that Amethyst had supplied, namely that the girl had felt unwanted and unloved and certainly her new step-mother had no interest in the girl being with her family. She had her two boys and anyone else was surplus to requirement and that included her husband. Having married him, she had never loved him and Dexter had come to the conclusion that she had married him for two reasons only: the first being that he was rich and the second her two boys needed both a father and a stable environment. Having achieved her aim and married him, she had had no intention of fulfilling her wifely duties and let him know quite soon after the wedding that sex, while she had to provide that, would be few and far between. She was no mattress and let him know that in many ways. Dexter soon saw which way the wind was glowing and retreated to his office in Austin. He did keep a very close eye on the ranch though, but he had two experienced cowhands that had been with him since the death of his father and he could rely on them to keep the ship afloat.

*****

Dexter was not happy and decided to do something about it. And that was to take the next plane to London and stay once again at the Dorchester, the very same hotel that had seen the disappointed Myra being told by her lover, that he had married her mother. Dexter of course had other plans. He needed to know if Amethyst had the kind of feelings for him that translated into becoming his third wife and for that phone calls were useless. He did not want to propose over the phone; he wanted to see her face to face and tell him that she loved him in the same way that he had fallen for her.

Amethyst was more than surprised but nevertheless pleased when out of the blue she received a phone call from Dexter inviting her to dinner at the hotel. Amethyst was pleased that he was in London for she had missed him and happily agreed to have dinner with him. But she was not altogether surprised when at the end of the dinner he had confessed that he had fallen in love with her and he wanted to know if he might hope that it would be the same with her. Before she even could reply he had hastened to add that he realised that even if she did say yes, he was still a married man, but he would see to it that Meryl would have a satisfactory income from him for her and the boys, so that would not be a problem. On the other hand he also realised that she too was still married but what he wanted to know was if she had feelings for him.

Amethyst had told him that she having lobbied her father into finding Lala-June all efforts to do so had so far been fruitless, but her father had told her that the possibility had to be considered in that she may have used different names that made detection very much more difficult. So far she had succeeeded but she said that her father was a clever man and whatever he undertook would eventually lead to success. As to her personal feeling for him she could truthfully tell him they were the same and that she had decided to divorce her errant husband in any case.

Dexter was over the moon that his love had felt the same way and together they set out plans what they would do together once both of them were free.

*****

Ysi had persuaded Max to try the heroin just the once to see if that client of Paul's had been right, and having tried it, it really did feel like they were wrapped in cotton wool and they floated away on dreams the like of which they had never experienced before. Pink Floyd had gone the way of Fleetwood Mac and Canned Heat and Bob Dylan had come in to help them reach nirvana and the strains of his nasal sounds helped them achieve that with ease. They had no idea that Max's father was hard at work to try and find Dexter Shelling's daughter and also had no idea that her real name, that of Lala-June, would eventually be discovered. Of any of that they were blissfully unaware as they descended into drug hell. Both of them were hopelessly addicted even though no syringes had been used but it was perhaps only a matter of time until that particular method would be tried along with free-basing, just as dangerous a method which had actually killed his parent.

Max spent less and less time at home and more and more time with Ysi – in fact, he had more or less moved into her flat. That it was a dump and in no way commensurate with what he had at home did not matter to him a jot. All he was interested was getting high and out of if with Ysi, have great sex and then sleep it off to the strains of Dylan.

He no longer attended medical school and Oskar who was in the same year watched from the sidelines as his cousin descended. Occasionally they still spoke but Max was now distant and distracted and actually unable to have the concentration for a long conversation of whatever topic and after a few sentences he would say he had urgent business and would depart. Oskar had looked at him and was amazed how a few weeks Max's countenance had altered. He looked wasted. Yet his cousin still thought fondly that he could kick the habit anytime he and Ysi wanted and they just liked getting high but they did consider themselves in no way addicted to the drugs they took.

Oskar of course reported it all to his mother and she in turn reported it to father and Tina and neither of them could understand what had happened to Max. Tina in particular remembered his first drawing of 'Shavany' as a young child and she wondered where she had gone wrong.

She realised that young boy had now grown up and despite their loving care had descended into narcotic hell. She had no idea how to rescue him. To tell him he needed to go into rehab was pointless because for one thing he was never home and for another he would still insist that he merely dabbled in drugs and could leave it anytime he wanted. Tina knew only too well that this was an illusion. Pelly had told her many times the same thing and she had to see him on a mortuary slab without every being able to convince him that life was worth living and with rehab he would have been able to that. She had failed with Pelly and Tina felt she had failed the same with Max.

*****

Chapter 31

Lala-June

Max and Ysi were now firmly in the grip of heroin. It was Max who had realised gradually that while that client of their dealer Paul had been correct about being wrapped up in pure cotton wool, he had not been right that particular brand of narcotic could be managed. It could not and Max finally accepted that he and Ysi ha become *junkies*. As yet neither of them had the awareness that what they were doing would and could lead to premature death, they had as yet too good a time with those packets of silver foil that still them float away into the deep yonder. They had amazing sex but afterwards, as they lay side by side, totally wasted, had descended into the kind of narcotic oblivion, only to wake from that strung out and craving another fix.

This business had become expensive, very expensive and while Max,'s monthly allowance was generous, it was in no way sufficient to keep them in heroin. Max who was paying for both of them and did not mind as long as they could get the next fix. Paul, their dealer who supplied them with safe and high grade stuff, was only too happy to be paid for what they bought. He had come to appreciate the young man Max and he had looked up the name. The family was rich beyond measure. Oh yes, whatever it took! He would be only too happy to supply the heroin and anything else they wanted for there was never any hassle with this client. He named the price and Max handed over the money. It was as simple as that and Paul thought if only all his clients were as liquid as that.

However, Max too had reached the limit of his allowance and after the last fix had sat at the rickety table and wondered how to get over that. He could go to his father and ask for more money, but that idea, just as it had formulated in his head was discarded. There was no way he could go home. He had not been home for quite a few weeks and to go home now would throw everything into jeopardy. He looked into the mirror, the grimy one over the shower sink and studied himself. There was no doubt that he was a different young man from just a few weeks ago. His clothes were hanging off him, he was no longer that concerned about his personal hygiene, nor was Ysi for that matter. The two of them only were interested in getting enough money together for the next fix, get high and wasted, then lie down and sleep it all off.

Now even sex was not that great anymore either. They needed higher and higher doses to achieve the same nirvana. Plus, some other side effects had started to gnaw at his young body. Of late he had experienced severe constipation and his gums had begun to swell and his teeth were yellowing. Ysi's periods had become irregular and to cap it all she told him she could not longer gauge anything. In fact she feared she might be pregnant, which turned out to be true. None of these things had been considered when they started on heroin and it was completely different from cocaine. The latter had been managable, this one managed them, no question, so much so that he finally had to admit to himself that he was no longer master of anything.

He was only looking for the next fix and anything else no longer mattered. It did not matter to him that he had dropped out of medical college, though, here he pulled a face at the mirror. He knew that all the aspirations he had to become a surgeon had now gone up in smoke; all that mattered was that next fix. It was a parlous state to be in he told the mirror, but he had to accept it that was so. In addition he no longer shaved and had grown a full beard that covered half his face and he also let his hair grow and scraped it back it into a pony tail.

Max turned away from the mirrow. It was enough truth to last him for a bit. Meantime he had to think about what to do about getting the next fix. Would Paul understand and give him some on tick? He did not know but he had no money and at least it was worth a try.

Max was thinking back to medical school and the warning about heroin. Of course hospitals use morphine of which heron is the modified version. Modified or otherwise it was a very addictive and the illegal opioid drug that was only available on the black market where it could be obtained through various scrupulous or unscrupulous dealers who grew quite rich with the supply to the hapless consumer. Paul always supplied good stuff, even Max knew that because heroin was a white powder, but because it could be mixed with substances such as sugar or even powered milk and other starches, even quinine, a bitter compound, the finished product is more brownish, or even like black tar heroin – a black and sticky substance. But regardless of the mixes the drug is readily and fast absorbed in the body and it is this speed that has such an addictive effect. The drug can be snorted, smoked or injected and in whichever way it is taken in, the effect and long term effect of heroin use is extremely harmful to the body.

Max knew all this from medical tuition, yet he had succumbed to it just as readily. As yet, neither he nor Ysi felt like injecting it as both of them were afraid of needles, and so snorting it had had just the desired effect until now. But Max realised that they had to resort to ever higher and purer stuff in order to get the same high they had the first time they had decided to try it because Paul's client had said that it would wrap them up in cotton wool and the feeling of well being was such that they would never again try anything else. And so it had proved but what the man had not said was how addictive it all was that they would no longer be masters of the drug but that the drug would be master of them. The man had said he had been on heroin for two years and would not consider anything wlse now. Max, now that he was on that stuff too, did not believe that bloke. Two years? He and Ysi had only been on that for a few weeks and it had wasted them. Yet Ysi, who had spoken to him had not mentioned that the man had particularly *looked* wasted. To her he had seen just a normal bloke. So how had they gone so wrong?

Max's rumination got him nowhere and on top he had now run out of money and needed another fix yet could not pay for it. Max had never run out of money before and he had to accept now that it was those heroin packets that depleted his allowance. He was not used to having no money because Pape had always given him more than enough, yet it was useless thinking that as now he needed urgently some funds he found he had none.

If Paul would not give him what he wanted on tick he he would have to go home and lay his cards on the table. Perhaps take Ysi with him for moral support. It was true the two of them looked a sight but it could not be helped. The time of wearing sun shades in order to pretend eye strain was long gone. It was time for a full confession.

Nevertheless the first port of call was still Paul. In spite of Max expecting a negative outcome, it was still preferable to be proved right that Paul would refuse, than go home and face a far more serious music. Paul's rejection as he saw it, was the less hazardous path.

To Max's complete surprise, Paul handed him
two silver foil packets on tick because he told him that he had not been home to collet his monthly allowance. Paul told him that it had to be a ‚one off‘.

„You see“, he said, „I only make a living because I have a few clients, but every day my being able to make a living hangs in the balance. To be sure you and Ysi are good and regular clients, but the guys who make the money in this racket is not me, but those who import large quantities. But even so, at ports and airports they now have sniffer dogs and ever bigger quantities of any stuff get found and confiscated, so you can see it is a precarious business. I am however one of a more scrupulous kind. I make sure that all the stuff that I buy is pure, because I cut it myself with quinine, which has healing properties and make it less likely, if proper dosage is followed, for my clients to die accidentally and so far nobody who has got their supplies from me has died".

Max had nodded, happy to have been proved wrong about Paul rejecting his request for a couple of packets on tick and with his two packets in his pocket he departed. The showdown with his parents had been averted for one more day. But he knew that would have to come, but tomorrow was another day and with that he headed back to Ysi.

*****

In the meantime Brendan had made progress with Fabienne Greystone. She had come up with five people on her list that had the same birthday, three men, so those could be discounted and two girls, one of which was in Scotland, so was probably not who he was looking for, yet would have to be followed up, but the other one was a girl with the name Ysenda Burrows. When Brendan heard that name he nearly dropped the telephone receiver, he was so shocked to hear that name. Ysenda Burrows. Was that not their son's girlfriend whom he refused to bring home? If he was right, then that girl had been living under their very noses so to speak and the whole time she was Lala-June, got to have been.

Brendan lost no time in telling Tina when he got home:

„You will never guess in a month of Sundays but I think we have found the elusive Lala-June for Amethyst's new man. And she has, by all accounts, changed her name which is why nobody could find her. And guess what the name is she had given to the Social Servicees? No, I can see you would never guess. The name is Ysenda Burrows. Can you believe that? It's our son's girl friend. The elusive Lala-

June has been going under the name of Ysenda Burrows. Remember, Max has refused to bring her home so we could have a look at her and form an opinion. I have an address and think that things have become a lot clearer. Max has not been home for weeks and I would not mind betting that he is holed up with that Ysi in her flat and both of them have become junkies. I have also only found out the other day that our Max no longer goes to medical college. He has dropped out which can only mean one thing and I am dreading it, which is he has become and junkie. And you know what they say. No junkie likes to be a junkie on their own. They need to know that whoever they are with have the same inclination, like alcoholics who need the company of other alcoholics to make them not feel guilty. Our son, my dear Tina is a cokehead and no mistake".

 While Brendan had been talking, Tina had sat down in her armchair with her head in her hands; she was deeply shaken. She had expected something like this to come, but now it was so very clearly spelt out to her what the matter was with Max, her brain refused to take it all in. All she could mumble over and over ‚so it was in the genes after all‘, our Max had gone the same way as Pelly, only Max was not dead yet. How much longer before an overdose would kill him. Was there time to rectify matters? She looked at Brendan who looked in some alarm at Tina's face. It had gone completely white.

 „Darling", Brendan said, „you know what they say and that it that the show was not finished until the fat lady had sung. As yet the fat lady was not due to sing and it may yet be time, just to save both Max and Lala-June, at least if it turns out that Ysenda *is* Lala-June. We don't know that yet, although in my mind I am almost sure that she has to be the girl that Dexter is looking for. I have an address and I shall hasten there. It will all be a lot clearer one I have seen face to face both Max and this girl. Iam equally convinced that our Max is living with her; we shall find out soon enough".

True to his word Brendan went to the address Fabienne Greystone had given him. He had asked Tina to come with him, but she had declined, saying she could not face it. He should go on his own and then come back and tell her his findings. She was still hoping that her husband had it all wrong, that Max was not there and the girl was not Lala-June. Deep down, however Tina knew that it was a forlorn hope and that she feared that what her husband had been told was fact.

Brendan had difficulty in finding the address. It was a run-down district, at leat in comparison with the area he lived in. The whole of Cranberry Street had block after block council housing blocks at least 25 stories high and he was looking for Cranberry Court. He found it set back from the street, behind another council block and he saw that all of the doors had intercoms. That was an unforeseen, for he did not want to press the bell then, if there was an answer, having to explain why he wanted entry. Brendan stood there undecided when the postman who had a special key to gain entry to the lobby in which to distribute his mail into several different boxes. The postman had no difficulty in letting Brendan in because the latter had mumbled that he could not find his keys. So he got in and quickly found that there were two lifts there, one reaching uneven numbers and one only even ones. There was no point in deciding as none of the lifts were in operation and so, having found that he had to get up to the eighteenth floor, had no option but to mount the stairs. There was a strong smell of urine hanging about the stairwell but Brendan disregarded that and eventually reached floor eighteen and knocked on the right door, 1847.

Brendan waited but there was no immediate answer and he was ready to leave again when he heard some shuffling behind the closed door and what seemed a long time, the door opened and a thin, dishevelled girl opened the door. Brendan was sure that this was not the girl he was looking for. This one looked middle aged with a pasty face, stick thin but with a rounded belly that clearly showed she was was pregnant. Brendan stood there for a moment unable to utter a word. He just looked at this girl than thought for a moment before he said:

" I am looking for Ysenda Burrows. The girl looked at him then said "And who is it that might be wanting her? She had an American accent and this gave him courage. He said he had some private words he had to say to this lady and it would be best if she would let him come in so he could explain it to her better. "Sure", she said, and with that Brendan entered the room. It was dismal and Brendan briefly wondered how people could actually live in a dump like that. Dump or no he was keenly aware that he had not come to measure the furniture but had come to find out if this Ysenda Burrows was in fact the Lala-June that all the world had been looking for these many months and had drawn a blank. He saw the grimy round table and two chairs and asked if he could sit down there. She nodded, waiting for him to speak. Max was nowhere to be seen.

Now that he was here he had not prepared what he might say to this girl an so silence hung in the room, Brendan sitting down and this girl standing up waiting for him to say what he had come to say. Finally Brendan had got his thoughts together as to what he was going to say to this woman who still stood before him.

„Your father is looking for you" he told her but the woman said:

„My father? I don't have a father that I recognise and my mother has been dead when I was small. I don't know what you are talking about"

„Well", Brendan countered: „I have it on good authority that you are not in fact Ysenda Burrows but that your real name is Lala-June Shelling". Ysi stared at him.

„And who says that? It happens to be wrong, my name is Ysenda Burrows you can ask Social Services about that". Ysenda pursed her lips and sat on the roll-up bed."My husband will be here soon and he will tell you who I am".

Brendan again: „You don't have a husband as far as I know but if you refer to your lover, his name I think is Max and he is in fact my son". Ysenda stared at him, dumbfounded:

„Your son?, How? You are his father? Well I am blowed, you must be Mr Easterwood then". Brendan confirmed that he was and then told her:

„So it is silly to play games with me. I have spent many many fruitless weeks trying to help your father, Dexter Shelling, to find you and it took all of my ingenuity to have finally found you. Your real name came up nowhere and it was only because I thought of tracing you through your actual date of birth which I obtained from your father, that I am actually here in this flat, talking to you. I see you are pregnant as well and I assume that Max is the father of your unborn child?".

Ysenda got off the roll-up and sat opposite him on the other chair.

„How is it my father is looking for me? Do you know that he abandoned me when I was still only small because he married again this woman who had two small boys and he only married her because he was kind and wanted to be a father to these two boys. I was in the way, so I was sent off to boarding school at the age of seven. If you have been told any different, it is a lie. What I am telling you is the bald truth, which is why I changed my name as soon as I could. Nobody in the world is called Lala-June. It is a silly name, though quite common in the southern states of North America. I found a newspaper that had the byline of one

Ysenda somebody and I thought it was a nice name. So I adopted it. Simple really and until you have turned up utterly effective. Max, the father of my unborn child does not even know my real name because I did not want to be found".

Brendan reached out across the table and took her hand. „I can see you are in a very bad state and I would venture that my son is in a not much a different state. He has not been home for weeks and now, of course, I can see why. The pair of you, or at least you, need help very badly and I am willing to help you if you want it, but you must want it as otherwise nothing is going to work."

Ysenda had not tried to remove her hand from his but now there was a key in the lock, the door opened and Max entered the room. He did a double take: for a moment he thought that his father was sitting at the table then realised it was indeed Papa who sat there holding hands with Ysenda. Brendan looked at his son and the sight of him made him want to weep. He no longer recognised the fresh-faced youth from a few weeks ago. Before him stood a skeleton; his clothes which were the same since he had seen him last had not been changed in god know how long and everything was hanging off him. He now wore a full beard that covered all of his lower face and what was not covered was covered in red pustules. His curly hair was scraped back and forced into a ponytail. It had obviously not been cut in weeks if not months. His beard seemed to be multicoloured, the lower half was red and the rest gold and black. Around his neck he still had the silver chain from which dangled his snake. He still had that, but his face was that of an older man, past forty, pasty and grey.

„You could do with a change of clothes and a bath, his Papa had told Max and, looking at Ysenda said that the same would be beneficial for her as well. This room smells terrible and the hygiene of the two of you leaves a lot to be desired"

Max grew petulant and told his Papa that if had come to criticise him and his woman, he could go again, but if he really wanted to help he, Max could do with a couple of hundred pounds so they could go and get fixed up again. The time for pretending, Max thought was over and it was time for plain talking now and what he needed right now was money to feed his habit.

Brendan listened to his son and was aghast. This was not the Max he knew but an alien being that was talking to him. Having got over his surprise at being talked to in that manner, Brendan told Max and the girl something completely different to what they wanted to hear. He said:

„Looking at the pair of you I know one thing and that is to look the way that you do it is not cocaine you are imbibing – for you to look as terrible and smell as terrible, you have gone several steps further in your cravings and I hate to think it but for my money you must be on heroin, nothing else makes any sense.

Max was about to answer his father, but Ysenda blurted out: „Yes, both Max and I are on heroin because we like it that way and we have Paul, our dealer whom we have used since we first started and he always supplies us top grade stuff and providing we keep to the dosage recommended there is no danger of our overdosing and coming to grief".

Brendan cut her short and told both of them that while it was true that he was a rich man and two hundred pounds were chickenfeed for him, he had decided he would doing them a disservice by giving them the money only to enrich their dealer, no matter how scrupulous they hold him to be. The fact was that heroin was a lethal substance and sooner or later both of them would come to grief. With heroin, which is deadlier than cocaine even, it is the case that more and more of it would have to be imbibed to get the same high as when first started and it most definitely was the slippery slope down to hell and he would be no party to that.

His last parting shot was that both young people, however ghastly and unsavoury their looks needed urgent help, go into rehab and get cleaned up. Turning to Max he said: „We have learnt that you have dropped out of medical school, Oskar told us and it is a crying shame to have done that when you have so much talent to make it in that profession. Do you remember still how you wanted to be a surgeon. Heroin has robbed you of that ambition and all you now want to do is take the drug and get wasted. I might remind you, however that you have responsibilities towards your unborn child and if nothing else you should be there for the new-born when it arrives in this world, instead of lying there and both of you wasting your young lives away.

I have come here because I wanted to find Lala-June. Instead I found two people whose lives matters so little to them that they are prepared to throw it all away in order to enrich some drug cartel who live high on the hog from the proceeds of street sales to dealers such as your Paul who is the low end of the market. The importers of this drug have money to burn, thanks to customers like you, whose bodies are ravaged beyond recognition. I would be failing in my duties as a father to give you enough money so you can kill yourselves". Addressing Ysenda he said: „Your father may not have been there for you when you were small but he is trying to make amends and has spent considerable time and money to try and find you. In the end he enlisted my daughter's help. He was reliably informed that you had come here to this country and he spent many weeks in a hotel, trying to find people who could further his quest in finding you.

People, and that includes me, you know, are not *born* parents – you are about to find that out – but we learn on the job, literally and I cannot pretend that we get everything right. God knows I myself have done a wrong to my first wife I had promised at the altar to be there for her and I had not been. Money had been more important to me and Marcus and Amethysts' mother died of drink and grief at too young an age. She was not yet forty, so I assume some twenty years younger than you. But children are harsh; they don't want to accept that parents have failings too and when they get older and have learnt that money does not bring the happiness everybody wants and want to make amends, the children sit in judgment over them and tell them they have never been there for them.

You are both at a crossroad. You can decide whether or not you want to be free of this insiduous death trap, want to get clean and have a proper life That is your choice. There is nothing else".

Brendan stood up. „Iam not making you go into rehab as I believe that we are here on earth to learn something. Everything we do carries a price; we have to decide if we want to pay the price or shop somewhere else. I leave you to decide." Then he walked to the door, opened it an closed it behind him. Cluttering down eighteen flights of stairs he wondered if he had done the right thing, whether or not he should have summoned people in white coats to come and take them away there and then. No doubt Tina would tell him that's was what he should have done. Once outside, he breathed the fresh air deeply. It had been a dismal hour he had spent in that dingy, smelly room with two people who no longer cared how they looked or if they were clean. Brendan went home depressed and downhearted. He had never thought that his son would turn out in the way he did. Tina though had told him endlessly in many conversations that she had had the same arguments with her brother and he too never listened until it was too late, way too late to rectify matters. Now he felt his son and that girl were going the same way.

Chapter 32

Max and Ysenda decide

After Max's father had left them they looked at each other. Max who had heard his Papa's assertion that Ysenda was in fact Lala-June asked her why she never had the confidence to tell him that she was born with a different name. But Lala-June aka Ysi said that she had ditched that name in favour of Ysenda because not only did she like Ysenda better as a name, but also precisely because she felt she had, once in England and the Social Services had been involved they had accepted the name. She could not change it back even if she wanted to because she was penniless. The Social Services were paying the rent on the bedsit and also were paying her council tax plus a small amount of money which did not actually allow her to live, but also did not allow her to die. What else was she to do?

Her father, as far as she knew had a new family and she simply had been surplus to requirement. Since that appeared to be the case she did not feel she owed anyone anything and she was now here in England and had to make the best of a bad situation. She never was of the opinion that the world owed her a living and since she was on her own, she made the best of what was available to her. It was really quite a simple story.

Ysi told Max that, when she first met him in that little shop she had figured that he still had tobe living at home, judging from the clothes he wore. Since he had been so generous to pay Paul for the both of them when she did not have the money she had accepted that generosity. And after a time she had simply viewed him as her husband, especially now that she was expecting his child and since she had thought of him as her husband she felt that husband and wives shared stuff with each other. As for the name it was, for her neither here nor there. She loved him and thought that he loved her too and so what was in a name? Nothing. What mattered was how people felt about each other.

Chapter 33

Tina weeps

Brendan arrived home in a very agitated state and Tina, looking at him was alarmed.

"Oh, darling", he said, flinging himself into the nearest chair, "what a mess it all has become". I have found the girl Dexter had been looking for, Lala-June. Max was there too and you would not believe the state of the two of them. They are both hopeless heroin junkies. That, my dear is the right word. I don't know what we can do about it and I fear greatly that we have discovered just how bad it all is, far too late to help them. Lala-June is pregnant, quite far gone and by the look of it and Max is the father. You would not recognise our boy anymore. He has grown a full beard, has not had a hair-cut in a long while and his hair is scraped back and held in a pony tail. They both reek, the room is terrible and neither of them have had a bath in weeks. Also Max is still wearing the same clothes and they are very grubby. Darling, I feel it is hopeless. I have left them to it, no point in doing otherwise. I told both of them that they urgently needed to go into rehab and if they decide that is what they want you and I will pay for the treatment for both of them, but it would be up to them to decide and with that I upped and left. I was glad to be in the fresh air again, it wa so very terrible in that dingy room. I don't understand how anyone could live like that.

Tina had listenend to Brendan without saying a single word, but tears were welling up and now she began to cry, so Brendan pulled her onto his chair and said he felt just as sad in the way that their Max had turned out, but he was of the opinion that all may yet come right, then he dried Tina's eyes and said „there is work to be done. We have to tell Amethyst that Lala-June had been found and that she should tell Dexter forthwith. At least that is one bit of of good news that would please at least one man.

Both Brendan and Tina resolved to say nothing about how they had found the two junkies but hoped all the same that they had now reached rock bottom and were intelligent enough to see that they needed help. By God they needed help, no two ways about that.

*****

After Max's father had left their room, Ysi and he lay on the roll-up bed. Of late that roll-up had been left flat; they had no longer bothered to roll-it up in the day time to have more room in that bedsit. Now as they lay side by side, they considered their position. Max's Papa had left without given hi son the regular allowance and now they were in that room penniless and they owed Paul about one hundred pounds, which the latter expected to have repaid.

Max was upset and angry in equal measure. It was the first time in his life that he felt he had no family to rely on for his upkeep and he had fondly believed that for as long as he lived he could draw a generous income from Papa, who had always set the amount, and who had now left without giving him any money at all. Max had not expected that outcome. He had been astonished to have entered the room and had found his father sitting there. He had had to rub his eyes to check if his imagination was playing him a trick, then found that his father was really sitting at that rickety table, holding hands with his Ysi before starting to pontificate that both of them lacked in hygiene and also that they should get themselves into rehab; that matters could not continue in this fashion if they wanted to live. Moreover that he would pay the fees for the rehab. Max thought about that. He felt that neither he nor Ysi needed rehab. What they needed was money to hand over to Paul for urgent fixes they both needed and that was all they needed. There was only one way to get the funds, now his allowance from his family had gone up in smoke, and that was to obtain that somehow. He thought about the snake and briefly thought to pawn it but just as quickly as he thought about that he discarded it. Gramps Liffet would not like the idea of letting that little snake out of his hands. It had been entrusted into his care and as a five year old, when he had received it, he still remembered his foster carer's words that he gave him the snake in order to remember him, gramps Liffet by. Also, that this little sliver of silver would keep him safe. And up to now it had done just that so there was no way that he could part with it. The tattoo on his upper arm was just a copy of the snake by way of indemnity should he ever lose the real thing. So, on the basis of that there was no way he could consider parting with it for any reason, long or short term. Another way had to be found.

*****

Over at the Easterwood house, Shayne realised that her time was up and that she had to go back home. She had been listing with mounting horror Brendan and Tina's woes over Max. She had liked Max on sight when she first met him and, realising now that he had become a junkie had made her very sad. She remembered when she had told Tina in the breakfast room some months back that it was rubbish that Max was wearing his Ray-Bans indoors because of eye-strain and she had told Tina then that Max was into drugs. Now he had become a real junkie on heroin, not just the soft stuff, but the real hard stuff. Not even she had realised how bad it was with Max. When he still wore the shades in order to deceive his parents about the real reason why he wore them indoors, she had observed that he was secretly dabbling in drugs. At that time she knew it was cocaine but had believed when he said he could manage that. Nobody in her family had ever used cocaine; she had told Tina that her grandfather had taken the magic mushrooms with its hallucinary properties, but she had resolved even then that stuff like that was not for her. She liked life as it was, real and sometimes harsh, but she felt that it was the only way one coud deal with reality and that was get a grip and come to terms with. Suni too had always said one had to look at life in a positive not negative manner and that her own mantra had always been; *change what you can and accept what you can't.* She always held that it was not what happened to you in life that was important, but how you reacted to it, how you took it.

She fully subscribed to that. For her it was a matter of getting a grip and even trying to change the unacceptable if that was possible, if not one had to bend to it, even if it was unsavoury. Fate dealt certain cards and one had to play with the given hand as best one could. That was *her* philosophy and anything else was wishful thinking.

Now she was at the end of one journey and was ready to go back home. Shayne thought about her aunt Suni and Max's snake. Suni had impressed on her that she had to bring that little snake back as Lightfoot had had no right to give it to Max. Lightfoot had given it to Max to remember him by but he had had no right to do so. Lightfoot may have instructed Max in the way of the Shawnee, but Max was no Shawnee and never would be. Now he had been living with his blood family in England from the age of five or six he had become English; in fact he had been English all along through his own father.

Shayne had decided now to depart for home without the snake. She had decided to leave it with Max. Whatever the reasons Lightfoot had, he had given that sliver of silver to Max; it had been an outright gift and she felt in no way qualified to take that away simply because her aunt said that it belonged with a Shawnee. Listening to Brendan and Tina expressing their sorrows over the descent of Max into drug hell along with that young woman, Ysenda, Shayne was aware that there would be no favourable outcome for these young people. She was aware that Max would not be going into rehab and neither was that young woman he was with, who it turns out had a father who had spent a good deal of time and money to try and find her, since he had not seen her since she had been a teenager.

Shayne's departure was now imminent and she did not want to depress Brendan and Tina any further by telling them that neither Max nor Ysenda would bend to the harsh cure of a rehab clinic. Shayne felt she had no right to be the harbinger of a bleak future, when that future had not happened yet and in any case she may yet be wrong.

So Shayne had said her good-byes and Brendan had taken her to the airport. His last words to her before she disappeared through the double doors, where non-flying passengers were not permitted, to write and come back anytime she felt like it, she would always be welcome; that it had been a pleasure to have her. Then she disappeared and Brendan headed home.

Chapter 34

Max and Ysi need money

Max and Ysi lay on the roll-up and considered their situation. Both were strung out and in bad need of a fix. Paul's client had been right about one thing: that heroin would wrap them in cotton wool and they would experience such a high feeling of well being that they would never consider any other drug after that. Ysi had come back to Max with that tale and Max had been dubious. He knew that this was the point of no return and he was not sure he wanted to go down that route. But Ysi felt that one should try everything once in one's lifetime and so she had won over a reluctant Max. At that point Max had plenty of money to pay for the vastly more expensive heroin and they had had a couple of week's pleasure out of that.

There was no doubt about it; it *did* wrap them in cotton wool and sex had been sublime – that part was certainly true. But not for long. After the third time, both felt that in order to achieve the same high they needed just a touch more. Paul had warned them and said that this was dangerous stuff and it was not a road one should travel on lightly. Nevertheless he was willing to sell them the drug and they were happy to take it. They came back to him with superlative words, both about the quality of it and the sublime high they had reached with this stuff. There was just a small thing they wanted Paul to know and that was that they needed a touch more of that than the last time. Paul knew of course that sooner rather than later he would have to sell them increased dosage and he absolutely knew where that led. He also knew that it was fruitless to tell Max that eventually it would lead to destruction but Max had not wanted to know about that, so he took the larger dosage and went on his way.

Two days later he needed more. Paul tried to cut it so that it looked like an increase but was actually the same, but Max had come back to say that what they had no longer satisfied. So Paul sold them the real thing in the bigger quantity. He knew they would be back before long to demand bigger still.

Now Max and Ysi lay on the bed and wondered what to do about getting stuff and paying for it. He was skint and Ysi's income via the Social circuit was so minimal that it had fallen to Max to pay the full whack whith his allowance. And that too had now gone into the ether. They both needed money badly to get fixed and Paul had been nice but adamant that he could not let them have anymore on tick, that he himself was scratching around for his living and he simply did not make enough to let out stuff for free. Max would have to see how he could obtain money in order to satisfy their craving for heroin. Max had turned it over in his head. Pawning the little snake on his chain was out. He would never be able to part with it. There was only one option and that would have to be considered. He would have to *steal* money in sufficient quantity to keep them in heroin for at least a few weeks. It would be a large amount of money and Max was now thinking of ways to get that.

Max rose from the roll-up and told Ysi he would be going out for fresh air for a bit to think things over. Ysi made no objection. Though strung out, she was tired and wanted to sleep. Her unborn baby had stated to tell her that ther was life in her belly and had started to kick. It woul be born soon and she wondered how she could cope. Even she realised that there was no way she could even think of giving birth to a baby while on heroin; the Social Services would come and take it away. She would have to give that some serious thought. But not now, now she just wanted to turn over and sleep for a bit and wait for Max to come back with something that might satisfy the both of them in the short term. For the longer term she would have to think about matters. Then she went to sleep. The last thing she heard was the click in the lock as Max had left the flat.

*****

Shayne having departed, Brendan had lost no time in telling Amethyst and Lala-June had been found. She had sent a telegram to Dexter and told him the same thing. Dexter lost no time in catching a plane and coming over. This time he did not stay in the Dorchester because Amethyst had insisted he stayed with her at her house. Dexter had come with good news as far as his own status was concerned. He had managed to get Meryl out of the house by buying her a house for herself and her teenage boys. Meryl had been quite happy and had accepte the generous offer from Dexter. She was happy to have now her own house, a real asset for her, considering she had come into his house with nothing but a suitcase and two small boys on either hand.

But now it meant that Dexter felt himself to be unencumbered, though not yet divorced, but getting there, which could not be said about Amethyst's situation. She was still very much married to Konrad, although their son Oskar lost no time in telling his father that Dexter had moved into the house and also into the marital bed. Konrad had winced when he thought wistfully, that a stupid bit of yellow paper with glue about the top end, had finished his marriage. He was as yet not ready to agree that it was not that yellow scrap of paper that had done the dirty on him, but his duplicity in having an affair with someone not his wife, which had ruined his marriage. Amethyst though had been quite clear, so clear in fact that Konrad could not have misconstrued her meaning.

As far as she was concerned she was getting a divorce because she considered her marriage finished. Konrad had of course understood but only in his head, in his heart he still thought there was a way of his coming back into the marriage. Now he knew for certain that this avenue was shut and that he had better get used to being a divorced man. Of course he had told Chum and the latter breathed a sigh of relief: finally there was movement. For months her lover had hedged his bets and evaded the issue; now he had to seriously address it. She wanted him, no question and she knew that he wanted her too, it was just that the marriage still stood in the way. However hard it was for him, he would not stand in the way of a divorce. His wife deserved happiness and he had betrayed her, so here was a way to make amends by granting her the divorce so she could marry her Texan lover.

When Dexter arrived and she had collected him from the airport she had lost no time in telling him that he could and should stay at her house and she would then drive him to the address where his daughter Lala-June was holed up with her father's adopted son Max. That was the plan, but in the end it did not work out like that, though that part where Dexter stayed at Amethyst's house and shared the marital bed, that part worked out exceedingly well.

Chapter 35

Fate takes a hand

Max had left the roll-up and Ysi with the firm intention to steal sufficient money in order to have no worries for the next two weeks, so they could enjoy their drug haze without having to worry if there were enough funds for the following day. Mainly, however Max decided to steal because he wanted to avoid the pain after he had come down. It was far worse then the hang-overs he had endured when he and Ysi had snorted coke. Quietly he cursed that man that had collared Ysi on the stairs from Paul's above by saying that heroin was so good it would wrap them in cotton wool and he himself had been taking heroin for near on two years and loved it. He still remembered how Ysi had said that one should try everything at least once. And this was the result. On coke he had sufficient regular funds – just – to pay for it, but heroin was vastly more expensive and since he had to pay for Ysenda too, his funds were depleted and he now had to resort to stealing.

How Max was attempting to procure the necessary funds by stealing was not formed very clearly in his head. Morally speaking he knew it was wrong to steal and his conscience told him the same thing, but needs must when the devil drives and he felt he had no choice but to satisfy this ever terri le craving craving in him and Ysi Moreover, it was a terrible disappointment for him that Papa had turned up to hold held them a lecture about rehab then departed without leaving the regular allowance that was due to him.

Max realised a bit late in the day, that he and Ysi had reached a point of no return, that they were hopelessly addicted. The man had been right about one thing: they *were* wrapped up in cotton wool and he was also rightabout sex which too was absolutely amazing. Max had never thought that sex could be so fantastic.

Max was aimlessly roaming the streets looking for asuitable premises to rob, while thinking about the sex he and Ysi had. If he was honest he had to admit that on heroin the first, second and third time had been out of this world. But after they got further into this drug, it had flattened out and in order to try and reach the ecstasy of those early snorts, they had to increase the dosage. And so it had gone on. Max realised it was becoming unaffordable. In the beginning when it had just been marijuana or even when he started dabbling in coke, he could cover it fine with the allowance his father gave him on a regular bases, and he had liked the fact that he never had to give any account as to how he spent the money. The set allowance would arrive regular as clockwork and he never had to ask for it; he was just given it and so he had come to rely on it.

Of course in the early days there had been no Ysenda and he only had to cater for himself, but when he got involved with Ysi he had felt honour-bound to cover her portion as well. Well he was the man and a man had to look after his woman. Ysi was pregnant now and neither of them had ever talked about what was to happen when the time came that she would have to give birth. Both knew that junkies did not make good parents and Max had remembered how Ysi had told him that she had been surplus to requirement once that stepmother had come on the scene; that the woman had only been interested in the welfare of her two boys and she had always found reasons to punish her for the slightest of misdemeanours, while the boys got let off. Ysi had told him all about it and Max had remembered his childhood and gramps Liffet and nana Akki and how his boyhood had been one of love and affection.

Max fingered his sliver of silver and it was still reassuringly hanging from that silver chain around his neck.

He would never never get rid of that however bad the situation got. That silver snake had been given to him on trust and even when gramps Liffet or nana Akki for that matter were no longer in life, he, Max would always honour them by keeping his little snake close by. The tattoo on his arm was only for if the worst should happen and he lost it, that the snake would still keep him safe.

*****

Ruminating in this way, Max had crossed steet after street, thinking and plotting how he could obtain the money but after a bit he simply realised he just was not cut out to be a thief. Despondent he returned to the flat. He dreaded having to tell Ysi that he had returned empty handed. As he entered the room the roll-up was empty and Max thought for a moment that she had gone out to get some funds herself, or even had braved the wrath of Paul and begged yet another small packet which she would share with him. That was what Max thought, but then he saw Ysenda lying on the floor. She had turned over on the bed, had turned a bit too much and toppled off the bed. Now she was lying there, prostrate on the floor, eyes open. Max grew alarmed. „Ysi you will be cold, get up off the floor and back onto the bed". But there was no response and Max knelt on the floor beside her to shake her. But Ysi felt cold to the touch and after a while Max realised that Ysenda Burrows aka Lala-June had died. And he had not been with her. He had left her to die on her own. That she was dead there was no question and Max did not know what to do. So he did what he always did when he was in deep trouble. He went out and called his Papa to ask him what he had to do to get his Ysi awake again.

Brendan who suspected that the girl was dead told his son to stay in the flat, he would be arriving shortly. So Max went back to the bedsit, sat down on the roll-up and stared forlornly down on Ysi who still was not moving. And she was also also not breathing and Max knew, just knew that she

268

was dead. His soulmate had died on her own while he had been roaming the streets looking to steal some funds to feed their addiction. He had dropped out of medical school, had not had a wash in weeks and had, moreover, not cared how he looked, not cared about his future and had looked no further ahead than the next fix. It was true though what that client of Paul's had said, that one did not get an hangover from it, but Max thought the addiction to that was worse than any hangover that he had endured, lying with Ysi on that roll-up, wasted and strung-out; a sigtuation that coud only be alleviated by having another fix. Max realised as he sat there, that it was no way to continue, then he heard the knock on the door and opened it to let Papa come into the room.

Brendan now took charge. He could see that Ysi had been dead a while and any kind of resusitation would be pointless. Nevertheless he went to call an ambulance who duly came and took the girl to hospital. Their first concern had been to to save the baby and for that they had to take her to a hospital.

In the end that too had proved fruitless. The baby died in the womb along with its mother. Max and Brendan had gone to hopsital with Ysi and after an interminable length of waiting they were told that nothing coul be done and it was best if both went home.

*****

It was in the end a cruel twist of fate for Dexter who had to be told that while his daughter had been found, he could be no nearer to make amends for all the years of neglect because his daughter, Lala-June had died, had been pregnant but fate had taken the baby at the same time. The only thing he could do was to visit the mortuary where he could view the body. It was Amethyst who had to be the bearer of these terrible news but Dexter lost no time to get to see Lala-June one last time. But when he saw here there lying so still and white on a slab he broke down and cried. In truth

269

he had not recognised the daughter he had last seen when she was fourteen, a freshfaced teenager, who had begged him to take her away and he, realising that there was no place for her at home, he himself had made a terrible mistake for which there would now be no atonement. He talked to her all the same:

"You have no idea my darling how much time and money I spent looking for you. I know it is now useless for you are lost to me, but all the same I want you to know that I tried everything. I know it is far too late; I should never have sent you away. When your Momma died, I did not know what to do, we had loved each other to bits and then she was taken from me along with your little brother. I had no idea what to do next, then Meryl came and I felt sorry for her and the two fatherless little boys. Since then I found out that her husband had not died, but he had left her because he just could not tolerate living with her anymore, though he had felt sorry for the boys. He had suggested that he would take one boy and she the other, but she would not hear of it, so he left, never to reurn. I have only found this out recently, so she married me while she herself was still married. I only realised after I had married her that all she wanted was a roof over her head and her two boys without having to work for it. I was rich and she could see that and worked it to her advantage. I Know now that I am not married to her, not legally anyhow. What I do know is that I sacrificed you in the process. I hope you can ever forgive me for that. You look terrible my love and I wish that I could make it all undone and we could have the time together again". Then he kissed her forehead and quietly left the room.

*****

Brendan and Max had come home from the hospital and were sitting in the living room, where Tina, not letting on how shocked she was to see her bearded son with a ponytail, served coffee and tea. Presently she too was sitting opposite

270

Max in an armchair and the three of them sat there together wondering to speak what was foremost in their minds. Max was the first to speak and said:

"I know I have gone very wrong, but if you were serious about rehab, I would like to take you up on that and the sooner the better. I feel terrible and I think that Ysenda, or Lala-June as we now know she was in reality it was a wake-up call. All the same I feel terrible because she died alone; I was not there when she died because I had gone out with the firm intention of robbing a store in order to have sufficent funds to get fixed up for the next couple of weeks.

I owe Paul about one hundred pounds for stuff he had given me on tick and I have to pay him. But, if I accept that I have to go into rehab then perhaps you might be willing to give me the money to pay Paul. I did not rob any stores because I am not cut out for that. I had always thought it was wrong and even though I had become a junkie, I still don't think it is right to rob people in order to feed a useless habit. So, it is not much, but at least I have stayed true to my belief and have not become a thief as well."

Brendan said that the money had never been a problem, as there was more than enough floating about in his family. He was happy to hear that Max had, through tragic circumstances, come to see that living on heroin was no life and of course he would only be too happy to pay whatever it cost to get his life back on track. And perhaps he could see his way to get back to medical school again and finish his exams.

"There is a future for you, Max, but you must want it", was what Brendan said to his son and Tina had nodded.

And so Max went into rehab and had been there for two weeks, when the dreaded phone call came to say that he had met another addict in rehab and he had given him a fix and Max had died in the night. The nurses on duty had no idea that illicit substances had been smuggled into their clinic but it had and Max and the person who had given it to him had both overdoses in the night.

When Brendan and Tina were told of their sons' death, they just stared at each other, unable to take in the enormity of what they were hearing. So, it had come to this after all; they had thought they had, just in time, managed to rescue Max from the jaws of death, only to find that in the very clinic they had put him in for his own safety, that he may recover, had not been vigilant enough and their Max had met with death after all.

Having got over the first shock and Tina being unable to handle the situation, Brendan had taken charge. He had organised viewing the body and both of them went to see him. The beard and the ponytail had gone; all that remained was the white face of Max, lying on a long table, hands down by his side, eyes closed, a faint smile around his mouth. Around his neck he still had the silver chain with the snake dangling from it and the clinic had asked Brendan what they should do about that. Brendan, after consultation with Tina had decided to leave it with him. It would stay with him in his eternal sleep. They had not found it within themselves to remove it. Like Shayne who also had decreed that Lightfoot had given it to him to remember him by and had felt it should stay with him, rather than accompany her on her journey back to her Shawnee family.

Now both Tina and Brendan had thought the same and so Max was buried along with that sliver of silver and Tina had remembered that as a ten year old he had specifically drawn the snake under his sloping name and she had been told that it was not a wavey line, but a snake of the sor that gramps Liffet had given him to remember him by.

Dying was such a terrible business for friends and relatives. And the worst of it was when parents had to bury their children. It was all wrong. Children should bury their parents, not the other way round.

But despite her grief Tina had to smile about that sliver of silver; let him take the snake to his final resting place. It should have kept him safe but there the snake had failed in its duty to do so. Maybe God would look more kindly on this boy, who was simply too young to die. And like his father and mother before him, he had gone the same way along with a young lady, Lala-June who had made it so difficult to be found that she had changed her name to Ysenda Burrows. Perhaps if she had not changed her name she would have been found earlier and so the grisly fate might have been averted for both of them. Change what you can and accept that which you can't. And so that little snake that represented the mambe for a man called Rooter, went with Max to keep him company in his eternal sleep.

Epilogue.

The death of Max affected Brendan and Tina deeply. Tina in particular because she could not help to compare Max's life with that of his father, Pelham or Pelly as she had called him when they were children, and now Max had gone the same way as his actual parents. So it was in the genes after all; he had all the care and attention and love and affection and it had all come to nothing.

Tina could not help but wonder whether or not he would have gone the same way if she and Brendan had left him with by Lightfoot and Akwase. Would he have gone the same way, or was it the Western way of living and growing up that had made this terrible difference. The ways of the Shawnee was a lot simpler and a lot more natural than the cosseted ways of the Western World. But such ruminations were now futile as both Dexter's daughter, Lala-June, masquerading as Ysenda Burrows, and Max had gone down the spiral of a wasted life at such a young age. Pelly was twenty-two when he died and Max was just twenty.

*****

There was one item of good news among the terrible tragedies. Amethyst had obtained the divorce and had married Dexter. She had agreed she would be moving to Texas with him in due course, when she had sorted the financial side of things with her husband as was, Konrad. She wanted nothing from him; he could have the house and the furniture and everything he wanted. Dexter had told her he had more than enough and money had not been his object of desire for a long while now. It was true that his father had left him the ranch, an asset of twentythousand acres and he had increased it to double that amount. But it was only because he wanted to see if he could do it. That he grew rich in the process had been a secondary consideration. Money always came in useful, that was a fact, but people had the wrong impression about money. If it was status they were looking for it was the wrong way up a ladder, for happiness and contentedness came first every time and since the tragic death of his daughter, if he had not known it before, it had been rammed home to him since.

The wedding of Dexter and Amethyst was a low-key affair in the aftermath of the tragedy of these young people. Dexter thought that they should wait until a suitable time had gone because he felt it would be wrong to marry when both his daughter and Max had gone to their untimely death. But Amerthyst would not hear of it. She told him that even if they waited it would not bring Lala-June and Max back, so there was nothing gained by waiting and so they got married, Amethyst in a light green outfit and Dexter in a dark lounge suit. Few people attended the wedding but Brendan, her father and Tina, did and they wished the couple every happiness.

It had turned out that owing to the fact that Meryl's husband was still alive, his marriage to her was judged to be nul and void, so the marriage with Amethyst could go ahead.

The honeymoon was postponed. The feeling was that they would stay to take care of the house and furniture which was left to Konrad, so he could move in with his lover and after the hand-over they would depart to Texas. Amethyst who had never been to America had briefly wondered what she would find there, but it was just a fleeting moment which she managed to dismiss. A new chapter was waiting.

*****

The Notters never had Hobson's Choice staged. In the end, everybody was taken up with other things, although there was another tragedy for them. Bugs had died. He and Jock were sitting at their usual spot outside the new Covent Garden, when Bugs just lay down and died. There had been nothing wrong with him – there had been no complaint about not feeling well. He had just been talking to Jock in French like he always did and Jock had obviously agreed with him for he had nodded and wondered why Bugs had not carried on with the conversation. Turning around he watched with mounting horror that his pal had changed his sitting position and had laid down flat. Bending over him he realised that Bugs was not breathing and in the way Jock knew, just knew that Bugs would never sit up again. Jock would have to carry on his own. He did and also became another Notter.

The Notter members had accepted him and meetings were still being held at Grant's pub on the first of every month and there was a new face in the shape of a woman who was introduced by Shuby; his new wife *Jocelyn*. He had quietly got married as well after a lot of deliberation and worry that it might turn out like his first marriage, but in the end he decided that life was too short to keep worrying and he liked Jocelin too much to pursue his single life. But there was something else as well he considered which was that it was pointless forgoing happiness because his previous marriage had ended in tragedy. He could not undo the past but he could try his best to have a better future and he felt that with Jocelyn's help he could do just that. And with that thought in mind they got married.

As regards Jock he had no intention of replacing Bugs by becming a Notter himself. Bugs was a one off and would be sorely missed. But he, Jock, could still make his presence felt and so he went to the meetings at Grant's pub where it was still very lively and all and sundry had different opinions on this and that and was not afraid to air them to their mates. To be sure it was not the same not having Bugs with his sunny nature there anymore but like when Fate had thrown them on the scrap heap and they had emerged from that, they felt that life was too short to worry about everything. One was dead a lot longer than one was alive and one had to take good fortune where one could. One would not forget those who had passed on, for sure one would miss them, but life was for living and dying came later. Jock remembered an old song he had heard when he was a boy that had started with:

The old streets still, the old houses still, and the old meadows still but the old friends and acquaintances they had all gone.

As to Fenella Gettevan, she never found her new recipe to riches after the loss of her fraudulent slipping and falling venture. After trying hard she had given up with bad grace, but not before getting rid of her unsatisfactory husband, Karl. But in the end Karl had at least the last laugh. Having told Karl that she was divorcing him, he looked crestfallen while secretly being more than pleased about it but did not want it to show on his face. He knew that Fenella would instantly make capital out of that so he kept quiet and pretended to be upset about it. Secretly too he had repaired his relationship with Mary-Jane who had decided to take him back and forgive him, chiefly because the duplicitous Fenella had urged her to divorce Karl simply because she had meant to marry him instead and that only, not out of love, but because she thought he would help to enrich her bank balane still further.

When Fenella discovered that her husband had taken back the life policy by putring it back in Mary-Jane's name for her and his children to benefit upon his death, hopefully many years hence, she was incandescent that that snake Karl had had one over on her, but since she never found out until after the divorce, there was nothing she could do about it.

Outwardly she told people that it was 'good riddance' while inwardly she seethed about having been betrayed. To the last Fenealla's interest was always just money and how she could get more of the same.

.....Then, like all the words that have fallen out from the story onto the sand, I will finish and the wind will take it all away".

Nisa, A Zulu

About the Author:
Ines C Rothen was born in Switzerland but now lives in Barnet. She started writing less than 10 years ago.

To date she has published: -
1. Her Autobiography, in three volumes:
    Vanished Times in 2014
    Walk into the Unknown in 2014
    Rollercoaster in 2015

2. Her first novel: -
    Tobias Stoller's Farm   in 2015 (blue cover)

3. A trilogy: -
    The Hat that Danced in The Wind, in 2016
        I – A Family
        II – Shattered Dreams
        III – Out of the Shadows

4. A Book of Shorter Stories: -
    Volume I   published   2016
    Volume II published   2017
    Volume III published   2017

5. **The Wayfarers**   2020

6. **A Sliver of Silver**
    (Sequel to Wayfarers)   2021